"Lyrical. . . . A well-wrought coming-of-age tale with an edge of magical realism: Carson McCullers meets Alice Hoffman . . . sharply drawn characters . . . tinged with allegory . . . startling. . . . Ship Sooner is an immensely likable, complex character who hovers above the chasm between childhood and adulthood that threatens to pull every adolescent into its merciless vortex. *Ship Sooner* is a strong, visceral, often violent novel, filled with the stuff of small-town life—secrets and lies and the dangerous and sometimes tragic paths those things can lead one toward." —*Baltimore Sun*

"You start hearing things as you read *Ship Sooner*. You notice the ticking of the clock on the wall, the hisses and pings inside the radiator, the footsteps in the apartment upstairs. What would it be like, you wonder, to have superhuman hearing like thirteen-year-old Ship Sooner? . . . Mary Sullivan paints a vivid picture. . . . *Ship Sooner* stays with you long after you put it down, as you continue to be a little more tuned in to the everyday sounds around you." —*Chicago Tribune*

"A Persian miniature of a second novel . . . ethereal and lovely . . . Sullivan's singular achievement is to make us feel what it's like inside Ship's head, where foreground sound and background noise all exist on the same overwhelming plane. . . . There's not a scene or action that doesn't reverberate with what Ship hears. —*Washington Post Book World*

"In this honestly rendered tale, Mary Sullivan gives us a protagonist we can't help but love: Ship Sooner, who hears far more than she wants to, including the cry of her own heart, and ours. This is a lovely and redemptive novel." —Andre Dubus III, author of *The House of Sand and Fog*

"Silence speaks volumes in this coming-of-age tale . . . [a] gripping journey from self-consciousness to self-discovery. . . . Thanks to her clear and convincing first-person narrative, Sullivan succeeds in making Ship's super sensitivity believable and her quest for connection palpable . . . a meticulously prepared dish. [Readers will] close the book with a new ear attuned to the world." —*Boston Herald*

Tess Walsh

About the Author

MARY SULLIVAN, author of *Stay*, has received a Rona
Jaffe Foundation Award, a St. Botolph Foundation
Award, and a Massachusetts Cultural Council Grant
in Fiction. She lives in Cambridge, Massachusetts,
with her husband and their two daughters.

SHIP
SOONER

ALSO BY MARY SULLIVAN

Stay

SHIP
SOONER

MARY SULLIVAN

Perennial

An Imprint of HarperCollins*Publishers*

A hardcover edition of this book was published in 2004 by William Mor-
row, an imprint of HarperCollins Publishers.

HarperCollins books may be purchased for educational, business, or sales
promotional use. For information please write: Special Markets Department, HarperCollins Publishers Inc., 10 East 53rd Street, New York, NY
10022.

FIRST PERENNIAL EDITION PUBLISHED 2005.

Designed by Nicola Ferguson

The Library of Congress has catalogued the hardcover edition as follows:
Sullivan, Mary.
   Ship sooner : a novel / Mary Sullivan.—1st ed.
     p. cm.
   ISBN 0-06-056240-4
   1. Teenage girls—Fiction. 2. Gifted teenagers—Fiction.
3. Hearing—Fiction. I. Title.

PS3569.U348S55 2004
813'.6—dc21
                                                        2003054116

ISBN 0-06-056241-2 (pbk.)
05 06 07 08 09 ❖/RRD 10 9 8 7 6 5 4 3 2 1

For CW and Tess

As all the Heavens were a Bell,
And Being, but an Ear,
And I, and Silence, some strange Race
Wrecked, solitary, here
                              —*Emily Dickinson*

acknowledgments

Many thanks to the Rona Jaffe and St. Botolph's Foundations for their generous assistance; to Jennifer Pooley, the best editor a girl could ask for; to my agent, Lane Zachary, for her faith and support; to my family for bearing with me; and to Chris Walsh, my eye, my ear, my heart.

Part One

THE
WHOLE WORLD
WENT QUIET

One

THE BRANCHES OF THE giant pear tree shake their last leaves into the December air. The stems snap off the ends of the twigs and the leaves are swept up in the wind, flying every which way before they skid down the roof slope and brush over the top of the grass. They blow backward and forward, rattling toward the Dodds' house. Then they are gone.

As night comes, the pear tree looms across the sky like it is ruler of the dark, its branches like great arms around our house. Of course, there are no pears now. They always fall in July before they're fully ripe because they're as heavy as stones. Every summer my mother, Teresa, is sure someone is going to get hit on the head by one of them, so she has us hang signs around the yard: BEWARE OF FALLING PEARS.

I sit at the foot of the tree between its stumpy toes and listen to Teresa and Trudy in the kitchen getting ready for my birthday party. Brian and I keep track of people in Herringtown— that's what we do. Otherwise I wouldn't know a thing because no one says anything around me. Teresa says you have to be careful what you do because it all comes back to you. Brian says it's important that we know more about them than they know about us. He has the softest voice of anyone I know. Like after the snow falls and covers everything.

A lighter snaps open, then a flame licks up, followed by the burn, the hiss, and the singe of Trudy's cigarette. Trudy is Teresa's closest friend, but she looks old enough to be Teresa's mother. I wait for her to exhale. Every third or fourth time usually ends in a cough, which racks up from her insides and wheezes out dry and raspy. She spits up into a napkin and Teresa pats her on the back, saying, "When are you ever going to quit?"

"Probably the day I die."

"Don't say that."

"I'm sure heaven has a smoking area."

"You so sure you're going to heaven?"

The freezer door squeaks open then shut, ice cubes plop, pop, and crack in their whiskey sours, and Teresa pit-pats back across the floor. Unless we have visitors, she goes barefoot inside. She'd never go anywhere outside without her high heels. She says the only reason men look at her is because of her legs. It's true—men are always dragging their eyes up and down her high-heeled legs. When we tell her she could be in the movies, she says, "Sure, if I got the part of an old lady."

She has the greenest eyes in the world. There's a photo at Jimmy Joe's, the only restaurant in Herringtown, of Ava Gardner standing with Frank Sinatra about to cut their wedding cake, and people always point to it and say Teresa looks just like her. I think Teresa is prettier. Her eyes are greener and sparklier in the light. Why would our dad ever leave her? She and Trudy clink their drinks together. Gold streamers are strung across the kitchen ceiling and balloons are tied to the backs of our chairs. I put them there.

"Guess who called?" Teresa asks.

"Jack?"

"Why do I make the same mistake over and over again?"

"You're too impulsive, I always tell you that."

"Desperate, you mean."

Trudy laughs.

"I'm already thirty-six." Teresa sighs. "I feel like I missed so much."

"You always get like this this time of the year."

"I do?"

"Yes, you do. It's the holidays."

"I guess you're right." She chuckles. "You should see his hair. He has twice as much as when we started dating."

"He's probably using some kind of hair-grow shampoo."

"It's like a bouffant now."

Helen walks into the kitchen, snapping her gum between her teeth. Something goes *twang!* Probably Helen punching one of the balloons with her fist. There is a faint high whistle of helium leaking. By tonight the balloon will be smaller, darker, harder to pop.

"Please don't snap your gum, Helen," Teresa says.

"Hi, Helen," Trudy says. "Where's Ship?"

"Good question." Teresa opens the back door. "Ship!"

"Why do you bother going to the door?" Helen asks.

I wait a few minutes, then step out from behind the pear tree and go inside. Whenever I'm around, everyone whispers or moves away from me. I can't help it if I hear everything.

"There you are, my wild child," Teresa says. She started calling me this because I spent so much time in the woods. "We were waiting for you."

"You're not the only one who's late. Brian is, too," Helen says. Of all the cheerleaders in Herringtown, Helen is the prettiest. She has green eyes like Teresa, but they're like pieces of glass. Everyone always stares at Teresa and Helen.

"Happy birthday, Ship," Trudy says, stubbing out her cigarette. "Come on over here and let me give you a birthday kiss."

"Thanks," I say. She's so nice and warm when I slide into her arms, I want to stay there. The flab on her upper arms jiggles as she releases me.

"What have you been doing?" Helen asks. "Your hair is all over the place. At least you could comb it for your own birthday party."

Teresa always says, "Don't let her bother you. She's just going through a phase."

"How long is a phase?" I ask. "Fifteen years?"

"I'll be right back," I tell them, dashing for the bathroom. My hair is such a tangled-up mess, I can't even get the comb through it. I grab Helen's hair spray from the cabinet under the sink. She'd kill me if she knew. I hold my breath and start to spray a wide circle around my head when I realize it's Lysol. What's the matter with me?

"Here he comes," Teresa calls. There are only two houses at the dead end of Hawthorn Street, ours and the Dodds', separated by a patch of woods. They must have been built by the same person because they're exactly alike, except ours is pale blue and the Dodds' is mustard yellow. There are also four empty lots, overgrown with brush and grass, where that builder might have planned to build four more houses just like ours, but never did.

"Finally," Helen mumbles.

"Looks like Mr. Dodd is with him." Then after a pause, she asks from outside the bathroom, "Ship, did you invite Mr. Dodd?"

"No."

"Well, he's here."

"Maybe he invited himself."

"How do you like that?"

At least the Lysol has done the trick, flattening my mop and shining it up some. I'm glad I'm not pretty like Helen and Teresa because it's plain too much work. As soon as Mr. Dodd walks in, I can smell his Old Spice.

Trudy says hello in her polite voice and Teresa says, "Make yourselves comfortable. How's Mrs. Dodd? Fine, I hope."

"Oh, she is," he says. He takes a deep whiff, claps his hands, and announces, "Sure smells good in here. I'm starving."

"You didn't have to bring beer. That was awfully nice of you," Teresa says, making a gesture to take the six-pack. Mr. Dodd keeps it at his side. His Old Spice drowns out the smell of the pizza, the birthday cake Teresa baked, and even the Lysol. Usually Mr. Dodd smells like the Gooey factory, where he works as a security guard—I think the chocolate has gotten right into his skin—but not tonight. If Herringtown is famous for anything, it's the Gooey Bar, chocolate and peanut butter over a crispy oatmeal and caramel nougat center.

We hadn't been in Herringtown a week when Trudy came over with a bag of Gooey Bars. She said we couldn't live here another day without trying one. According to Teresa, that was the first sweet I ever ate and I devoured the whole thing, including the wrapper, in seconds. After that, every Sunday after church, we marched over to Rexall Drug to buy a Gooey Bar. But the first Gooey Bar I remember tasting was right after I got my ear caps, which I've been wearing since I was six. With my caps on, I could taste each separate flavor, without the trace of metal I was used to tasting when I ate. All week I'd smell them being made at the factory and wait for Sunday to come.

When Brian said he wanted to work at the Gooey factory, Mr. Dodd said, "Oh, no, you won't. I'm doing it for your uncle, but my son isn't going to work on any factory line. Leave that for those Herringtown kids who'll never leave this town. Understand?"

"Yes, sir," Brian said. "But I thought he got you the job?"

Mrs. Dodd's brother owns the Gooey factory. In the lobby of the factory inside a glass case, there is a picture of him holding up a Gooey Bar. He looks like Mrs. Dodd, except he's smiling and I've never seen her smile, and his nose is red and bulbous. His bow tie is gold, the same color as the print on the Gooey Bar wrapper. Even though he's named after him, Brian has met his uncle only twice. He's what Teresa calls filthy rich. He lives in a mansion on the shore farther north.

Brian pulls on the pocket of his green suit jacket. There is a tear between the lining and the wool in the right sleeve where he hides Gooey Bars.

Trudy whistles to Brian. "Hey there, handsome."

"What are you trying to do, make us look bad?" Teresa asks him.

"I had to," he mumbles. I stare at his polished black shoes like two boats on our kitchen floor. Brian is already half a head taller than his father. I am the same height as Mr. Dodd, which is exactly five feet, six and a half inches. Brian's face glows pink as if it has just been scrubbed with a scouring pad, and his hair is slicked back behind his ears, making them stick out more than usual. Sometimes, like now, he blushes and pulls on the end of one of them.

"Guess I'll have a beer." Mr. Dodd sets the six-pack on the dinner table. He shifts his legs and slips one hand into his pocket and scratches. Coins clink.

"Sure you don't want a whiskey sour?" Teresa asks him. She slides an extra plate on the table along with one of the special wine goblets, made of thin red glass on a long red stem.

"Oh, no, I don't drink the hard stuff."

"What about you, Brian? A whiskey sour?" Teresa winks at Mr. Dodd.

"I guess I'll have one," Trudy says. "Just to be sociable." Her doctor said that she has to cut down on drinking, smoking, and eating or she'll have a heart attack, but she keeps right on as if he never said anything. There is a layer of fat over her eyelids like a clump of foundation. When she blinks, I hear a tiny fleshy sucking sound.

Mr. Dodd twists a Budweiser from the plastic ring, pulls off the tab with a snap, and leaves the other five beers on the table.

"You look like you're going to a funeral or something," I whisper to Brian. His heart goes *thump thump shhh*.

"No whispering, Ship," Teresa says. "Not even on your birthday."

"How old are you again?" Mr. Dodd asks. "Maybe this year we'll go sailing, huh, Ship?"

This has been his joke since the day they moved in two and a half years ago. People who know me call me Ship, the name Helen gave me when I was one and a half. We were in the bathtub together when Teresa stepped out of the bathroom to answer the phone. When she came back, Helen was holding my head up out of the water while the rest of me floundered and splashed. "Ship. You're a ship," Helen said. From then on, she called me Ship, and so did everyone else. People who don't know me call me Sheila, my real name.

"Thirteen," I answer, "same as Brian."

"Just a few years younger than me." He gulps his beer. "Oh, I forgot to tell you, President Carter called me this morning and said your birthday was canceled." He puts his hand over his chest and laughs.

When we're all seated at the table, Trudy says, "Did you know Ship was born in the back of a Cadillac?" She glances at Mr. Dodd. Everyone else knows. Teresa tells this story every year.

"She hasn't combed her hair since either," Helen mutters.

"They should have called you Car instead of Ship." Mr. Dodd laughs.

"Tell him what happened," Brian says. "Do you want to know, Dad?"

"Sure, why not?"

"We were living in Waterfalls, Rhode Island then. I was

driving to my husband's job site to tell him today was the day.
The Caddy skidded out on a patch of ice and we got stuck on a
back road. We were there for twelve hours before anyone found
us." She pauses, straightening her back, then says, "I delivered
her myself. Luckily there was a newspaper and some water in
the back of the car. It was ten at night before the police finally
found us."

"Well, Ship was born in a car." Mr. Dodd opens his mouth.
After a minute he says, "It's good she didn't die."

Teresa and Trudy look at each other. "Yes," Teresa says, "it's
good."

"I was there, too," Helen says.

"That's right, Helen was there, too."

"Now look, thirteen," Trudy says. "I can't even remember
being thirteen. Who does?"

Helen sighs and says, "Teresa finally let me get my ears
pierced."

"Well, it wasn't as fun as you thought, was it?" Teresa says.

Helen tosses her long blond hair over her shoulder.

"I can't even remember my *last* birthday." Mr. Dodd turns to
Brian. "Tell them about Mossy."

"Everyone knows I got a shotgun," Brian says. It was just
last summer. That day was the only time I was inside his house.

"That's right," Mr. Dodd says, wiping the back of his hand
across his mouth, then folding in a second piece of pizza. "This
pizza is damn good."

"I hate guns," Trudy says.

"Me, too," Teresa agrees. "They're too dangerous."

"That's right." Trudy nods. "No need for them either."

Mr. Dodd chuckles.

"When I was thirteen," Teresa says, "my mother gave me my first pair of stockings."

"I don't think you've taken them off since," Trudy says.

Mr. Dodd looks down at her legs as if to see whether she still has them on or not. "What's your brand?"

"These are regular old Hanes."

"For twenty-one years I sold Tippy Toes panty hose. I did all right, but if I could have brought you along to model, I bet I would have done a lot better." His eyes flit up and down her legs.

"What percent would I have gotten?"

"Twenty?"

"I wouldn't have taken any less than forty."

"How'd you get into the business?" Trudy asks.

"Family."

"Why'd you get out?" Teresa asks.

Mr. Dodd shrugs. "We had to move."

"Why?" Trudy asks.

His jaw starts working, going to the right and then to the left. "Mrs. Dodd needs the sea air."

"Oh," Trudy and Teresa say.

In the center of the table, where Teresa has set a bowl of gold Christmas bulbs, I see our faces reflected long and skinny, then fat and wide. All of us are there inside the bowl on the center of the table. The pear tree scratches the side of the house to remind us it is there. I lean closer. In the distorted image on the bulb, even Trudy is skinny. Teresa's mouth is like a big slice of melon. Helen's face is squeezed up next to Brian's and I can't see Mr. Dodd. He cracks another can of Budweiser.

"Oh, well, it looks like I got a little extra cheese on this one," Trudy says as she takes a piece of pizza, dragging half the cheese from the next piece. "How's cheerleading going, honey?"

Helen was the only tenth grader to make varsity. I went to all the home games, not because I wanted to either. "Do I have to go?" I asked Teresa.

"Don't you want to support Helen?"

"No."

"Ship," Teresa said as if she were surprised. "Well, you're going whether you like it or not."

The band, the announcer, the clapping—all of it was so loud, we had to stand at the end line so my ears wouldn't break. We could still see Helen, but if you ask me, it's a big waste of time going to all that trouble to jump up and down for a football team. I have to admit, I did try on her baby blue sweater with an H on it and the short pleated skirt—only for a second, though; I didn't want her to see me. It was sort of pretty, but I felt like an idiot. I'd much rather wear jeans and a T-shirt.

Brian went to the games with us, too, and it was then that I first noticed him looking at Helen the way he's looking at her now. Everyone looks at Helen that way, I tell myself, but why does Brian have to? I have one best friend in the world and that's Brian. People always think Brian and I are brother and sister. When they ask Teresa, she says, "Practically."

"Cheerleading?" Helen says now. "Don't ask me."

"Why not?" Trudy asks.

"Because"—Helen pauses—"I quit."

"What?" Teresa blinks. She shuts her eyes. Her bottom teeth rub against her top teeth. She opens her eyes. "What'd you say?"

"I said, I quit."

Teresa's mouth snaps shut. Trudy's hand holding her pizza halfway to her mouth freezes. Mr. Dodd gulps his beer. Brian finally looks at me.

"When?" Teresa asks. "Why? Why didn't you tell us?"

"I did. I just told you," she says. She scrapes the cheese off the top of the crust and pushes it to the side of her plate.

"Helen," Teresa says.

"What? I didn't want to do it anymore."

"I'm surprised you didn't say anything before this. I'm surprised you didn't let us know."

"Well, it's not like you tell us much," Helen says, leaning forward, squinting at her.

Teresa stiffens. We know what's coming.

"We don't even know where he is," Helen says, her voice rising.

She sticks her chin in the air like she did the other night when she was talking to us in French. Even though Helen was mad at Teresa, as soon as she went out, Helen tried on her black night dresses, highest heels, lamb's wool sweaters, scarves, and makeup—mascara, eye shadow, eyeliner, lipstick—the works. With her chin in the air, she strutted around the living room where Brian and I were watching *Charlie's Angels,* swinging her hips all over the place. Propping her elbow on her hip, she started speaking French, telling me and Brian something, like to get her a drink, I think. We didn't.

Teresa says, "That's enough, Helen."

"I'll say," says Trudy.

I hear it coming like the air leaking out of my birthday balloon. Mr. Dodd leans in his chair, then reaches out for the last piece of pizza as if nothing has happened. A smell like boiled cabbage rises up around the table.

Teresa says the best sign that a meal is good is that there is nothing left. I'm still hungry, so I ask Helen if she's going to eat the cheese piled on her plate. She pushes the plate toward me and I eat the whole greasy lump. She has hardly said a word to me since I heard her telling her friends that she saw our dad over the weekend. Later she said to me, "Remind me never to say anything in front of you again. You should learn to close your ears."

I can't help it if I hear everything.

"I want to spend more time on my singing," Helen announces.

"Your singing?"

"Yes."

"What do you mean?"

"I want to be a singer," she says like we should all know this.

"Oh," Teresa says, "you do have a good voice."

Helen is always singing along to the radio, and I've seen her in front of the mirror holding a pen like a microphone. But a *singer*?

"Owen says I can sing."

I hear her singing along to Carly Simon, and I remember feeling like the whole world was pressing between my ears.

"Who's Owen?" Mr. Dodd asks.

No one answers him. Owen Hart's family owns half of Herringtown. The first time he came over to pick up Helen, he came inside and did two things Teresa said were unforgivable. First he sat on the counter where Teresa makes her pies. Then he didn't have anything when Teresa offered him something to eat.

"He's too damn full of himself," Teresa announced as soon as they left.

Trudy shook her head. "Did you see Helen? I've never seen her like that before."

"He didn't want any pie."

"Well, he can get it free at Jimmy Joe's whenever he wants."

"Still," Teresa said.

I don't like him either. Last summer we were on our way home from the Gooey factory when Owen pulled up in his father's silver BMW. "Aren't you Helen's sister? The one who can hear everything?"

At first I thought he had an English accent, but when I asked Teresa later, she told me he got it at private school. "That's what you call *affectation*," she said. "From being rich." She and Trudy laughed.

Owen leaned toward the open passenger window.

I shrugged.

"Want a ride home?"

"No, thanks."

Brian elbowed me.

Owen's dark hair was slick with gel and he wore black Ray-Bans. His shirt was unbuttoned so I could see the dark hairs at the top of his pale chest. He pressed his foot on the gas. "Sure you don't want a ride?"

I nodded.

"Okay, tell Helen I said hi."

As soon as he drove off, Brian groaned. "I've never been in a BMW."

"I like how he assumes we know who *he* is."

"Well, we do."

"Still," I said.

"Let's hear you sing something," Mr. Dodd says to Helen. "Know this one? 'My bonnie lies over the ocean, my bonnie lies over the sea'?"

"No," Helen replies, "I don't know that one."

There is a pause now—silence for them, but not for me. The kitchen faucet drips, the overhead light hums, Trudy pulls on the cigarette she's not supposed to be smoking, Helen rubs her hands together, Mr. Dodd swallows a burp, the heat sifts through the walls, Teresa grinds her teeth, in the cabinet a pan settles into another pan, Brian's heart beats. I listen to the thump-thumping beneath his green jacket until it's all I hear. That's what I do when the noise crowds my head. *Thump thump shhh*.

I was four when Teresa decided to test my hearing. She stood in different places of the house, each time further away from me, and spoke in her regular talking voice. "Ship, I'm next to the bathtub. It looks like it needs a good scrub. Can you hear me? Here I come!" I told her what she said and she said, "I knew it. You do hear everything!" The second time I told her what she said, she shook her head and held me to her. The third time, she said from the garage, "What am I going to do with you, Ship?"

She took me to Dr. Gould, who told Teresa that I had exceptional hearing, which is why I have to wear ear caps. A maroon headpiece connected to two black foam pads, the caps fit exactly over my ears like the headset I wore at his office. He said I could hear sounds only dogs could hear. Helen said to Teresa, "I think something happened to her brain when she landed on her head that time."

"Don't be silly, she was born like that," Teresa answered.

"Like what? Weird?"

"That's enough, Helen. She was born with exceptional hearing, that's what Dr. Gould said."

When I was two, Helen was on one side of the wooden horse swing set in our yard, pulling and pumping, and I was on the other. I couldn't hold on. I flew. But I could hear everything before that happened. And after.

The first sound I remember was a hissing like steam coming out of the radiator. The second sound was the rocking of my cradle, squeaking as it went back and forth. The third sound was Teresa whispering that we had to go now. And the next sound I remember was a pear hitting with such a thud on the roof that I thought the sky was going to fall down on us.

Teresa asks, "What's everyone so quiet for?"

No one answers her.

"Listen to me," Mr. Dodd bursts out. "As soon as he's in office, Reagan's going to get those hostages released, just you wait and see. Carter hasn't been able to do anything."

"How do you know?" Trudy asks.

"I just know. He's going to change this country."

"That's what I'm afraid of," Trudy says.

"He's going to turn it around, you'll see."

"Like I said, that's what I'm afraid of."

Teresa tries to hold in a laugh, but it comes out her nose. "Guess I'll go get the cake ready."

"I'll help you," Trudy tells her.

Teresa starts clearing the dirty plates, then stops and says, "Helen, can you clear, please?"

Brian starts to get up, but Teresa puts her hand on his shoulder. "You and Ship stay there. You're the guest and Ship's the birthday girl."

Helen sighs and rises quickly, sending her fork clattering to the floor. As she reaches down to pick it up, the front of her blouse falls open. They're huge, almost like Mrs. Hayes's, whose are bigger than anyone's in Herringtown. I thought they had become as big as they were going to get, but they're definitely bigger. I wonder if Teresa knows Helen isn't wearing a bra. Brian's mouth opens, and so does Mr. Dodd's, whose eyes don't budge from Helen's chest, even when he brings his Budweiser to his mouth and drinks. She doesn't seem to notice or care. She doesn't even look at us. Her Sassoon jeans are so tight, we can see the square outline of a folded piece of paper in her back left pocket as she walks to the kitchen.

I said to Helen once, "Think your blue jeans are tight enough?"

She said, "They're not blue, they're indigo."

Mr. Dodd takes a deep breath and leans back in his chair, his eyes glued to the open door leading to the kitchen where Teresa and Trudy are scraping dishes, opening and closing the refrigerator, and laughing. Trudy's laugh is low and raspy like her cough. "I ate too much. Look at me," she says. "I'm bursting out of my pants."

"Stop," Teresa says.

She's always saying how fat she is. She just looks like Trudy to me.

Brian pulls at his earlobes.

"You have a nice house, nice house." Mr. Dodd pauses and turns to me. "Very, very nice."

There's something in Mr. Dodd's voice that I don't like. When he talks, everything gushes out; then he stops and repeats what he just said as if his tongue is stuck. He's not thinking about our house. "What's so great about it?" I ask.

His eyes flit around the room. "That's a very pretty piece." He points to the dark mahogany cabinet with a glass door, in which Teresa has arranged her best dishes, including sterling silver baby spoons, crystal salt and pepper shakers, an antique tea set, a vase hand-painted with white irises, and most important, her photos. Almost everything in here came from her grandparents. These things are all I know about my relatives.

In an oval gold frame, there is a photo of Teresa's mother in a floppy hat, standing beside her husband. Teresa's father, a cigarette in his mouth, looks up at his wife, laughing. Teresa says they did everything young—married young, had children young, and died young. In a simple wood frame, the picture of Mum and Pop shows them at the ocean, wearing white bathing caps and dark suits, with ten-year-old Teresa laughing between them. The photo of her brother, Peter, was taken when he was small enough to fit in the kitchen sink. Four-year-old Teresa stands on a chair with a washcloth in her hand and soapy bubbles covering her bare chest.

Teresa was six when her parents died in a car crash, and her brother was three. She thinks soon after she was born her mother had a premonition of some sort, because she wrote up a will stating that Teresa's grandparents were to be Teresa's guardians should anything happen. Her mother and father died before they thought to name a guardian for Peter. Because it was too much for Teresa's grandparents to take them both, Peter went to live with his uncle in upstate New York. From then on, Teresa and Peter saw each other just once a year in the summer.

Because Peter now lives in Japan with his wife, who is Japanese, they visit only every three years. Peter's wife wears long skirts that rustle like tissue paper when she walks, and when she talks it's like she's taking soft, sharp breaths. If our school had a Japanese class, I'd take it. Instead I'm taking Spanish, because all those nasal sounds you have to make in French rub the insides of my ears.

Everyone is in that cabinet except for my father. His first name is Charles, but everyone called him Mack. I guess they still do. I just call him Dad. He left when I was two and Helen was four. I mean, he just got up and left one day and never came back. We don't know why. We know that Teresa met Mack when she was in high school. He was older and lived in Waterfalls, Rhode Island. We never got past the usual questions, which went something like this. I'd ask, "Why did they call him Mack?"

"They just did."

"Did you call him Mack?"

She'd nod.

"Did he look like me?" Helen would ask.

"Yes," Teresa would say. "And like Ship."

"How could he look like both of us when we don't even look alike?" she'd protest. "Why don't you have any photos of him?"

Teresa would shrug. "He didn't like his picture taken."

"There must be one."

"If there was, it's lost now."

"What was he like?"

"Handsome." At that point she'd usually look away or out the window. "And quiet. He did construction."

"What'd he build?"

"Everything."

"Tell us something else. A story."

"Not now." That's what she'd always say, "Not now. Later."

"When?"

"Someday."

That's how it used to end when we started asking about him, but not anymore. Lately Helen says, "It's not fair, we have a right to know who our father is. Everyone else has one." Teresa doesn't say anything.

Helen's always saying that she was his favorite. "That's why he left me the blanket and that's why he called me his Pineapple Princess."

"Helen," Teresa says, "your father didn't have a favorite. You were both his best girls."

"How could he have two *best* girls?"

When we were little, Helen and I used to go everywhere together. When she was only four, she'd pick me up and carry me, half her size, and we'd collect shiny things like pennies, bits of glass, stones, scraps of metal, buttons, and beer caps. We'd spread them out in a sunny spot, then put them into jars. Sometimes we'd glue them into a glob and give it to Teresa. We did everything together.

I stare into the Christmas candle, wondering what happened to Helen. On either side of the cabinet a gold Christmas candle lights up a window. It's my job to plug in and unplug all the candles in the windows every night, except tonight. The rule is, I don't have to do one drop of work on my birthday.

Helen steps through the door with an armful of plates and a fistful of forks. Trudy follows, flicking off the light, and Teresa parades in behind her with my cake, candles crackling on top. "Happy birthday," she begins to sing and everyone joins in, with Mr. Dodd's voice booming over everyone else's. Teresa sets my cake down. "Go ahead, make a wish and blow out the candles."

I wish there was a photo of my father in the cabinet. I want to know what he looks like. I stare at my sparkling cake while the wax sizzles from the candles into the frosting. I wish every day was my birthday and I wish I didn't have Helen for a sister and I wish Brian wouldn't look at her anymore and I wish Mr. Dodd would stop being so loud about everything. *I wish, I wish, I wish*. They are all breathing around me, huddling closer. Outside, a raccoon or skunk scratches through the milk cartons, cereal boxes, candy wrappers, egg cartons, soup cans, and whatever else it can find.

"Help her blow them out, Brian," Mr. Dodd says.

They are all too close. I wish they knew what it was to hear all this. Sometimes it's too much. It never stops, not even when I'm sleeping. My head keeps filling up. I wish I was normal. I wish we had a father like everyone else. I wish I could hear Brian's heart beating. I wish he'd always be close enough for me to hear his heart beating.

Helen's hair drops over her shoulders as she leans over me, blowing a little so the candles flicker and drip onto the white frosting with green letters that say, "Happy Birthday, Ship!" I spread my arms around my cake to guard it.

"What are you waiting for?" Helen hisses. "Your next birthday?"

The candles sparkle. Everyone looks on. I have to make the

right wish. Mr. Dodd eggs Brian on. "Give her a little help, don't be shy."

"Make . . . a . . . wish," Helen says. I hover closer to the cake.

You're supposed to wish *while* you blow out the candles. But I know from last year and the years before that as soon as I start to try to blow, I forget the wish. One flame flutters and dips with a gentle pop, almost going out. As I lean closer, narrowing my wish down, there is a crackling spark, then a sudden burst of yellow light, and the whole room flares into oranges and reds. Flames explode around Helen and Teresa, and it seems like our whole family is on fire. I am burning up! I yelp, a high, piercing bark. Helen's mouth freezes open, screaming. In that second, she stares at me like she always does, like I'm an idiot. I realize she's not on fire, only I am—or my head is. At the same time, Brian goes to whip off his jacket, but his arms get caught in the sleeves. It sounds like my head is cooking in a frying pan.

"Put it out!" someone yells—Trudy, I think. She snatches a napkin from the table and waves it in the air. Mr. Dodd throws the rest of his Budweiser in desperate jerks, and more flames lick up around me. Teresa whips her apron from where it hangs at her waist, pushes me back down in my chair, and wraps the apron around my head. The flames are out. The stink of burnt plastic and smoke overpowers even Mr. Dodd's Old Spice. Teresa slowly peeks around to look at my face, dripping with beer. Her breath streams out of her mouth in relief, then she breathes in through her nose. My ear caps slip around my neck. Everyone waits for Teresa to lift the apron still tied around her waist. Her heart is beating as fast as mine. She massages my head through the apron.

"Are you all right, Ship?" Trudy asks.

"Yes," I say. *Now* I bet Brian's looking at me.

"What the heck happened?" Mr. Dodd asks.

"I don't know, her whole head just caught on fire."

"How?"

"That was pretty cool," Brian says. "I was going to put it out with my coat, but I couldn't get it off."

"What'd it look like?"

"Like fireworks or something."

Teresa laughs. I laugh, too. "One, two, three!" She lifts the apron. "Phew, you can't even tell." She holds up a clump of my stinking hair. "Look at that, just a few singed ends. Trudy will give you a trim and then you'll be like new." Trudy cut my hair once before when I had gum stuck in it. Otherwise, I've let it grow.

"Beer's supposed to be good for your hair," Helen says, pinching her nose. "How'd it happen anyway? Did you use my hair spray or something?"

"No."

"Sure. I told you to ASK." She barks that last word at me. That's what she does if she really wants to get me.

"Luckily that's all that happened," Teresa says, wiping down the bench beside me. "Helen, open the windows in the living room, please."

"I'm glad you're all right." Trudy rubs the back of my head. "Come on, let's go wash it out."

I glance back at Brian, who smiles at me. His eyes follow me out of the room.

With her palm on the back of my neck, Trudy guides me

into the bathroom to the sink. She takes off my ear caps, then bends over me, running the water through my hair, massaging my scalp. I'm supposed to take off my ear caps only when I have to get my head wet. When I do, I still hear the faint *ssssss* I used to hear all the time, like a tire losing air. Trudy's fingers work Teresa's conditioner through the tangle of hair, swishing, combing out the knots, washing out the beer. I wish it were that easy to smooth out everything.

Or maybe it's me. Maybe if I were normal, Teresa and Helen would be, too. Maybe our dad wouldn't have left. Instead, something like this is always happening. Through the water pouring over my head like Silver River, I hear them in the living room.

"We better eat the cake before the beer seeps in," Teresa says gently.

Mr. Dodd says, "It must be a sign."

"Of what?" Helen asks.

"Of something, I don't know what." I can hear him chewing. "It's good, isn't it, Bri? I like it with the beer."

"Yeah, it's really good, Teresa."

"Oh, it's the easiest cake in the world to make," Teresa says. "I could make it with my eyes closed. I bet your mother makes one that's just as good."

"She doesn't cook much," Brian says.

"Sure she does," Mr. Dodd looks hurt. "But not cakes and things."

"Oh, like what?"

"Spaghetti and pancakes and stuff," Brian tells her.

"I bet you're a good help around the house." Without waiting for him to answer, Teresa turns to Mr. Dodd and says, "I

don't know what I'd do without Brian helping me take my pies
to Jimmy Joe's."

"You know I'm only doing it so I can steal your recipes,"
Brian says.

Teresa laughs.

Trudy combs through my hair, pulling it straight down to
my waist, then just like that, she snips a good four inches off all
around. Snip, snip, snip. It's like being in Hair Camp. That's
how Teresa met Trudy—getting her hair done at Hair Camp
when we first moved to Herringtown. On busy Saturdays, I
sweep for Trudy. On those days, Trudy washes and conditions
my hair, then puts it into a ponytail. Helen used to sweep when
she wanted to be a hairdresser, but she stopped when she started
dating Owen. Now she wants to be a singer.

Some of the hair around my face is burned right up to my
chin. "I'll layer it a bit in the front," Trudy says, careful not to
cut too close to my ears. "There, that should do it. Let me look
at you. Wow. You look like a movie star. I'll just give it a quick
dry."

Holding the blow-dryer an arm's reach from my head, she
feathers my hair with her fingers spread like a comb. Then she
cups the hair on either side of my face, fluffing it up. "Wait until
they see this. Come on, let's go back and have some cake."

I slip my ear caps back on, and just like the first time, everything settles around me. The day they arrived special delivery
in the mail, it was warm and we were eating lunch outside. As
soon as I put them on, the whole world went soft. The hissing
stopped, and for the first time I heard nothing—the perfect
sound of nothing at all. I thought I was falling like I do some-

times in dreams and grabbed the sides of my head until I saw Helen and Teresa sitting beside me eating their lunch. Then the wind crinkled the bubbly wrapping in the box my ear caps came in, and I heard that and only that one thing.

I touched my fingers to the caps, and I felt like someone else. Even my tomato sandwich tasted different—like tomatoes, mayonnaise, and Teresa's oatmeal bread with none of that metal flavor I was used to. Their voices weren't sharp anymore either. And Helen's hair stopped shining the brightest gold so I could look at her without my head hurting. She was scowling at me then like she is right now.

"Oh, Ship, your hair looks fantastic. Isn't that something?" Teresa says. "It's so glamorous." She holds a glossy white box with a gold ribbon.

"You look older," Brian says, staring at me. Heat rushes to the top of my head. He pops the rest of his cake into his mouth, then stuffs his hands deep into the pockets of the green coat.

"It's very nice. Nice," Mr. Dodd says, tossing back the last of his beer. He turns to Trudy. "Maybe I will have a little taste of one of your famous whiskey sours."

"All right, sure." Trudy laughs. "Just to be sociable, Joe?"

"You are lovely, lovely ladies," he says. His watery eyes fall on Helen. "We haven't been in a room with so many pretty girls in a long time, have we, Brian?"

"No, sir." He blushes.

Joe-Dodd, I say to myself, rolling the words around. *Joe-Dodd, Joe-Dodd, Joe-Dodd*. I can't help laughing.

They all turn to me. "Ship," Teresa says. "What's so funny?"

"Nothing," I say.

Trudy pats Mr. Dodd's shoulder as she hands him a whiskey sour. I hope she doesn't start bawling like she usually does at the end of parties.

"I have a present for Ship. And Helen has something, too, don't you, Helen?" Teresa says, placing the box in front of me.

"What?" Helen asks.

"Do you feel all right?" Teresa asks, reaching for Helen's forehead.

"I'm fine." Helen ducks her head.

They turn to watch me, opening my present. This morning I unwrapped two pairs of the straightest blue jeans ever made, and this afternoon Brian gave me a Moody Blues record, *Seventh Sojourn*. He has all the Moody Blues. Now I open the white box with a gold ribbon. Underneath the tissue paper I find a pink sweater with tiny pearl buttons. I think it must be the most delicate, silkiest thing I have ever touched. I press it to my face.

Trudy whistles. "Hold it up."

"It feels like Rabbit," I say. Brian's rabbit, Rabbit.

"Let me feel." Brian touches the sleeve of the sweater.

"Is it cashmere?" Helen turns to us.

"One hundred percent pure cashmere." I read the tag.

"Well, I didn't think it was ninety-nine percent."

"Helen," Teresa says, "I want to talk to you when we're done with Ship's party."

Everyone stares at the sweater for a while, then Mr. Dodd announces, "Well, Bri, let's call it a night."

"Wait one minute," Teresa tells them. "I'll wrap up a piece of cake for your mother."

When she comes back, Teresa hands Brian the cake, then

presses her hands against his cheeks and kisses him good night. There is a faint wet suction of her lips leaving his skin. "See you tomorrow, kiddo," she says.

After they leave, Trudy goes, and then Helen and Teresa drive to the end of the driveway to sit inside our Lincoln Continental and talk with the windows rolled up. I go to my room, take off my beer-soaked T-shirt, and slip on my new pink sweater. In the mirror, I don't even look like myself. I try to make the sound Teresa made when she kissed Brian by puckering my lips and slowly letting them part. I wish I could do that. My lips brushing the air, I look at myself from every angle. The sweater is too pink, too pretty. I fold it up and put it back into the box. Then I sit on my bed beside the window with a view of the pear tree and the woods that separate our house from the Dodds'.

My room is almost bare because too much clutter gives me a headache. When I was little, I'd bring home leaves, pine cones, stones, feathers, bird's eggs, bugs, frogs, and whatever else I found. I'd keep them in my closet, my drawers, or under my bed. Then Teresa found a broken-winged sparrow in my sock drawer. "Ship, a bird can't live in here," she said. "It looks like the woods in here. Why don't you just move your bed out there. What on earth is this?" She lugged a big gray rock with a copper ring around it from underneath my bureau.

After a few minutes I said, "Okay."

"Okay what?"

"Okay, I'll move my bed out there."

"You will do no such thing, young lady. You're seven years old. You're not going to live in the woods." After that she made me put all my collections in shoe boxes in the closet.

The raccoon or skunk is still scavenging through the trash outside of the kitchen. I lift my window and stare into the dark night, breathing in the cold air, the chimney smoke, and the smell of pine. A faint hum rises from deep in the woods. At first I think it's Mr. Dodd's TV or the radio inside the Continental, but it's a steady, hollow humming. It must be Brian sending me a signal from his window. I try to stare through the branches of the pear tree to Brian's window, but whatever is calling seems to be coming from farther away, from far, far away.

I remember that day, when Brian Dodd moved next door. I thought the pears were falling early. I thought it was a pear storm and the pears were smacking onto the roof, then thumping down, bouncing and knocking until they hit the ground. But I followed the sound next door where Brian was hitting stones from his house into the woods. A streak of sun followed his hand as he picked up the stones from the pile by his bare feet, tossed them in the air, and swung. I couldn't stop watching and waiting for another stone to shake our house down. Every few swings, he'd hold the stick behind his head at the base of his neck, his arms hanging over it. His dark blond hair was messy and thick, but not enough to cover his ears, which stuck out like saucers on either side of his head. When the next stone ripped into the trunk of the pear tree, I went marching right over to him. "What do you think you're doing?"

The sun made the sweat drops lining his forehead sharp and white. His blue-gray eyes flickered at me, but he didn't answer. The smell of blooming lilacs reminded me of the Willgohs baby who I used to hold while Mrs. Willgohs was doing her housework.

"Well?"

He half smiled, then shrugged, tapping his stick on the ground. "Why's that tree so big, anyway?" His voice was like velvet in my ears. Almost everyone talks too loud. Something warm spread across my chest.

"I don't know, it just keeps growing."

"What is it?"

"A pear tree. The pears are so big they could kill you."

"Pears can't kill you." He laughed. His face was pale, with light freckles across his cheeks, and he had a wide mouth. I don't remember if it was on account of his ears, but I couldn't stop staring at him.

"Yes, they can. My mother's best friend was almost killed by one." That was a lie. Guilt wedged up into my throat. If Trudy died, it would be my fault. "Where did you move from?"

"Rhode Island."

"I used to live there."

He tilted his head to the side, smirking. "What are those?" He pointed to my ear caps.

I flinched and lifted the caps off my ears, thinking he was going to rip them off and toss them around. From inside his house, a man's voice said, "I said we'll see him every Sunday for now. That's all there is to it."

"Is that your father?"

"Who?"

I pointed. "In there."

"I guess. Why?"

"I just heard him talking."

Cocking his head to the side, Brian stepped back into the shadows of a juniper tree. "What do you mean," he asked slowly, "you heard him talking?"

I shrugged.

"What's he saying?"

I lifted my ear caps again. "'That Patrick McCarthy I was telling you about from the Gooey factory is selling rabbits. What do you say we get one for Brian? Where is he, anyway?'" I turned to Brian.

"How do you do that?" Brian asked, his eyes circling me. "What are those things?"

"They're ear caps, and I hear more without them."

"Cool. I wish I could do that."

"You do?"

The back door of his house slammed. "That's my dad." Brian looked down and kicked the pile of stones. A thin white scar arced beneath his right earlobe along the base of his jaw.

"There you are," Mr. Dodd said. Small and scruffy, he looked like a gnome, but he spoke fast and loud. His words seemed to slip out of his mouth.

"Hi, Dad." Brian tugged on his right earlobe.

"Who do we have here?"

"Ship. I live right there."

"Ship? What kind of name is that?" He frowned, looking me up and down.

"No kind. It's my name." I frowned back at him.

"She heard you talking to Ma."

"What are you talking about, son?"

"We were standing right here and she heard you talking inside."

"That's a crock of shit." He frowned and turned to me. "How could you hear what I said? Is it because of those things on your ears?"

"No."

"Come on, now." He scratched his chin. "All right, what'd I say, then?"

"That you were going to get a rabbit from Patrick McCarthy."

Mr. Dodd shook his head. "Were you spying, son?"

"No, sir."

"You know how I feel about that."

"I swear, Dad, she heard you inside the house."

He picked something off his grayish-white T-shirt. "All right, let's try it again if you're so sure." He sighed and walked back to the house, holding his head up, muttering.

Kicking the stones at Brian's feet, I took my ear caps off and held them in my hand. I was nervous. He was testing me.

In a quiet, scratchy voice, Mr. Dodd said, "This is the stupidest thing I ever heard. There's no way on earth she can hear me all the way over here. And if he has anything to do with this, I'll knock his head in."

"Did you hear him?" Brian asked.

"Yeah," I said.

Mr. Dodd snorted and coughed all the way back to us. "All right?"

I told him, adding the snorting and coughing.

"Is this some kind of trick?" He felt up and down his sides, as if we had bugged him. Then he searched Brian, patting up and down the inside and outside of his legs and arms. He looked at me like he wasn't sure what to make of me. "Come on, Brian. We have to go now." He yanked Brian by the arm. Brian was beaming.

The inside of my chest burst. I breathed in the lilacs. They started toward their house. I slid my ear caps back on, then picked up Brian's stick and smacked a stone into the woods. Blackbirds rose and fluttered off into the blue of the sky. Brian turned, and when he saw me he smiled, and I knew I would see him tomorrow and the next day and the day after that.

Two

LATER THAT NIGHT, A car sputters up our driveway. Someone takes his time getting out of the car, then knocks on
the back door. "Hi, Teresa."

"It's late, Jack."

"Listen, all I want is my jacket back."

"What jacket?"

"My leather jacket, Teresa." He sighs. "The one I said you
could wear the night you forgot yours."

"Oh, on the 'Ladies for Free' night," Teresa says. "How
could I forget?"

"Why don't you just give me the jacket and I'll leave."

"I have to look for it."

"I can wait."

"It's already ten. The girls are in bed."

Helen's door creaks open and she tiptoes to the top of the
stairs. We both listened the last time he came over, too—not
that Helen talks to me about it. But I heard her listening.

"How have you been?" His voice goes soft. "I've missed
you."

"Please, Jack. Don't start."

"You look great." His sentences sound like questions.

"You do, too. Your hair has grown."

"Thanks."

A quick, choking laugh escapes Helen. A month ago, Jack was practically bald.

"I've been using a new shampoo."

"Really?"

"Yeah, I feel like a new person."

"I'm glad for you."

There is a pause. Then Teresa says, "Come on, Jack, it's really over. I have a busy day tomorrow. I have a ton of orders this week."

"Pies? You're thinking about your damn pies right now?"

"I'm always thinking about pies." Teresa laughs. "Good night, Jack. I'll let you know if I find your jacket."

"I bet you will. Why don't you mail it to me?"

Something thuds, then slides across the floor. Teresa bolts the door.

The last time he was over, I heard Jack groan. Then Teresa told him, "I'm still married, Jack."

"You have a funny way of showing it."

"Stop," she said. "The girls will hear you. I told you about Ship."

Jack groaned again, more pathetic this time, a higher pitch. I remember thinking, What if our dad came home and found Jack?

When it was quiet again, Teresa said, "You need to go now."

"What? Now?"

"I have to get up early and I don't want the girls to see you here."

"I'll get up when you do."

"No, I don't think so."

"Teresa."

"Please, Jack."

Jack slipped out of the house and, without starting his car, backed down the driveway over the long snaky skid marks another boyfriend before Jack had left. I wanted to ask Helen if she heard what I had and what she thought Jack was doing to Teresa, but she was already back in her room. Downstairs, Teresa sighed, then laughed to herself. I lay in bed, wondering if our dad left because I could hear everything.

The morning after I heard Jack groan twice, Teresa asked us how we slept. We stared up at her as she cracked pecans between her fingers, letting them fall into a white bowl. "I had a friend over," she said carefully. "I hope we didn't wake you."

"A friend?" Helen asked.

"Well, Jack."

"I slept fine." Helen spooned a section of grapefruit into her mouth.

"How about you, Ship?" Teresa asked.

Before I finished chewing my bacon, I blurted out, "Why did you let him come over?"

"Oh," Teresa said, catching her breath. "He won't be coming over anymore, don't worry." She turned to check the pies in the oven, then said she had to go put on her face.

That afternoon, I stopped by Hair Camp to talk to Trudy. I can tell her anything. Along the wall lined with mirrors is a long, low bureau with drawers full of brushes, combs, hair clips, barrettes, and curling irons. Holes have been cut into the top of the dark wood to fit the heads of blow-dryers. On either end of the stations, there are two big jars of lavender bath salts. I always leave the lids on because their sweet smell makes me sick.

Trudy's station has photos of me, Helen, and Teresa taped to the lower right-hand corner of her mirror. There is also a photo of her pushing her father in a wheelchair in front of his nursing home on Long Island, but the picture is stuck behind the plastic container of combs soaking in sterilized water and she has cut out her body so her head appears to float over him and the wheelchair. Even though he doesn't recognize her anymore, she visits him once a month.

Behind the hair dryers on the other side of the salon, magazine pictures are pasted on the wall, showing all sorts of haircuts someone could choose from. Dorothy Hamill is up there and Farrah Fawcett. There is even one of Bo Derek with all her braids. Trudy says she is going to put a photo of me with my new haircut up there, too.

No ladies were gossiping under the hair dryers that afternoon, just Trudy blow-drying a woman's long hair with a round brush. The dark puffs seemed to grow higher and higher. Then Trudy hair-sprayed the giant mound and held up a mirror so the woman could see the back of her head where all the feathered hair met in a line like duck feathers.

"It's gorgeous," the woman said. "I love it. I wish you could do my hair every day."

Swiveling the mirror to the right, then the left, Trudy tucked a piece of loose hair under, then stepped back. Light spread across her face as she admired the woman's hair. She looked the happiest when she had gotten a cut just right. She turned to me. "Hi, Ship. How's school?"

"Fine."

"Anything the matter?"

I didn't answer. The woman with the new hairdo was staring at my ear caps. I was glad I didn't have to sweep up her hair.

Carol, the owner of Hair Camp, shuffled past the black basins for washing hair and sang out, "My God, you're a new person!"

"I almost didn't recognize myself!" The woman laughed. "Isn't it amazing?"

Carol stood behind the register.

"I'm going outside for a quickie," Trudy said. She took my hand.

While she blew long lines of smoke, I blew cold gray air. "Jack came over last night," I told her.

"I bet he won't be coming over anymore."

"What was he doing?" I asked. "Why would Teresa want him to come over? I thought—"

"He won't be back, don't worry." Trudy's cigarette crackled as she inhaled. "She does the best she can, Ship."

"Why doesn't she ever talk about our dad?"

"Shhh. She will, don't worry." She slid her arm over the shoulders of my bomber jacket. It's way too big, but the dark brown leather is worn in just right with scratches and rub marks and there is fur on the inside and around the collar. "At least you got his jacket."

"That's true," I said. I found it hanging on the back of the kitchen chair one morning and put it on. Teresa was happy because I usually went without a coat. "You can have it. Go ahead. He said he never wore the damn thing. I only took it because I was cold," she told me. "It suits you."

Teresa pulled up in front of Jimmy Joe's then. "Thanks," I told Trudy, kissing her good-bye. I looked back as soon as I stepped inside Jimmy Joe's to see Trudy drop her cigarette on an icy patch on the sidewalk. It hissed and went out.

THERE ARE only ten days before Christmas, which means Teresa is baking as many pies as she can. Bags of sugar and flour, blocks of butter, eggshells, pans of melted chocolate, and bowls of whipped cream are spread over the kitchen counters along with pecan, blueberry, lemon meringue, and Boston cream pies. Teresa makes five dollars a pie, and on average sells about forty to fifty pies each week, plus rolls and bread and special orders. Next week she has triple the orders, but there have been weeks when she has baked only ten or fifteen pies, like during the hot spells of summer. When the pies are cool, Brian and I help her take them to Jimmy Joe's.

Trudy scrapes her chair on the linoleum floor, then holds the edge of the table to stand. "I've got to get back. I left Mrs. Ryan under." Under the dryer, she means. Her voice is like pouring gravel in my ears. The more she and Teresa drink, the louder they get. Luckily they have only one whiskey sour. "I put your photo on the wall," Trudy says about the Polaroid she took of me with my new haircut. She takes my chin in her hand and kisses me on the mouth with her smoky, whiskey breath. "Right beside Farrah Fawcett. You look better than she does."

Who would think a haircut would make such a difference? But I guess since I've had the same hair my whole life and since it's usually a huge mess, people would notice when it changed. Even Helen's friend Margie, who's a lot nicer when Helen isn't there, said she liked my haircut when I passed her in our driveway on my way to the bus stop while she was waiting for Helen.

"We're going soon, too," Teresa says. She stops separating egg yolks from whites to pat across the kitchen floor and check her pies in the oven. Her feet leave flour prints on the black squares of the checkered linoleum.

Brian decides to play the Moody Blues record he gave me for my birthday. When I go into the living room, he's holding the framed photo of Helen in her cheerleading uniform about two inches from his face. She's shaking her pom-poms and doing a scissors kick so you can see her belly button and her blue underthings. She smiles like she is waiting for someone to come along and take a picture of her. Her blond hair is white in the sunlight. My chest tightens. I want to tell him to put the photo down, that Helen hardly notices him, that he should look at me standing right beside him. Here.

There used to be a photo of me, Mr. Dodd, and Brian at Silver River after we went fishing. I'm holding a largemouth bass, the first fish I ever caught. *Remember that day?* I want to ask him now. *Remember when I fell in?* My feet reached for the ground and my hands for the sky as the swirling current carried me away. Then just like that, I was standing in a clear blue pool next to Brian. He had jumped in after me.

But Teresa tucked that photo away somewhere after Mr. Dodd called us a broken family. I heard him talking to Brian, telling him that he shouldn't be spending all his time with me, since I came from a broken family. Every few minutes his voice would go down a level and he'd add, "She's probably listening right now." He'd peer out the window, searching for me. Then he'd forget and start up again, talking louder than anyone else in Herringtown. Sometimes I'd hear him say, "Did you say anything to anyone, Brian?"

"No."

Then his feet shuffled around the floor and I peeked in to see his arms combing the air, swishing this way and that. "You're not just saying that, are you?"

"No, sir."

"Stay on your feet, son. Don't duck." His fists swung through the air. "What do you say you do on Sunday afternoons?"

"Go to church in Osprey and then for a drive."

"Watch your chin. On your toes. If I find out otherwise, you know what's going to happen, don't you? Watch it—a quick right. This guy's still got it—yes, he does. They don't call Dodd a dangerous man in the ring for nothing. Come on, hit me back, go ahead. Go ahead and watch it on the left."

This would go on for a while. Then Brian would say, "Okay, Dad, can we stop now?"

When I asked Brian if his dad was afraid I'd spy on him, he said, "He doesn't give a rat's ass." I never told Brian what I heard and he never told me what he wasn't supposed to say about whatever they did on Sundays, but I was going to find out somehow. How could he have something he couldn't tell me?

When I told Teresa Mr. Dodd called us a broken family, she was furious. "What right does he have!" she screamed to Trudy on the phone. She pulled the telephone cord all the way into the basement where the washer and dryer were running, but I could hear her like she was right beside me. "He should talk," she said. "His wife never even leaves their damn house. He probably has her chained to the bed. No one in the entire town has met her except for Ship once, and he's talking about us? Besides, that never stopped him from coming over and eating every single thing I put on the table," she yelled. That was true.

"He doesn't know one thing about it either. *Broken!* Do we seem like a broken family to you? I mean, technically I'm still married. I'm a married woman raising two girls by myself, and I'm not ashamed of that." She didn't say anything to me. She just put the photo of me and the Dodds away somewhere.

With the photo of Helen in his hands, Brian sings, " 'I'm just a singer in a rock—' "

"What are you doing?" I ask him.

"Nothing." He blushes as he sets the picture of Helen back down beside the stereo. His voice is deeper than when I first met him, but still easy on my ears.

"I'll put on my face and then we can go," Teresa calls. The water runs from her bathroom sink through the pipes, streaming and groaning through the house. She unscrews the lid on a jar. Then she is sliding her closet door open, fishing through her high heels. Brian keeps singing along with the Moody Blues, his heart pounding like the thumping of the bass.

Brian and I slide Teresa's pies into crates, separating them with flats, and carry them out to the Continental to take up to Jimmy Joe's. On the way to town, we pass Jack in his souped-up Mercedes. His hand hanging out the window, he flicks his ash but doesn't wave as he cruises by. If he had looked, he would have seen that I'm wearing the bomber jacket he came looking for last night. "I know I shouldn't have kept his jacket, but that was the best thing about him. I'll never date another salesman for as long as I live," Teresa says.

The wind pressing against the windows fills my ears like a wall of noise. A voice on a passing radio reports "major delays on I-93 South due to an overturned car at the Milton exit." I try not to let anything else slip through. I hold my hands over my caps and concentrate on the thick blur of sound. As we get closer to town, trees bend over the road like hooded old men. Their shadows darken into the creeping vines and tangle of overgrown blackberry bushes. Father Hannah whistles as he strolls alongside the scrubby trees, his black willowy robes puffing up, clinging to his legs. We all wave to him and he gives us the peace sign back.

Trudy can hardly talk when Father Hannah is around. When Teresa teases her, Trudy says, "Please, stop! I know it's awful, but you know if there were any decent men around here, it'd be different." The last time Trudy cut his hair, I was dusting the jars of lavender and listening to Trudy suck in her breath, then slowly let it out. She breathed faster and harder until she had to take another deep breath, up through her nose, closing her eyes and puckering her lips before she let it out.

Father Hannah's short brown hair needs only the littlest trim, but Trudy spends forever cutting all the gray edges. Afterward, she has me collect the tiny trimmings in a bag for her to take home. "Don't you dare tell a soul about this, Ship. Except Teresa." She makes me swear. Later she drops shampoo off at the rectory for him.

The bell clangs four o'clock at the town hall. At this time every afternoon, all of Main Street smells of Jimmy Joe's roasted garlic and fresh bread. At exactly 5:10 P.M., the train will come wailing into town, stopping at the station on the other end of Main Street. Ever since I stood too close to the train track while the train was passing, I brace myself before it comes thundering through town at noon, 5:10, then 10:30 P.M.

A yellow Volkswagen sputters by, coughing exhaust. Its bumper stickers read: "JESUS LOVES YOU. EVERYONE ELSE THINKS YOU'RE AN ASSHOLE," and "VOTE FOR CARTER! REAGAN BELONGS IN HOLLYWOOD." Knowing full well she voted for Jimmy Carter, Mr. Dodd told Teresa, "I like Massachusetts, except for all the damn liberals. This state is packed with them."

"Here we are," Teresa says, pulling up in front of Jimmy Joe's. She got the Continental, which is big enough to hold about a hundred pies, for cheap because the front end is all smashed in. Laura knocks on the window of Jimmy Joe's, then waves with the cloth she's using to wipe down the checked, waxed tablecloths. She works lunch and dinner Tuesday through Sunday all year including holidays. On Mondays, Jimmy Joe's is closed. After I wave back, she turns and walks toward the bar, her left foot scraping the floor.

It happened at the pear tree when Laura was a girl. She was swinging too fast on a wooden board that hung from one of the higher branches, and fell off. For days she was afraid to tell anyone, which is why her leg healed all wrong. That's the reason Laura won't ever come to visit us. Sometimes at night I dream the pears are falling like hailstones—thousands of them pounding down, and no matter how much I cover my head, they land right on me, splitting my skull open. On these nights I think about what happened to Laura, but she won't say anything. "It was a long time ago, Ship honey," she tells me. "Don't you worry about it."

There are about a dozen regulars today. Laura wipes the sweat beaded over her lip with her sleeve, then starts fishing through her huge leather purse. She smooths the sides of her sky-blue waitressing dress with the scoop neck and pearly white buttons down the front. Her fingers flutter over her pockets as she sings along with Frank Sinatra, "Let me love you . . ." She pops the top off a beer bottle. "It's for sure—" She slides the bottle across the bar and leans toward the customer. "All the way, all the way." I bet Laura knows more about everyone in Herringtown than anyone else, even Father Hannah, who listens to confessions every Saturday afternoon from two to four. Everyone, that is, except maybe me and Brian. But we don't know anything about Laura. When she's not working at Jimmy Joe's, she's in the room above it, where she lives. Once someone scratched, "Call Laura—Get SOME To Go!" on the bathroom wall at Jimmy Joe's. There is only one bathroom. Brian saw it, too, and said, "So?"

"So?"

He shrugged. "I thought that's what waitresses did."

"Laura?"

"Why not?"

As we carry a crate of today's pies—blueberry, apple, Boston cream, chocolate meringue, lemon chiffon—to the dessert case at the front of the bar by the register, Teresa calls out a big hello and everyone says hello back. The men's eyes follow Teresa as she walks around the bar.

"I'll settle up." Mr. Grant, our bus driver, pulls out his wallet. When we come in with the last of the pies, he is shuffling out. He pretends not to see us.

"See you tomorrow, Andy," someone calls.

Laura slides two root beers and a whiskey sour across the bar to us. She whistles. "Great haircut." She pushes my hair behind my ear. "You beauty."

"Very funny," I say.

"C'mon, Ship." She opens the cash register with a *ching!* and snaps up two dollar bills. In the other hand, she holds a Virginia Slim. "Ship and Brian, do me a favor—don't ever start smoking."

"That's right, Ship, did you hear that?" Teresa agrees.

"No," I say, rolling my eyes. She knows I hear everything. "Did she say something?"

"All right, all right," Teresa says.

Laura exhales.

"I guess that's all for now. I'll call you in the morning to go over the rest of the Christmas orders," Teresa says.

"Good. Are you all set, then?"

"I think so. This week flew by." She puts her hand on the side of her head as if to hold it on.

"I know it."

Deeper than—pop—*blue sea*, Frank sings. All they play at Jimmy Joe's is Frank Sinatra. I hear every time the tape pops or skips. *That's*—pop—*how*—pop—*deep*—*it's real*. In the afternoon when Laura is getting ready for the dinner shift she plays her favorite love songs.

I tell Teresa that Brian and I are going to walk home. "Dinner's at six," she says. "Be careful and don't be late."

I check to see if Trudy is smoking a cigarette outside Hair Camp. Joy Tucker is carrying her baby down the sidewalk. I elbow Brian. "Joy Fucker," Brian whispers. We haven't seen her since she dropped out of high school last year. She slides into the passenger seat of a gray Ford Escort and the driver pulls away. Even after the car has vanished, I keep seeing the head of her baby like a lightbulb bobbing over the back of her shoulder.

"Wanna go to the bridge?" Brian looks down to the end of Main Street.

"Yeah." We bolt past Chuck's Hardware, Rexall Drug, and the Mobil across the street. Past the Missing Sock, where the washers and dryers shake the sidewalk with their spinning and whirring, and past the town hall. Typewriters go clack, clack, and a sharp voice says, "He can't talk to you right now, sir. I'm sorry." A toilet flushes, phones ring, car engines squeak, a tire scrapes against the curb, and Frank Sinatra keeps on singing. Our feet smack the pavement as we pass Herringtown Savings Bank and Hart Insurance, echoing the loudest when we pass the library, which is so quiet I can hear pages turning. I know what I have to do—filter through all these sounds—but sometimes I think my head's going to snap before I get to the sound I want to hear. *Thump thump shhh*. We don't stop until we get to the walking bridge that no one uses anymore.

The space underneath the bridge where water used to run is filled in with tall grass and weeds, trash and broken glass. There is a hole in the cement wall that goes straight through to the inside of the earth. When I put my ear on the wall, it sounds like an ocean is pressing against the other side.

Brian's breaths are clouds of white air. "You go first."

I close my eyes and put my right thumb inside the hole and turn my hand around once, turning my fingers like a pinwheel. I forget about everything except making a wish. A tight band forms around my chest, making it hard to breathe. I can't think of anything I want except for things to stay exactly like this. When I open my eyes, there is a sliver of light around the hole, then it goes dark.

"What'd you wish for?"

Tiny reflections of me flicker across the blue-gray of his eyes. "I can't tell."

He puts his thumb into the hole and turns, pinching his mouth shut and squinting hard. The train whistle blows as it gets closer to town. Brian turns his hand, making his wish. His lips are moving, but I hear only one word: *Dad*.

"Dad?" I ask him. "What about your dad?"

"Nothing," he says, opening his eyes. "Nothing about my dad. Who gives a rat's ass anyway?"

I know if he told me whatever he's not supposed to and his dad found out, he'd get killed. But I wouldn't ever let Mr. Dodd know I know. The thing is, I tell Brian just about everything, so I don't know why he has secrets from me.

"Come on, the train," he says, grabbing my arm.

While the train is stopped in Herringtown center, we cut up over the bridge through the woods to the tracks. I balance on a single rail, keeping my eyes on the line of steel. When the train starts again, the vibration travels through the railing up into my feet. It rings like the tuning fork our music teacher uses. The whistle blows, closer this time.

Brian bends over and howls. Then he pulls me by the hand

off the rail and we run down the center of the tracks, over the wooden flats and sharp rocks. His skin on my skin is like electricity shooting through me. The train chugs and screeches, sending a knife pain through my head. The whistle blasts and metal scrapes against metal. His fingers press tight around mine, and in that second I catch Brian's eyes and I think we are the same—he and I are two halves.

We've run in front of the train before, but it seems louder, closer this time, almost right on us. The top of my head is going to come off. Before it explodes, Brian steers me hard to the right. We are flying. We can do anything.

Then we're falling, rolling onto the hard ground over the brush and grass. Something covers my head and everything goes still. The train passes, and I start breathing again, rocking slowly back and forth. My head is tucked against Brian's chest. He is spooning me, pressing his hands against my ears. A *thump thump shhh* moves through my swollen head—my heart beating or Brian's. My skin goes warm, then cold and prickly. I push my caps back on to stop the ringing. I want to stay this close to him, but I'm afraid of the heat pushing through my body. His right ear wiggles, making the softest clicking. He slowly unfolds himself, then rolls back on his elbow, away from me.

He starts laughing. "You okay?"

"Think so. My head hurts."

"What was it like? Hearing that?" His voice is even softer now that the train has passed. A leaf partly frozen in the dirt flutters loose.

"This screeching getting louder and louder, crowding my head, and I can't stop it. My head gets so full, I can't do anything." I don't tell him that when he's here it's different because I try to listen for the thump of his heart through all the noise. I say, "It's like a bomb went off inside my head."

"I feel like that sometimes."

"You do?"

"Yeah. My head gets all crowded like that. Like right now I can hear my dad telling me what to do, Ma crying, Mr. Doherty asking me why I didn't do my homework, Susie Long saying something about my ears. I can even hear stuff from before we moved here, like things Johnny said . . ." He looks down.

"That's what it's like," I say. "Who's Johnny?"

"Don't you just wish it would stop?"

"Who's Johnny?" He mentioned Johnny before, but he didn't want to talk about him.

"No one."

"No one?"

"No," he whispers. His fingers scrape along the top layer of dirt. Then he sits up. "Should we go to Mr. Gray's now?"

I started spying on Mr. Gray on Brian's dare. Even though it's the same thing every time, it's not like there's a lot else to do in this town. He picked Mr. Gray because he is the only man in Herringtown with a ponytail. Worse, it's gray and scraggly. You'd never know from looking at him, but Mr. Gray used to be a gym teacher in Farmington.

After we brush the dirt and leaves off ourselves, we cut back over the track to Main Street and walk half a block to Persimmon Street. I think besides Dr. Gould, Brian's the only one who likes that I hear everything. Sometimes I think I hear everything for him.

The day we went to Dr. Gould's, Helen wanted to stay in the car, but Teresa made her come in. While Teresa and Helen sat in the chairs by the window, Dr. Gould took my temperature and my blood pressure. Buzzing fluorescent lights shone down on his bald head, the porcelain basin, and his silver instruments. He whapped my knees with a rubber hammer. The thump wasn't that loud, but the room was so quiet I jumped back, bringing my knees to my chest.

"We don't have to check reflexes now," he said. He made humming noises as he flashed a light down my throat, into my eyes, nose, and ears.

"Very good," he said. "Now let's check your heart."

I could hear the beating of my heart vibrating through the cold silver piece he pressed to my chest, my back, and the base of my neck. My heart beat all over the room. Teresa smiled up from her *Good Housekeeping*. Helen looked out the window. The sunlight made a square on the floor between them.

After he checked my eyes, he said, "Good. Now I'm going to put some earphones on you. Raise your right hand when you hear a sound in your right ear, and raise your left hand if you hear a sound in your left ear. All right?"

The first sound I heard was so piercing, I whipped off the earphones and threw them to the ground.

"Ship, that's not nice," Teresa said.

"Nice?" Helen giggled. "Ship, nice?"

I closed my eyes and rocked gently in place.

"Let's try again," Dr. Gould said.

The sharp beeping rang through the inside of my ears and I had to lift the foamy ear caps about six inches from my head to continue. It went on for a long time, lifting the earphones, raising one hand, then the other until the beeps didn't hurt anymore and I could simply raise my hand. I forgot all about Dr. Gould, Teresa, and Helen until Dr. Gould said, "Oh, thank you, Sheila. This is very interesting. Excuse me while I make a few notes." He stared at me, then turned, smiling, to his paper. His face flushed and his eyes widened.

"She hears everything, doesn't she?" Teresa asked.

He removed his glasses and began chewing on one of the rubber-tipped ends. His eyes fixed on me, he explained. "At first I thought there was something wrong with her hearing, but as the tones lessened, she picked them right up. She hears exceptionally well. She can hear frequencies humans can't normally hear. Those, for example, only dogs can hear. I'm shocked, to tell you the truth. Shocked and delighted!" A quick laugh squeaked out of the corner of his mouth.

Teresa nodded.

"I knew there was something wrong with her," Helen blurted.

"That's enough, Helen. Why don't you wait in the car." She added, "Ship, you go, too. I want to talk to Dr. Gould alone."

After that Helen started screaming into my ears, or mouthing words as if she were talking out loud. When she was asked in English class to use the vocabulary word *anomaly*, she said, "My sister, Ship, is an anomaly." That's all I heard for weeks—that I was an anomaly. It got worse when Father Hannah announced in the church bulletin that I was "blessed." The *Herringtown Weekly* had a write-up about my exceptional hearing and a photo of me. Trudy said I was famous, but if that's what being famous means, I don't know why anyone would want to be. Mostly people looked at me funny and lowered their voices when they were around me. I heard them anyway.

Besides Dr. Gould, Brian's the only one who is really glad about my hearing, and that's because I tell him most everything I hear. Teresa says you're lucky if you have one best friend, so I guess I'm lucky. I think we're the only ones who know what Mr. Gray does in the afternoon in front of the mirror. The only ones who know Mrs. Hayes—wearing only a bra—rides her stationary bicycle and listens to her spiritual tape. The only ones who know Father Hannah was watching *The Godfather*, who know Trudy was talking on the phone with a psychic and Officer Robinson was yelling at his wife for eating too much. The point is to know more about everyone else than they'll ever know about us, but the truth is, most people are boring, at least in Herringtown, so we've crossed them off our list.

From the back of Mr. Gray's house, no other houses are visible, but we duck anyway as we cross his lawn, past the sandbox with sand pouring out its splintered sides and with a pink flamingo standing on one leg in the center. We step up on the cinder blocks we've set under the back window that looks into his bedroom.

Sometimes we have to wait up to an hour for something to happen. But not today. His back to us, he is already talking into the phone in front of his mirror. Every few minutes he draws spit up from the back of his throat like water being sucked down a drain. "Are his eyes closed yet?"

"Not yet, stay down."

"What's he saying?" Brian asks.

I slip my ear caps around my neck. " 'That's right,' " I repeat.
" 'Nice. I like that. What would you do to me?' " I stop when
Mr. Gray does.

" 'Yeah. I'd like that. I already am. Really hard. And then
what? Hot like your—' "

I whisper, " 'Yes, nice and tight.' "

I take a deep breath. " 'Perfect.' "

I want to be back at the railroad tracks with Brian.

Mr. Gray unbuckles his pants and lets them drop in a puddle
to the floor around his ankles. He holds his hand over the bulge
in his tight white underwear before he yanks these down and
spreads his legs as far as they will go. His feet get caught in the
leg holes. He spits into the palm of his free hand, grabs hold of
his thing as if it's going to escape, and starts jerking it up and
down. He seems grosser than usual. This is the last time.

"What's he saying now?" Brian lifts his head.

" 'Tiger. Not cougar. Just say tiger,' and he's moaning a lot."

When Mr. Gray steps out of his underpants, he's sticking
straight out.

"Should I time it?" Brian turns to his watch.

"Okay."

"More or less than a minute?"

"Less."

"One Gooey Bar."

"Okay," I say. I like betting with Brian, but I'm sick of Mr.
Gray.

"Go." Brian glances from his watch to Mr. Gray. The front
of his head is shiny where it is balding, but the back is the thin
gray ponytail, which bobs up and down as his hand jerks faster

and faster in slick slaps. I think he is holding his breath. His mouth opens and in the mirror becomes a dark hole. He leans back, his face to the ceiling, and drops the phone onto the bureau. It used to be funny. When I turn to Brian, he blushes. I can't look at him either. I wonder if Brian does this and if he thinks about Helen when he does. The idea makes me sick.

Mr. Gray's whole body goes taut; then a shudder runs through him. He screams a polite scream, and next thing a white glob splats on the mirror. Then a smaller glob on the floor. His face falls, and for a moment, he looks as if he is going to cry. I think *I'm* going to cry, too. A weight presses down on my shoulders, pushing me toward the ground. I slide my ear caps back on. "Done," I say.

"Fifty-three," Brian whispers. "Crap."

Mr. Gray picks up the telephone from where it dangles by the cord and places it on the receiver. He takes off his socks, and with one of them cleans the white mass trickling down the glass, then turns the sock inside out. He uses his other sock to wipe himself.

I take off running back toward Main Street and Brian follows me. I slow to a walk and say, "I don't want to go back there." I just want to be with Brian.

"Why not?"

"Well, why do we have to?"

"We don't have to."

"I thought you wanted to. He's just so gross," I blurt out.

Brian laughs.

Long shadows fall around us, making all of Herringtown small and cold. Brian doesn't say anything about stopping at

Mrs. Hayes's. Her TV hums as we cut across her yard. Some people say she has fake breasts because they're so big and as hard as rocks. I know because I bumped into one of them when we were waiting in line at Rexall Drug. The only other breasts I ever felt besides my own, which are too small to say anything about, were Teresa's, and hers were soft like pillows.

"Look," I say, waving my hand in front of him. In the meaty center of my palm is a thin cut smeared with blood. My heart beats faster and sweat lines my forehead.

"Cool." He holds me by the wrist. "Does it hurt?"

"No," I lie.

"I had fifty-two stitches after the accident," Brian says, letting go of my hand to finger his scar, which has turned blue in the cold. Running along his jawbone, the scar seems to separate half of his face from his body. "My dad called me Frankenstein."

"You always talk about the accident, but you never say what happened."

"You know, the car accident—when I split my chin open," he says softly.

"What else?"

"Nothing."

"Nothing?"

He tosses a rock into the trees.

Doesn't he know that I'd never tell his father?

"My mother broke both her legs."

"Is that why she never leaves your house except on Sundays?"

Brian stares at me.

The cars whoosh by on Main Street. I start counting them and get up to nineteen before he finally turns and says in a rush of breath, "It happened on Christmas Eve," and he takes off through the woods. Maybe that's why he got only three pairs of socks last year. I want to follow him to tell him I'm sorry for asking, but I don't.

Right after the Dodds moved here, I started hearing these cries at night and I knew they were Mrs. Dodd's. I thought it must have been because of the accident, but I didn't know how to ask him. What could I say, "Does your mother scream out in the middle of the night? Is it because of the car accident? What is the matter with her?" Some nights the cries are much louder than other nights. By now I've not only grown used to them, I've come to expect them just like I expect the train to blow through Herringtown three times a day.

I could try to find Brian at the Gooey factory, but it takes eleven minutes to walk from Jimmy Joe's to the factory, then thirteen more to get home. It takes fourteen minutes to walk home from Jimmy Joe's and I'm already late. The wind blows the Christmas lights strung around the lampposts on Main Street, swings them back and forth, turning the sky red, green, and white. Sinatra keeps singing and Trudy's laughing cuts through the steady whir of the hair dryers inside Hair Camp.

The door of Hoodie's Ice Cream Parlor rings as Officer Robinson steps out with a cup of steaming coffee. He tips his hat to me, then turns and slurps. When he pours the top of the coffee onto the street, a few drops splatter up onto his black shoe. He sits inside the cruiser, sipping his drink. The problem with listening in on some people is that I can never look them in the eye again. When I see Officer Robinson, all I see is him yelling at his wife for eating so much chocolate pie when she was supposed to be on a diet. Static crackles over his radio.

I start home, passing houses decorated with lights and wreaths, plastic snowmen and mangers. When I get as far as Harry's Bait and Tackle, I cut through the woods, where someone is splitting logs. *Chuck, chuck.* When I reach the clearing halfway home, a bright shadow crosses my path. Then something in the dark sky reaches down and takes hold of me. Bands of light sift through the trees. The wind sweeps past and birds swoop by. Heat creeps up my legs and my mouth goes dry. It's as if there is a thick sheet of glass between me and the rest of the world.

I smell the fur of a dog, feel his warmth running through me, hear his heart beating next to mine. I was in woods like these before. It was day and then it was night and the wind moving through the trees and the dog's breathing pricked my ears. Nothing else mattered. I remember it like remembering a dream. I have to tell Brian.

When the shadow goes, the branches of the pear tree soar out of the dark sky ahead, marking the distance between here and there.

Three

ON CHRISTMAS EVE MORNING, I wake early to the radio in the kitchen playing Christmas songs and Teresa rolling out pie dough. The wooden pin slaps the table as she pushes the dough out and flips it over, smacking it gently from one side to the other. She sets the dough in the pie tin and slices off the extra with a knife. Then her fork works around the pie shell, indenting it—*phht, phht, phht,* like a cat walking. It smells of coffee and pecan pie. Teresa has been working straight through the nights ever since Trudy had a heart attack exactly five days ago.

Except when she is baking, Teresa stays with Trudy. Today she is taking her home from the hospital. The doctor told Trudy she was lucky this time. Teresa keeps saying that Trudy's not going to die. "She just has to take care of herself. Doctors always make everything worse than it is," Teresa tells us.

When Teresa dropped me and Helen off to visit her at the hospital, Trudy had tubes going in and out of her and she was wearing one of those hospital gowns like a tent. Her hair was limp and matted to the sides of her head, and under the bright hospital lights, it was an awful bleached-out orange-yellow. I could hardly stand to look at her, but there was nothing else to do as she took turns laughing and crying and coughing. Even though she wasn't smoking, that cough was raspier than ever.

I didn't know what to say. I said, "You look skinny."

"That'll be the day." Trudy snorted. "But I already lost fifteen pounds." Nurses and doctors rustled by in a constant patter of footsteps and clinking of carts and trays and machines.

"No wonder, with the food they serve in here." Helen made a face. With her arms folded across her chest, she stayed a good three feet away from Trudy's bed as if she was going to catch something. From behind the tan curtain separating Trudy's bed from her roommate's came the voice of a game show announcer and the *ding!* of answers being revealed.

"You'll disappear," I said. The machine she was hooked up to ticked like a typewriter over the droning TV voices.

Trudy laughed, combing my hair with her fingers. "Look at your hair. You're the prettiest one on the Hair Camp wall, you know."

"Sure," I said, thinking she must be delirious from her medication. Helen grunted like she was thinking the same thing.

"It's true, Ship." Then her eyes filled with tears and she said, "Oh, I guess I won't need you to sweep on Saturday."

The crying, the rattling and ticking, the echo of footsteps in the hallway, doors opening and closing, and this endless hum— all of it reminded me of a fly buzzing, trying to get out through a closed window. I couldn't wait to leave and Helen couldn't either.

Coming out of the elevator, Helen asked, "Skinny?"

"She is skinny for Trudy."

"Trudy will never be skinny, okay?" She shook her head. "I'm never going back there."

"What if it happened to Teresa?" I asked her.

"Shut up."

On the way out, I caught my reflection in the glass door of the gift shop and wondered if Trudy was lying about my picture on the wall. If I'm so pretty, then why is Brian looking at Helen instead of me?

ONE AFTERNOON, when Teresa doesn't need me to go to Jimmy Joe's with her, I study myself in her makeup mirror lit with movie star lightbulbs. First I take my ear caps off; then I feather my hair back with my fingers like Trudy did, fluffing it up. I heat up Teresa's curling iron and curl my hair so it falls around my face and down my back in soft waves. We're not supposed to touch Teresa's makeup, but I roll her cherry lipstick over my lips—first the bottom, then the top. The dark red makes my skin pale enough to count the freckles spread across my nose. I cover them with globs of foundation, then rub red powder along my cheekbones like I've seen her do. When I brush on mascara, my eyelashes look fake.

I start to color my eyelids blue when the wind rattles the window, shaking the glass. Something like a high-pitched whistle or the far-off shriek of a seagull is calling out there. That band of shadow and light in the woods—what was it trying to tell me? What's out there?

I drop the eye shadow in the sink, leave the makeup and curling iron where they are, and run out of Teresa's dressing room to follow whatever it is. I race through the woods trying to find the call of the wind or an animal until sweat is pouring down my face. What is it? Walking in a circle, I push back my flattened hair. I wipe my face with the back of my hand, streak it red and black. I'll never be pretty like Teresa and Helen.

Something is the matter with Helen—I mean more than usual. When Teresa spends the night at Trudy's, Helen locks herself in her room, playing the radio as loud as she can, probably just so she can break my ears. The other night when I asked her to turn it down, she stared at me until I was sure she could see right through me. Her eyes are like the broken green glass under the bridge. Teresa insists Helen's going through a phase and that it'll happen to me when I'm Helen's age.

Every day Helen has a new question for Teresa. "About Dad," she starts, which is Teresa's cue. Yesterday Helen asked Teresa how he asked her to marry him.

"He just asked me," Teresa said.

"Did he get on his knees?"

"No." She laughs. "We were dancing at the White Horse. He said, 'Let's go to Las Vegas.' I said, 'For what?' And he said, 'To get married.'" Her voice drops to a whisper.

"That was it?"

She nods.

"Did Mum and Pop like him?"

"They didn't really know him."

"Did they go to the wedding?" Helen leans forward.

"No, they didn't go." She laughs again.

"Did they want you to marry Mack?"

She winces and draws back. "Not exactly. They thought I was too young. And they wanted me to go to college."

"What was the date?"

"Why do you want to know all this?" She looks hurt.

"Because he's my father," Helen says. "Why did he leave?"

"I don't know." Teresa rises. "It doesn't matter now."

"How could you not know? Did he just disappear?"

"That's enough," Teresa says, blasting the kitchen faucet. "Interview's over."

Another thing: Helen has been wearing the long blanket our dad gave her like a shawl around her shoulders—probably to remind me that he didn't leave me anything. Made of soft cotton, the blanket's covered with faded gold stars and bleached moons. I don't know how many times she has told me that he gave her this blanket and that he used to sing her the Pineapple Princess song. "He sang lots of songs to you, too, Ship," Teresa says.

"Like what?"

"Oh, lots of them."

Helen doesn't know that I have a few things that were his. About three years ago, I found a guitar pick stuck between the pages of Teresa's *American Heritage Dictionary*. I knew it was his from the way Teresa's mouth opened, then snapped shut, and from the way her eyes got watery when I showed it to her. I wish I asked her then if it was our father's.

Same thing when I found the ruby ring in her jewelry box a few months later. She was trying on outfits for a date that night when she saw me wearing her ring, holding my hand up to the light, spreading my fingers apart, then together. The only ring I've seen her wear is a plain gold band, her wedding ring. Teresa stopped in front of the mirror, half dressed.

"Why don't you ever wear this one?" I asked.

She said, "Please take that off now, Ship, and put it back in the box." Then she went into the bathroom and stayed there for a long time. I left the ring in the box, and the next time I checked, it was gone.

After that I decided to search the rest of the house. In Teresa's shoe box of odds and ends, I found two leather buttons like the tops of turtle shells, which looked way too big for anything Teresa would wear. Then on the back shelf of her closet, I found a black-and-white photo inside a handkerchief. It was of a boy, dressed as a cowboy, one hand on his hip and the other shooting a cap gun. He is in front of a fireplace hung with Christmas stockings. A white burst of light covers half the boy's face.

Brian didn't think much of the buttons, and when I showed him the photo, he said what I was thinking. "If it is him, why would she save this photo? You can't even tell what he looks like."

"Maybe it's the only one she has." We spent a long time staring at it, but didn't come up with any other answers, so I put it back on the shelf in her closet. Every once in a while when Teresa is out on a date, I take the picture down and study it again. I wonder if Trudy knows about it.

Next, in a box of old tools in the basement, I found a worn-out man's navy blue wool sweater splattered with yellow paint. I wondered if he painted our old house this color. When I asked Teresa what colors the rooms in our old house were, she laughed and said, "Gray. Plain old cement gray."

"The whole house?" I asked.

"It was a garage."

"A garage? The one on Cotton Street?"

"Yes. We lived there for four years to save money."

"Oh." I had thought about going to our old house plenty of times, but I had no idea it was a garage. There aren't any buses that go directly from Herringtown to Waterfalls. The closest station in Rhode Island is twelve miles from Water-falls, and by the time I got to Cotton Street and back, I would miss the return bus. And if I didn't find him, then I don't know where I'd stay. I could hitch with Brian to Waterfalls, but Teresa made us promise her we'd never ever hitch because there are too many creeps around.

The man I spoke to at Classy Cab said it would cost a hundred and ten dollars, not including the tip, for a cab ride from Herringtown to Waterfalls and back if there was no traffic. I have seventy-two dollars saved up now and Brian said he could chip in, so we think we should have enough to make the trip soon after Christmas. I tell Brian that even though my dad's not in information, I think he must live in Waterfalls because Teresa said he left everything he owned there, including his truck.

"Does he know where you live?" he asks.

"No," I say. "Or he would have come here."

IN THE early morning kitchen, the branches of the pear tree look like gray fuzz, barely visible through the steamed-up windows. Racks of chocolate drops, walnut squares, hermits, meringue kisses, macaroons, and butter cookies in the shapes of Christmas trees, wreaths, and bells cover the counters, and cardboard flats are piled on the kitchen floor. Date-nut, raisin, cranberry, and special Christmas bread and knotted sweet rolls are spread over the top of the refrigerator, on the cutting board over the sink, and on all the chair seats. Pie shells line the kitchen table. It doesn't feel like Christmas, though.

Dark strands of hair have fallen loose from Teresa's ponytail and her eyes are bruised and puffy. Even when she's gotten no sleep, she's the prettiest in the morning without makeup. She smiles and gives me an end piece of date-nut bread. It is warm and chewy. While she chops pecans, melts chocolate and butter, whips egg whites, I fold the cardboard flats into boxes. I want to ask her why we don't have a Christmas tree, but instead I say, "How's Trudy?"

"Pretty good. She'll be here for supper, you know. There'll be no talk of diets, either. She keeps talking about this new vegetable and fruit diet. You know she doesn't eat any more than I do. Doesn't seem fair." Teresa sighs. "She said the first thing she was going to do when she got out was have a cigarette. I told her I'd kill her if she did, but I think she'll take care of that herself." Teresa piles dishes in the sink. Upstairs, Helen crosses the floor, then the bathroom water runs. "Go ahead, you better go get ready or you'll miss the bus," Teresa tells me.

In my room, I slip on a pair of straight blue jeans and a T-shirt. I brush my hair a hundred times on each side, which I've been doing since I got my new haircut, then slide on my ear caps. Sometimes when I'm getting ready for school I remember what Teresa said right after I started first grade.

What happened was, two boys from Helen's class grabbed my ear caps during recess and started playing keep-away with them. Someone was trying them on and others were laughing and grabbing at them. I didn't want to wear them anyway. The wind was a shrill hum rising above the crickets buzzing. I walked past the jungle gym, across the soccer field, and into the woods, listening, not wanting to leave. There were no human voices. I wanted to stay back there all afternoon, but then a train came thundering by and I thought I was going to die. I rocked back and forth, grabbing the sides of my head until I couldn't bear it anymore and ran home.

My mouth watered as soon as I smelled the steaks they were cooking, but I couldn't let Teresa and Trudy see me here in the middle of the school day. Teresa was saying, "He wants to do all sorts of special testing. He's practically begging me. I told him absolutely no. All I want is for her to have a normal life and that's what she's going to have."

"You can't trust those doctors. He probably wants to write an article about her for a medical journal. 'Special testing,'" Trudy said. "I'd like to say a thing or two to him."

"Anyway, the ear caps are working out fine. I just want her to be happy. Normal."

"I know you do," Trudy said, chewing. "Steak's good."

"Is it cooked too much for you?"

"Perfect, nice and bloody."

That's when the school called to say that they had found my ear caps on the playground and that I had left the school property. When she got off the phone, Teresa cried, "What if something happens to her? She's only six. What if she doesn't come back?"

I lifted myself into the crook of the pear tree and started shimmying up.

"Don't worry, we'll find her. I'm sure she's close by, behind the school or at Jimmy Joe's or somewhere. Come on, I'll drive."

"And here I am talking about *normal*. Who am I kidding? Damn it, it's my fault. She needs a father."

"We've been through this before, Teresa. I'm sure Ship is fine. Believe me and stop worrying."

"What if she isn't?" Teresa's voice became high and wobbly. "It's all my fault."

"Stop blaming yourself for everything," Trudy said. "Come on, let's go."

The word *normal* kept ringing through my head. If we were normal, I thought, then we'd have a father and I wouldn't be climbing this giant pear tree. I climbed higher.

By the time Trudy and Teresa were out the kitchen door, I was about thirty feet up and climbing. Just as they were about to get inside Trudy's Dodge, I yelled down, "Here I am."

"Oh, Ship, there you are." A sob escaped Teresa's mouth. Her high heels went clickety-clack across the driveway and then she squinted up at me. "Ship Sooner, what on earth are you doing up there? That's dangerous. Come down this minute."

"No," I said.

"Why not?" Teresa asked. "You're not going to get in trouble. Please come down."

"Look how high up she is," Trudy squealed. There were tears in her eyes. "I can't watch. Ship, please come down. You're going to give me a heart attack."

I stopped.

"Ship, I don't want to call the fire department. Now, come on down. We'll have some ice cream. And I'll call the school and tell them you're here and everything's fine."

"I don't want to."

"Okay, you don't have to go to school tomorrow if you come down. We'll do something special, whatever you want. Now, please, come on."

I came down after she promised that I didn't have to go to school for the rest of the week. She told them I had the flu. Helen was sent home with my ear caps, and after that the teachers kept a close eye on me when I was out at recess.

Even now, I think that all Teresa wants is for me to be normal, but how am I supposed to be normal? No other mothers in Herringtown are married but don't have husbands, go on dates, and wear high heels everywhere. I arrange my hair to cover my ear caps.

WITH WET hair and shoes untied, Brian runs to catch the bus at the end of Hawthorn Street like he does almost every single day. Mr. Grant revs the engine and nods, the white ball of his Santa Claus hat bouncing with his nodding. Sometimes I smell alcohol on his breath—maybe whiskey, because he smells like Teresa and Trudy after they have their whiskey sours. Brian is gasping by the time he slumps down beside me. Wisps of his hair are frozen. When he finally catches his breath, he says, "Did you read that poem?"

"Which one?"

"You know, for English."

"I forgot. What was it about?"

"A bird or something. I didn't read it either."

"He shouldn't have given us homework on Christmas Eve. He'll probably give us a quiz, too."

"I did a snow dance last night, but it didn't work."

"It's supposed to start today."

"That figures."

Mr. Grant jams on his brakes, sending us flying forward. In

the front of the bus, a white box skids across the floor and breaks open, and bright-colored candies scatter in every direction. A girl, a first grader with blond pigtails, cries out, then stands in the aisle and starts picking up the candies. All I see is the back of her bobbing head and the red, green, and yellow candies sparkling in the sunlight.

"Sit down!" Mr. Grant yells, swiveling in his seat, his pom-pom whapping him on the cheek.

The girl totters down the aisle and reaches for the empty box, which has slid under the seat two rows up from us. An orange whizzes by me, smacking a boy on the shoulder. He stands and hurls the orange back. It hits a boy behind us on the head. "You're dead!" he screams.

Laughter ripples up from the back of the bus. "Hit him again!" someone yells. "Shut up, Johnson. You loser!"

They yell over Mr. Grant, who repeats, "Sit down on my bus!" The girl with the empty candy box seems to be running backward down the aisle. I can't keep track of anything. I press my ear caps to my ears.

"Are you all right?" Brian nudges me.

I nod. *Thump thump*—

Brian stands up, waves his arm, and yells, "Stop, everybody, stop!" He ends in a squeak.

They do—for a second they stop, turn to him, and stare. Then someone cracks up and soon the bus is rocking with laughter. Brian laughs a little, too. *Thump thump shhh.*

A football player in the back stands up and waves his arms around like Brian. "Get off the bus, Dodd!" Someone else smacks him on the back. "Way to go, Dodd."

Mr. Grant swerves the bus to the side of the road, pulls it to a shuddering stop. He rises halfway out of his seat and yells, "That's it! If you want to make noise on my bus, you can get off right here and walk to school." Just like that, it goes quiet again. "All right, then. That's better."

When the noise stops, it's as if it was never there at all. Brian shrugs, tugging on his ear. Cellophane crinkles as the little girl wraps the candies back up. My head is free again.

ENGLISH IS first period with Mr. Doherty, whose olive suit looks especially drab next to his red tie with green Christmas trees. I pretend to focus on the poem in front of me so he's not tempted to ask me any questions. I keep track of his shoes gliding over the classroom floor, up and down the rows of chairs with his hands behind his back like an ice skater. At the desks of certain girls, he stops to stare at their feet, his eyes moving slowly upward. Ever since I got my hair cut, he's been doing it to me, too.

Brian keeps his eyes close to the page. If Mr. Doherty calls on him, his face will turn the color of a beet. The ends of his ears are already red.

"'Hope is the thing with feathers—'" Mr. Doherty says, gliding away from me. "Who would like to read the poem? Anybody?

"No one?" He pauses. "All right then, I'll read it.

> *"Hope is the thing with feathers—*
> *That perches in the soul—*
> *And sings the tune without words—*
> *And never stops—at all—*

And sweetest—in the Gale—is heard
And sore must be the storm—
That could abash the little Bird
That kept so many warm—

I've heard it in the chillest land—
And on the strangest Sea—
Yet, never, in Extremity,
It asked a crumb—of Me."

" 'Hope is the thing with feathers—' What do you think that means? What is the author saying?"

No one says anything.

"Vicki? Did you read this poem last night?" When he talks to the girls in the class, his voice turns soft.

She nods. "Uh-huh."

"What do you think Emily Dickinson means?"

"I dunno. It's like a bird or something—hope."

"Okay, hope is like a bird. How so? Can you read the first stanza again, Vicki?"

" 'Hope is the thing with feathers that perches in the soul and sings the tune without words and never stops at all.' "

Mr. Doherty looks like he's going to laugh, but instead he says very seriously, "Why do you suppose Dickinson chose to use those long dashes? George?"

"They're like periods or something."

"Good, she's telling us to stop and take a breath."

"Why doesn't she just use periods, then?" George asks.

"Good question, George. We'll get to that. First, why don't you read the poem for us?"

He stops for a good three seconds at each dash, looking up at Mr. Doherty each time.

"Thank you, George."

"What do you like about this poem, Brian?"

"I never said I liked it," he says quietly.

Everyone laughs.

"All right, then. What *don't* you like about the poem, Brian?"

"Just kidding," he says. "I like that it perches in the soul."

"Be specific. What is a soul?"

"I don't know exactly. Something way down inside. Past your stomach." Someone laughs. Brian blushes. "You can't see it."

"Okay." Mr. Doherty lifts his eyebrows and slides around Brian. "So, what's going on there?"

"Hope is a bird, singing in the soul." He keeps his eyes on the page.

"Okay." Mr. Doherty raises his voice and his hands. "Why?"

"I don't know—because that's what it does."

"Yes, that's what it does. And why? Why does it?"

"So we have something...something...something—" His voice breaks. He looks at me. "And don't just hear the other stuff."

"Good. Class, the opposite of hope is despair, something Dickinson knew well." He looks around the classroom. "Yes, Stephanie, did you want to add something?"

"I don't think it's a real bird," Stephanie says.

"What do you mean?"

"Well, it's like a metaphor."

"Yes, remember similes and metaphors, class? The bird stands for something else." Mr. Doherty stops and skates over to me. "Is something funny, Ship?"

"No," I say. I try to stop smiling. The poem reminds me of being in the middle of all that racket on the bus this morning, waiting for the quiet to come.

"All right, why don't you tell us what you think the bird stands for, then?" Mr. Doherty stands over me.

"Well," I say, trying to figure out how to say it. "To me . . ." My face goes hot as everyone waits for me to answer. "To me, the bird is what makes everything better when the noise is too much."

Mr. Doherty takes off his glasses and puts the end that fits over his ear into his mouth. "Okay, go on. What is Dickinson saying?"

"The quiet, it always comes. Hope, I mean. Even when it feels like it's never going to and your head is going to explode."

Someone giggles.

Mr. Doherty spins around. He walks around me. "Good. Was there something else?"

"No."

Mr. Doherty frowns. "All right, class, let's take a look at the grammar of the poem." He glides off.

In Mrs. Garvey's classroom next door, the chalk scrapes against the chalkboard—stopping, dotting, underlining, grating—and the eraser brushes and claps.

THE THING about the cafeteria is that everyone is always chewing so loud. It's like they're doing it on purpose, like Helen does right in my ear. Sometimes my own chewing gives me a headache, especially when I eat apples or potato chips or ice cubes. Brian and I are at our usual table at the back near the door, two over from Helen's.

Helen carries her lunch tray to sit with the other cheerleaders, some of them juniors and seniors. Most of them have feathered hair and wear blue eye shadow. Helen drinks her Tab, which she brings wrapped in tinfoil every day, and picks at her pizza crust. Brian has finished his slice and is working on the cherry Jell-O.

As she walks by, Susie Long says, "Think your ears are big enough?" Then with a slight turn of her head, she adds, "I'm talking to both of you."

"Shut up, Susie," Brian says.

"I should pin her again," I say. In second grade right here in the cafeteria, I knocked her and her tray over and pinned her to the floor after she said, "Why don't you have a dad? Is it because of those things?"

Brian says, "Yeah, why don't you?"

"I promised Teresa I'd keep my hands off her."

"Doesn't she ever get sick of herself?" Brian asks.

Helen gets up, tosses her lunch, and leaves the cafeteria.

"Come on, let's go, too," Brian says. I know he just wants to follow Helen. When we walk by her table, Margie smiles at us, showing her teeth. Brian and I amble down the hallway, listening for Helen. She's not in the girls' bathroom, the auditorium, or the library. We walk around the entire square of corridors until we see her on the pay phone. I can't hear her, but I see that her eyes are wet. When she sees me, she turns her back to me and hunches over the mouthpiece. We walk by her as if we're just passing.

"Who is she talking to?" Brian asks.

"Probably Owen," I say.

"Maybe he broke up with her."

"Maybe." Part of me is glad, but now she can go out with someone else.

Later that day, I help Teresa finish boxing up all her desserts to take to Jimmy Joe's. Brian had to meet his dad at the Gooey factory. The trees along Main Street are strung with colored and white lights, and garlands of plastic pine are wound around the street lamps. At Jimmy Joe's, Laura has looped white lights along the bar and around the perimeter of the ceiling. "Life is so grand," she sings along to Frank. Even while I am in Rexall, I hear her singing, "A fabulous fairy land," and for the first time I wonder about Frank Sinatra. Does he really know what he's talking about? Does he have any idea?

I buy Teresa and Trudy Chanel No. 5, and for Brian's present I go to Harry's Bait and Tackle for a Crazy Crawler with a frog pattern, light on the bottom and dark on the top. By the time I start home the sky has darkened and tiny flakes have started to fall. A tinkling like far-off wind chimes fills my ears. I decide to take the long way so I can see all the Christmas "spectacles," as Teresa calls them—lighted plastic mangers; full sets of reindeer, Santa, and sleigh; families of snowmen; and flashing lights crisscrossing whole houses and yards. I cut behind the Gooey factory to see if Brian's still waiting for his dad. As soon as I walk into the woods to head home, the sky turns a thick dark gray. The snow leaves a white layer like a veil on the sleeves of my bomber jacket. I love when it snows—it's like the world is wearing one great big ear cap.

Muffled voices come from the shed behind the Gooey factory, where high school kids go on weekend nights. The lopsided walls of the shed are rain-colored, and the whole front roof is caved in. Inside, there is a stained mattress and a few candles stuck in beer bottles. On Mondays, Brian and I find condoms, sticky and turned inside out.

"Why'd you call me, then?" a voice says. I stop.

"I wanted to talk to you." It's *Helen*.

"Then talk." And *Owen*. What are they doing back here?

"In private."

"No one will see us."

"What about him? Can't we go somewhere else? I want to really talk—about everything. You know." They are standing in the doorway of the shed.

"I thought we already talked about that," he says. He touches her lip with his finger. "It's Christmas Eve and I have to leave in about twenty minutes. Everyone's waiting for me. Do you want me to just go now? Do you want to just forget it?"

"No."

"Here, have some. I got it for our jam session." He pushes a bottle in a paper bag into her hands as he pushes himself up against her. "You can come next time."

"Really?"

"Yeah."

"Well, what's he doing back here?" Helen whines, smiling as she passes the bottle back. "With his stupid rabbit."

"Shhh." Owen laughs, taking a big swig. "It's only Brian Dodd. He's not going to bother us. Are you, Brian?

"Here, have some."

Brian is standing behind a tree like I am. With his arms crossed over his waist, holding Rabbit inside his jacket, he steps up to them. What is he doing?

"Right." Helen flips her hair over her shoulder. "Is Ship with you?"

"No."

"Where is she?"

"I don't know."

"Come on," Owen whispers and pulls Helen against him in the doorway. "I know you want to."

Owen presses Helen against the doorjamb. They make disgusting, wet noises for what seems like forever. He stops to lift a gold chain around her neck with his finger. Then he runs his hand down her side, over her backside, around to the tops of her thighs, reaching between her legs and back up. Goose bumps are running up and down and all over my skin and this buzzing starts in my ears. I wish I could see Brian.

Owen's hand stops at Helen's waist and then disappears into her jeans. She stands straight, pulling at Owen's hand. "Owen," she cries out, "what do you think you're doing?"

"Come here," he tells her. "I'm not going to see you for two weeks."

"I know, that's why I wanted to talk to you." She stamps her high-heeled boot.

"Go ahead, talk to me." He puts his mouth on hers again.

Helen giggles. "Why does he have to be here?"

"Who cares? Come inside." He kisses her chin. "Besides, it's a free country, I can't make him leave."

"Well, what if he says something? Like to Ship?"

"Brian, are you going to say anything?"

"No."

"What?" Owen stands straight and juts out his chin.

"No."

"Make him swear," Helen tells him, shifting her weight from one foot to the other.

"Do you swear, Brian?"

"I swear."

"What? I can't hear you."

"I swear."

"See," Owen says, dropping his hands, taking a step inside.

"Make him swear on something." She drinks too much and chokes, spitting up the alcohol. Owen licks it off her mouth, her chin, her neck.

"Okay, Brian, do you swear on your rabbit?" Owen smiles.

Helen giggles again.

Brian nods. "Yeah, sure."

"Well, say it," Helen demands.

"I swear I won't say anything, I swear on Rabbit." Now he has another secret.

"Happy now?" Owen laughs and guides Helen inside the shed. "That's better. Now just relax. Take another sip, a little one."

I creep over to the far side of the shed and clear a circle on the snow-covered window.

Brian has stepped into the open doorway. Owen says, "Okay, that then."

The snow is coming down harder now. Owen is pushing Helen's head down until her face is at his pants zipper. One of them kicks over a candle propped in a Budweiser bottle. The snow has made Helen's gold hair white. I'm shivering, and not because of the cold. I never get cold. What am I so afraid of?

Owen sucks in his breath and half closes his eyes. He unzips his zipper. She puts her mouth there. His hands guide her head back and forth, faster and faster. He thrusts forward, his mouth open and his head tilted back. She is on her knees now, with her head bobbing to the rhythm of Owen's hands pushing her. The noises are terrible. Heat spreads across my face. She looks so stupid. I'm embarrassed for her—I cover my ears, but I can't stop watching her. Inside, the snow on top of her head melts, and outside, the snow falls over everything.

With one hand, Brian holds on to his crotch, rocking on his heels, and Rabbit in his other hand rocks with him. Heat licks through me. Owen breathes faster and Brian, too, and Helen breathes a little through her nose. I try to hear Brian's heart beating. He should be with me. I mouth his name.

Then Owen half grunts and half yells. He jerks forward into Helen's face. His body caves in at the waist, then slumps over. After a few seconds, he straightens, tucks himself in, zips his pants, and stands there smiling. Helen wipes her mouth with the back of her hand, then smiles at Owen, I can't look at her— as if *I've* done what she did. I inch backward. Next thing, she is snapping her gum, blowing bubbles, laughing with him.

What's wrong with me? Why do I feel like I've done something wrong? Maybe because I listen to them, I'm just as bad as they are. I wonder if Joy Tucker got pregnant in here. Years ago one of the Gooey factory workers had her baby in this shed. A couple found the baby dead a week after the worker had left Herringtown. At least that's what they say.

Helen and Owen take turns drinking from the bottle in the paper bag, then Owen passes it to Brian, who takes a long swig. "Can we go back to your car and talk now?" Helen asks.

Owen says, "Bet you want a turn, huh, Bri?"

Brian chuckles and takes another drink.

Brian.

"How about giving Brian a turn?" Owen says, cracking his knuckles.

"Very funny."

"I'm not joking."

"Owen," she cries, "that's not funny."

"I'm not trying to be funny," he says. "Come on. Why not?"

"Yeah, right."

"Just do it for me."

"No way, Owen. Forget it. Anyway, I thought you had to go?"

He puts his mouth to her ear.

She laughs at whatever he tells her, and then he kisses her long and hard. When she looks over at Brian, it is so quiet I can hear the snow landing on the ground. Helen has changed her mind.

"You're gonna owe me, Brian," Owen says. "Why don't you put the rabbit down first?"

"She'll escape."

Rabbit scratches the inside of his coat. Please don't do it, Brian.

"Oh, my God," Helen says.

"Let's see," Owen says. "Pass me the rabbit."

"Owen," Helen whines, "do I have to?"

"Yes. Remember what I said." His fingers cup her chin. He whispers, "And close your eyes if you want to. Pretend it's me."

He scoops Rabbit out of Brian's arm, clutching her like a schoolbook.

Brian just stands there, fidgeting with the pockets of his coat.

"Well, what are you waiting for?" Owen asks him.

"Nothing." He pulls on the end of his ear.

I see the back of Helen's head as Brian unzips his jeans. She burps and laughs, then tosses her hair and shakes her head like she does when she's mad. She doesn't know what she's doing.

I press my head against the wet clapboards, wishing the snow collecting at my feet was deep enough to bury myself in. Helen is making the same noises as before, only it's worse, because where Owen was is Brian, breathing hard and fast. As it happens I want to erase it from my mind. I hold my ear caps to my head as tight as I can, but the sound gets through.

The snow is closing in all around me, and I try to hear him, his heart, but I can't. I can't. I trace a circle in the snow, trying to find my way out. Then another, and another inside this. I am drowning in snow, going deeper and deeper into its swirl.

Then it stops and Helen says, "Don't touch me."

Brian stops breathing. Owen laughs.

"Sorry," Brian whispers.

The word floats by me. I can see the letters written out in a string. I see the word, but I can't make sense of anything. Does Brian want me to do this to him?

Owen stands behind Helen watching and drinking, smoothing out her hair, which is damp where the snow melted. Brian's heavy breathing starts again. I keep my face on the side of the shed so I don't hear him. I wish I never had to hear anything again. A few flakes slide down my shirt and burn into my chest. Brian, I want to call out, it's me, Ship. What are you doing?

Heavy footsteps are coming fast through the snow toward us—Mr. Dodd's. I flatten myself against the side of the building. "Brian, where the heck are you?" he calls.

"Holy shit!" Owen drops Rabbit, who scrambles into the far corner. He grabs Helen by the arm and they stumble past Mr. Dodd in the doorway and past me. Owen doesn't see me, but Helen does. Through the flakes of white her eyes meet mine for a second, then she's gone.

"For crissake, why aren't your pants buckled? What is going on in here? What were you doing with that Sooner girl?"

Brian doesn't answer.

"I was waiting for you back there, you know? I thought we were going to get your ma something nice for Christmas. What's this?" He kicks Owen's bottle in the paper bag. "What are you doing in this place, son?" His voice drops, disappointed.

"What were you doing in here?"

A bottle smashes against the wall where I am on the outside, sending me reeling backward. I rock myself back and forth.

"And what the hell is Rabbit doing here? By the time we get to the truck, you better have something to say for yourself." With Rabbit under his arm, Mr. Dodd walks out of the shed, heading back to the Gooey factory.

Tucking in his shirt and combing his hair back, Brian stumbles after his father. Did he say something? Was he talking to me? Is my hearing failing me just as I wished it would? Was Dr. Gould right—I'll hear less in time?

Before I open my mouth to say anything, Brian disappears into whiteness.

Four

I LAY THERE, LETTING my arms and legs turn white until the town hall bell rings five times. When I stand up, I can't feel myself. About to sneeze, I listen to my heart stop for a split second and wish it didn't have to start beating again. As soon as I sneeze, it does.

I trudge home and wait underneath the pear tree until the Continental pulls into the driveway. A door opens and slams shut. "Just wait right there, I'll help you," Teresa says.

Trudy's breathing turns into coughing, and her coughing into choking. Teresa pats her on the back. "Okay?"

"Okay," Trudy says.

The snow falls between me and them, thicker and thicker. I am bringing a whole new set of secrets into our house. Are they all going to just pile up on top of each other?

"Almost there," Teresa tells her. I can barely hear her high heels clack-clack through the powdery snow while Trudy shuffles up the walkway to our house.

"Good." Trudy gasps.

I want to tell them what happened. The problem is, the

more I try to forget, the more I remember—all of it. I have to go inside. I wish I could turn things back, I wish I wasn't me. Only an hour ago, things were regular. Why can't that one little hour disappear?

Teresa is cutting potatoes when I finally come in. "Look at you—you're covered!" she says, and she and Trudy laugh.

"Merry Christmas, Ship," Trudy says.

"Merry Christmas," I say. "Welcome home, Trudy."

"It sure is good to be here. Take off your coat and give me a nice big hug."

"Are you all right?" Teresa asks.

I nod. "Just cold."

"Cold? You're never cold."

Trudy's hair is curled around her face like it usually is and she wears a lot of makeup. Her foundation is lumpy in spots and the rouge heavy on her cheeks. "You look nice," I tell her.

"You're sweet, but I know I look terrible. I lost eighteen pounds, but I'm still such a tub. Look at this flab." She pushes the fat hanging beneath her upper arm.

"No, you aren't." I want to fold myself inside of her.

She brushes the snow from my hair, fingering it into place. "You still look like a movie star," she says. It's only been a week since I've seen her, but now that she's sick, I can't tell her that it's just a stupid haircut and it hasn't made anything better. I almost believed what she said about my picture on the Hair Camp wall, but not now.

"Give me your hands," Trudy says. She rubs each of my hands inside hers. "They're like ice cubes. What on earth have you been doing?"

"I was outside."

"I'd say so."

The front door creaks open and Helen tiptoes upstairs. She's so good at this, I can barely hear her. Teresa opens the oven door to pull out the pan of roast beef. She pours spoonfuls of the juices collected in the pan over the top of the meat and quarters of potatoes around it and slides the pan back into the oven. She washes the asparagus spears in the sink and cuts off the ends. Cold water hits the sides of the sink harder. It rings more than hot water.

"No broccoli with cheese sauce?" I ask.

Teresa shakes her head.

"No Yorkshire pudding?"

"Not this year."

"Or pecan rolls?"

"No, I'm simplifying. Besides, we don't need to have the same thing every year."

"That's true," Trudy agrees. "But at least we'll have our usual toast, right?"

"You're not supposed to drink. Then you'll want to smoke and you just promised you wouldn't."

"One little drink on Christmas Eve won't hurt anyone."

"One drink? Is that possible?"

"Just one," Trudy says, "to be sociable. I've been trapped in that awful hospital for ten days. Let's celebrate, for heaven's sake."

"I thought we were going to stop?"

"It's Christmas Eve," Trudy says.

"It is."

Through the window the snow is white on dark, blocking even the pear tree from view. I want the snow to fill my head until I'm frozen numb and I can't see anything but pure white.

"It's really coming down, isn't it?" Trudy says.

"You'll have to stay over." Teresa drops the asparagus into the boiling water.

I listen to the sound of their voices until Trudy takes hold of my shoulder. "Ship? Are you all right, Ship?"

"Yes."

"Did you hear what I said?"

"No."

"Your ears must have frozen."

"I think they did." I smile at her.

"I was wondering if you were going to put on another magic show for us this year."

I can't put on a magic show now. Don't they know anything? "I haven't done it for so long."

"Oh, go ahead, cheer up your old friend Trudy."

"I don't know, Trudy. You really want me to?"

"We'll pay admission. A dollar each. Come on."

That's two dollars toward the taxicab to Waterfalls. I get two dollars for a full hour of sweeping at Hair Camp. "Okay, just one trick."

"Deal." Trudy turns to Teresa. "It sure is good to be out of there."

My eyes tear up at the sink and I have to set the eggs down and splash water on my face. Helen and Brian shouldn't have done that. Is that what I get for listening to them? After a few minutes, I am ready. I have to do something.

I hold out two eggs, one in each palm. "Here I have two plain brown eggs. See—one, two." I look at the eggs, rolling them in my open hands. I look into Trudy's eyes, then Teresa's. "The thing that is particular about these eggs," I continue, "is that they will do exactly as I tell them to." I clear my throat.

"I have two glasses of water here, exactly the same. I'll drop the first egg in here and tell it to sink." *Plop!* I wave my hand over the top of the glass. "Sink, egg! Voilà! And the second egg, I will order to float. Do as I say and float, egg." Plunk goes the second egg into the clear sugar water, bobbing up and down as I hold my hand like a wand over it.

They applaud wildly at first, but ease up when they see me cringing at the noise. I bow, holding out the eggs again.

Trudy asks, "Where's Helen?"

My whole body freezes.

"I think she's in her room," Teresa says. "Ship, can you call her down to set the table?"

When Trudy gets up, Teresa says, "You sit right back down. You're not doing a single thing."

Trudy sighs. "I'm going to get lazy."

"Enjoy it while you can. Go ahead, Ship."

My hands make fists and I can feel my face distorting. I stop in the hallway at the bottom of the stairs where Teresa has propped our Christmas tree against the coat rack. It must have been the last one. Its branches are straggly and the tip of it only reaches my chin.

I force myself upstairs, where Helen is snapping her gum. Footsteps cross the hallway and water runs in the bathroom between our rooms.

"Hel-len," I call, hating the sound of her name. Heat rushes to the top of my head.

She doesn't answer.

"Did you hear me?" I yell into the bathroom. "Teresa said you have to set the table."

She flings open the door. "Why don't YOU? Because you're too busy spying on everything I DO?"

A shaking works its way from my head down through my limbs to my feet, but I keep standing there until Helen goes blurry. "Why did you do that?" I yell so loud my ears ring. I rock myself back and forth.

She laughs, then slams the door as hard as she can, locking it. I throw myself at the closed door, punching and clawing it.

"Helen and Ship," Teresa calls from the kitchen, "what's going on up there?"

I stop. I can hear Helen laughing to herself, then humming her Pineapple Princess song.

"Helen and Ship!" Teresa yells again. "Ship, did you hear me? Ship?"

"Yes."

"Well, answer me, then."

"I did."

"Say something before I have to ask you."

"All right."

"What are you doing up there?"

"Nothing."

"Nothing?"

"No."

"Well, come downstairs. I don't want any fighting tonight. Come on."

I come downstairs. "What about Helen? She's supposed to set the table."

"Never mind Helen."

"But, Teresa." I want to tell her about Helen—about what happened this afternoon, but I can't say it. I can't say the words. "She always does exactly what she wants," I finish. When I lift my hand to protest, it seems disconnected from the rest of me. It's like I am outside, looking in at them. My palms, neck, and back are sweating and the back of my mouth is dry.

"Don't let her bother you so much." Teresa empties the steaming asparagus into a colander. The water splashes against the sides of the sink. Trudy pours whiskey into the sour mix, adds ice cubes, and stirs again. Teresa opens the oven door, slides out the roast beef pan, the gravy and fat splattering around the roasted potatoes. When Trudy fills their glasses, ice clinks. She and Teresa set out the good plates, the sterling silver, and the special holiday wineglasses. They don't ask me to do anything.

All the sounds echo in the way back of my head. What I hear is Helen padding around her room, Helen snapping her gum in and out of her mouth, Helen laughing, Helen barking at me, Helen sucking and breathing and giggling. She doesn't even like Brian. When Teresa calls "Supper's ready," I close my eyes and press my ear caps tight. She's coming.

She fills up the whole room. I hear Owen groaning, Brian's heart beating, Rabbit scampering into a corner, Mr. Dodd's footsteps. I know it's Owen's and Brian's fault, too, but I can't stand looking at her. She wishes Trudy and Teresa a "Merry Christmas," and then we all sit down at the table like nothing at all has happened.

"Ship," Teresa asks, "do you want roast beef or not?"

"Yes, please."

"Look at me, then."

I do. She places two thick pieces of roast beef on my plate. We also have a basket of sweet rolls, asparagus spears covered in lemon sauce, roasted potatoes with rosemary, and cranberry muffins.

"Everything looks delicious," Trudy says. Her upper lip trembles and her eyes are already watering. I wonder how long it'll take her to start her holiday bawling.

"Phsst, it was nothing," Teresa tells her.

Trudy sighs and takes a big helping of potatoes and passes them to Helen. "It sure is good to be here."

"It's good to have you back." Teresa squeezes Trudy's arm.

"It is," Helen agrees.

"I'm so glad to be done with all my orders, too. Every time I close my eyes I see trays of cookies. I don't want to see another sweet for a long, long time," Teresa says. "Well, at least a few days."

I eat my roast beef without looking up. If only they knew what I know. If only they heard what I heard. Helen's chewing and smacking her lips as she sits there smiling makes my body turn into a fist. I have to grab onto the sides of my chair to keep from throwing myself at her.

"What'd you do this afternoon, Helen?" Teresa asks.

"A little Christmas shopping."

"Shopping?" I ask, finally looking at her. "Shopping for what?"

"Christmas presents—if that's all right with you." Gold sparkles around her neck.

"Christmas presents?" My lungs fill. I let out a shrill howl.

"What's going on here?" Teresa asks.

"Yeah." Helen laughs. "Christmas presents."

I catch my breath, then hum like I used to before I got the ear caps, like a vacuum cleaner.

"Ship?" Teresa asks. "Is everything all right with you?"

I keep humming.

"Can you stop that, Ship, so we can enjoy our dinner?" Teresa sets her fork down.

"Your mother went to a lot of trouble to make this dinner," Trudy says quietly.

Helen pushes back her chair. "I'm going to get a Tab." That's all she drinks. "Anyone want anything?"

"No, thanks."

"I'm good."

I wait to hear her footsteps, the swish of the kitchen door, the creak of the refrigerator opening, but she doesn't budge. She shifts her weight from one leg to the other, folds her arms across her chest, and breathes slow and even. I concentrate on the white wall of snow outside.

"Ship," she says, dragging out her words, "can I get you a drink of anything?"

I don't care how many times she asks me, I'm not going to answer. The wind blows the snow against the window, each flake pelting the glass with tiny cracks. That's what I hear—crack, crack, crack—as I pick up my red wineglass of milk and hold it tight. *Crack, crack*. How can the window bear it? I wonder, and I hold the glass tighter.

"Ship?" Helen repeats.

"What is going on here?" Teresa asks. "Will one of you answer me?"

I don't hear anything after this except a pounding, which must be my heart becoming louder and louder, thump-thumping as if it's going to burst right through the skin. Where is the thing with feathers now? Where is Brian? I keep humming, letting the storm build around me. I don't move until the red wineglass I'm holding shatters and milk splatters everywhere. Trudy screams. A sudden pain runs through the center of my hand. I clutch it into a ball and smell blood.

"Are you all right, Ship?" Teresa is beside me.

When I open my hand, my palm is a pool of red.

"Good Lord," Trudy says. "I'll get a cloth."

"Oh, Ship." Teresa grabs my bloody hand at the wrist and holds it like a flag in the air. She touches the ends of my fingers. "Come on, I'm taking you to the hospital."

"I'm going with you," Trudy says.

Helen comes back to the table with her Tab as we're leaving.

"Hurry," Teresa says, wrapping a clean kitchen cloth around my hand, "and keep it elevated."

I turn once to see Helen's blank face following us as we parade out the kitchen door, Teresa holding my hand above my head and Trudy putting my jacket over my shoulders. I wish Brian could see me being rushed off to the hospital like this. When we're almost to the Continental, which is a mound of white, Teresa says, "Oh, I didn't even say good-bye to Helen."

"Me either."

"She'll be fine. We better hurry. I've got to brush off the car."

"I never thought I'd be going back there so soon," Trudy says.

I've ruined Christmas Eve dinner, but it's worth it.

LATER THAT night, I examine the bandage that covers the seventeen stitches in my palm, wishing I could show them to Brian, but he seems like a different person now—the one who did *that*. One of the doctors at the North Goodheart Hospital recognized my name. "Oh," he said, holding the needle over my head, "you're the one with the hearing?"

"Her hand." Teresa pointed. "We're just here for her hand tonight, Doctor."

"But she *can* hear everything," Trudy said proudly.

"Shh," Teresa told her.

"Well, she can."

I open my window, letting the storm blow in. The snow is thick and heavy and coats the windowsill in seconds. The cold air makes my hand feel better, but a dull pain throbs through my fingers. And my mind is like a scratched record, playing back what happened this afternoon over and over—Helen putting her mouth there, Owen laughing, Brian breathing like he was dying, Mr. Dodd finding him. I don't understand it. All I want is to stop thinking about it. I sit in the window with the wind and snow whipping around me, feeling like my skin is being peeled off strip by strip, the way Teresa scrapes carrots and cucumbers.

A branch snaps. There are footsteps. Nothing is visible through the snow, except for the dark. I take off my ear caps and lean out the window. He's going to tell me what happened. He's going to tell me why. He's waiting for me.

Brian.

I creep down the stairs, stopping at the landing to hear water running in the kitchen, dishes clanking, and Teresa and Trudy laughing. I push the front door open and step into a blast of cold. Then, holding my bandaged hand under my shirt, I run toward the Dodds'.

I think he is going to meet me halfway, in the woods between us, but no one is there. I lift my ear caps off and keep going. A jackknife opens, then shuts. I am close. He is circling around Rabbit, who is hopping from one end of the raised cage to the other. The snow collects on Brian's head, shoulders, and arms. He flicks open the knife. She wriggles her nose into the meshing in front of him. Snowflakes fall on the blade of the knife. The snow swirls around me. My whole body shudders. Should I tell him to stop?

"Hi, Rabbit," he says softly.

I stop breathing.

He traces a square in the meshing with the point of the knife. "Here's a window for you." Except for my eyes following the gleam of the blade, I stand there unmoving. He cuts a perfect rectangle. "There," he says out loud. He tosses the piece of meshing into the snow and snaps the jackknife shut. I didn't even know Brian had a knife. I want to yell, *Why? Why did you do that? And why Helen? Why this?* But my mouth is frozen. It seems to be filled with snow. Without a sound Brian walks away through the snow falling through the trees. He could have opened the cage and pulled her out.

Before he reaches his house, Rabbit has pinched her body through the opening, has jumped to the ground, and is hopping through the snow toward whatever calls her in the night. I watch her hop away, white on white, wiggle and sniff, then vanish into nothingness. Just like that, they are both gone— Brian and Rabbit. Cold and nausea hit me at once. I stare into the dark, letting snow cover my head and arms. Blood has seeped through my bandage and frozen into a red star. I wave my hand through the air, trying to forget all of it, then walk home with my ear caps on. I don't hear anything in the storm.

Nobody notices I was gone. Back upstairs, I shut my bedroom window from the snow, like silent waves crashing on our house. Water runs and splashes in the tub, where Helen is listening to the radio. Maybe she'll electrocute herself. I think of every time she and Brian could have been together. I wonder how many times he spied on her and if they met behind the Gooey factory and what other things they did I didn't know about. Did Brian tell her secrets he didn't tell me? Did he tell her about Johnny and about where they go on Sundays? Is Helen getting back at me for listening in on her all those times? How will I ever find out?

Teresa's and Trudy's voices float up from the kitchen. I lay there for a long time, thinking that Helen is going to come in and cut off my ears like she used to say she was going to. Downstairs, glasses clink, and somewhere outside, Rabbit is hopping through the woods, but I can't hear her. It's strange—I can't hear anything out there.

F i v e

ON CHRISTMAS DAY I wake instantly, remembering something terrible has happened. A weight presses down on me like a huge hand, pinning me in place. I know. It did happen, it did, *it did*. I have to see Brian, I have to ask him why. Something else is happening to me, too—*it*. I knew I was going to get it and still I'm not ready. Inside, blood stains my sheets. Outside is pure white. In the bathroom before anyone else is up, I watch the blood drip out of me drop by drop. It is Christmas Day and no one is going anywhere, including me. Everybody's shut in, shut away.

Everyone else sleeps in while I listen to the radio in the kitchen, waiting for them to get up. Last night's storm took a strange turn, hitting the entire north shore of Massachusetts. By the time it stops snowing tonight we should have twenty-two inches. The Cape and islands didn't get a single inch. The temperature has dropped twenty degrees, the phone lines are down, and every few minutes an enormous gust of wind whips against the clapboards, rattling our house to its bones.

First Teresa comes in, then Trudy and Helen, saying "Merry

Christmas" all around. I even say it to Helen. When they ask about my hand, I show them my bandage and tell them it's fine. They have coffee and juice and look out the window at the snow. No one bothers to take a shower or get dressed. At noon we all go into the living room, where Trudy slept on the pullout couch, to watch *Hud*, Teresa's and Trudy's favorite movie.

On top of the stereo are photos of us and on the wall behind it is Helen's painting of a bowl of apples and bananas—a perfect imitation, her art teacher said. Though there is a rocking chair, we all wrap ourselves in afghan blankets and sit on the sofa to watch Paul Newman on the TV that Teresa keeps in the closet.

"This is what I call a good Christmas," Trudy says.

I look out the window at the snow coming down until my eyes grow heavy. I wake once when Helen goes up to her room. Then again when Trudy bursts out, "Don't tell anyone I said this, but Paul Newman is God's gift to women. Listen, listen, I love this line: 'I like to interpret the law in this lenient sort of manner,'" she drawls, gazing at the TV. "'Sometimes I lean to the right, and other times I lean to the left.'"

She laughs. "Well, close enough!"

Pretending to be asleep, I peek at the TV. Under the blazing sun, Hud stands cool.

"Why can't I find someone like that?" Teresa sighs. "Jack was so useless."

"You can say that again."

"He never even took me out. We split it every time. Even the early bird special. The cheapskate."

"And that stupid hair."

"Don't remind me, all five pieces slicked down—until he started using his new shampoo. How do you find a decent guy?"

"That's easy. You don't. You can't rely on them anyway."

"I can't argue with that," Teresa says.

"Look at him walk." Trudy doesn't take her eyes from the TV.

Teresa whispers, "He reminds me of Mack, you know."

"I know," Trudy whispers back.

At the commercial, Teresa says, "Well, I know one thing, if Paul Newman came to our door, I'd pack my bag so fast." They laugh quietly.

Teresa's hand smooths my hair over my neck, down my back. "Poor thing," she says, "she's exhausted."

I wonder if one day I'll like Paul Newman the way they do. I hope he never comes to our door.

LATER, TERESA goes down to the basement to find the tree stand and the box of tinsel, the colored bulbs, the strings of white lights, and the salt dough ornaments Helen and I made when we were little. Trudy and I decorate the puny tree while Teresa heats up the roast beef to have with a fresh batch of pecan rolls. Trudy's going to break her new diet because it's Christmas. After the tree is decorated, we'll open our presents.

"We don't want to overload the poor little tree," Trudy says, winding the white lights around and around. "I feel like I'm strangling it."

Still we add more tinsel, glass bulbs, stars, and flashing lights until the tree looks like it's going to topple over. "Where's Helen? She should see this."

I shrug. The tree glitters, but it's the falling snow that catches my eye, and I find myself gazing out the window in the direction of Brian's. I try to hear something—anything—from his house. I slip off my ear caps. What I hear is Trudy's breathing like a clogged-up sink, as if sand is caught in there and is being pulled up and down her throat. I hear the tiniest tinkling of the decorations brushing against the pine needles and the wind's steady thumping on the windows. I used to think when it was windy or stormy that the windows were going to shatter. I listen as hard as I can, but beyond the window, beyond the pear tree, all the way to Brian's house, I hear nothing.

Dr. Gould told Teresa that with time and exposure to the environment, my hearing would lessen, and I wonder if this is finally happening. Or maybe I'm getting what I wished for—to never hear again.

"Are you going to see Brian today?" Trudy asks.

"Not unless he comes over." I put my ear caps back on. I'd like to know if he got me a present.

"There's always tomorrow," she says. She twirls the tinsel around the tree. "Frankly, I think men are overrated."

"What about Paul Newman?"

She laughs. "Well, except him. And you know who."

"Anyway Brian's not a man," I say.

"He will be soon enough." She fluffs up the flattened sides of my hair. "There," she says.

"Trudy?"

"Yes?" She walks around the tree to plug in the Christmas lights.

"I got *it* today. You know—"

"Oh, Ship!" she exclaims, pulling me close, almost strangling me. "Have you told Teresa? We have to celebrate. Teresa!" She marches me into the kitchen.

"How's the tree coming?"

"Well, I think we overdid it, but that's not what we came to tell you." She smiles at me.

"What?" Teresa asks.

"We need three small glasses of the *reddest* wine in the house to toast Ship."

"My little wild child!" Teresa puts her hands on the front of her jeans, leaving two flour prints, then throws her arms around me.

"Don't call me that." I wait to start feeling different.

THE DAY after Christmas, I wake to the sound of shoveling from the Dodds' house. There is a thunk, followed by a scraping sound, the brief silence of snow heaved, arcing through the air, and then the thump of it hitting more snow. It is so white it hurts my eyes to look outside. A clump of snow slips off the tree branch outside, plopping onto the piles below. The morning birds are whistling and chirping, their tail feathers dark against the white. I am going to Brian's.

I got forty dollars from Trudy for Christmas, which means we could take a Classy Cab to Waterfalls this week. Brian said he was going to go with me, but now I don't know.

When I get to the edge of the Dodds' yard, the driveway is shoveled, but no one is there. All the shades are drawn, even in Brian's room. Inside, someone is dragging something down the stairs. It lands with a heavy thud on each step, then is hauled across the floor. I'm about to throw a snowball at Brian's window when all three Dodds come out, dressed in dark wool coats that go all the way to their feet like Father Hannah's robe. Mrs.

Dodd's fur hat sits on her head like a cake. Every Sunday the Dodds leave in the pickup, but they're never dressed up and today is Thursday. I crouch behind a tree.

Mr. Dodd locks the back door while Brian pulls an old black trunk by its leather strap across the porch and over to the truck. Together they lift the trunk into the snow-filled bed of the pickup, shaking the whole truck. Next thing, Mr. Dodd is backing out the driveway, with Mrs. Dodd and Brian beside him in the front seat. I think Brian's going to turn to see me waving to him, but he doesn't and the truck disappears. I stand on the edge of the strip of woods between our houses, waiting for him to come back. The plastic snowman in the middle of their backyard glows white except for its red bulbous nose flashing on and off.

For days the Dodds' house stands dark and dead quiet except for the lit-up snowman and his blinking nose. I am shaken out of my sleep each morning by the *Boston Herald* thumping onto their front porch, followed by a bicycle coasting down the driveway. One morning the paper hits their front door. I carry the *Herald*s from the front porch to the back porch, peering through the shaded windows as I do. But I don't see anything. Did they go wherever they go every Sunday or somewhere else? Curtains are drawn over the front and back doors.

Every afternoon I wait for Brian to come back. I wait while the melting snow drips, turning their backyard into a pond, and I wonder why he didn't tell me he was going away. They haven't gone on a vacation since they've been in Herringtown. But they used to, I know that.

Last summer Brian told me, "We used to go to Cape Cod

every July. My dad took me and Johnny—" He stopped and stared at his sneakers. "I mean *me*, he took me to the go-karts and trampolines."

"Who's Johnny?" That was the first time he talked about Johnny.

He blinked twice, shoved his hands into his pockets, and started digging into the dirt around the root of a tree with his toe.

"Was he your best friend?"

He shrugged.

Maybe he still is. "Did he always go on vacation with you?"

"I guess."

"Did your mother talk to him?"

"Of course." He laughed.

She's never said a word to me. "Did he go fishing with you, too?"

"Ship," Brian said, finally looking at me, "can you do me a favor?"

I nodded.

"Can you stop asking me questions about Johnny?"

I nodded.

"At all, especially if my dad is there."

"Why?"

"Because. Okay?" He sucked in his breath and held it in.

"Is he still your best friend?"

"No, he's not."

"Okay," I said.

Johnny must have had something to do with Brian leaving the way he did. I should have done something; I should have found out about Johnny.

. . .

TERESA BAKES the whole week, filling all her orders for New Year's, and Trudy keeps her company. Helen wears her new Walkman and sings "You're So Vain." It sounded much better when she sang along to a record; at least we could hear the real song. She borrows Trudy's Polaroid to take photos of herself in the mirror, then hangs these photos on her wall next to pictures of Carly Simon, Cher, and Joni Mitchell. "I need to get a microphone," she tells Trudy and Teresa.

"They must be expensive," Teresa says.

"I'll make it back with my first hit." Teresa and Trudy laugh, but Helen doesn't.

Teresa will probably buy it for her like she always does. A few years ago when we were food shopping at A&P, I asked Teresa if I could get a Gooey Bar. "No candy," she said. "You know the rules." When Helen asked if she could get one two minutes later, Teresa told her, "No candy. We're having a nice roasted chicken tonight." As soon as Teresa turned to unload the groceries from the wagon, Helen put the Gooey Bar on the conveyor belt next to her six-pack of Tab.

"Teresa!" I yelled. The cashier was ringing in the Gooey Bar.

"What did I say, Helen?"

"It's for my field trip. Everyone else will have candy."

Teresa sighed. "What am I going to do with you?"

This is the way Helen is with everything. She still thinks she can have whatever she wants.

All week I hold my ear caps close to my ears.

"Ship," Teresa says, "she doesn't sound that bad. And at least she's enjoying herself."

"Are you going to buy her a microphone?"

"Maybe for her birthday, we'll see."

I groan. "It's bad enough without a microphone."

"That's not very nice, Ship. Maybe *your* phase has started." Of course Teresa doesn't know what I know about Helen.

"You know, the Dodds have been gone for three days. They left the day after Christmas."

"They're probably on vacation."

"Brian didn't say they were going anywhere. Besides, they never go anywhere."

"They'll be back soon, Ship. Don't worry, things will work out. They always do." She slides a pecan pie into the oven.

On the fifth day, the snowman's nose stops flashing. On the seventh day, the Dodds' pickup swings back into the driveway. Mr. and Mrs. Dodd get out and walk quickly up to their house. Mr. Dodd scoops up all the *Boston Herald*s I've piled there, looks suspiciously around, mutters, "That's the last time," grunts, unlocks the back door, then disappears inside with Mrs. Dodd. *What's* the last time? The last time they get the *Herald*? The last time they go away? The last time I'm allowed in their yard? Or what? I don't know how long I stare at the empty truck before I realize that Brian isn't getting out of it. He's not here.

When I call their house, the phone rings and rings, so I stand on the edge of the woods, watching their shadows moving inside. The house seems darker without Brian in it. I ring their doorbell, but no one answers. All afternoon I stand there, staring at the white light on the melting snow as if I could make him reappear.

I do. I see him standing there holding the squirrel his father shot with the Mossberg last summer, the day Brian turned thirteen. That was the only day I ever went inside their house. Mr.

Dodd said to Mrs. Dodd, "Just this once," and then he called me from the backyard. "Come on, come on, Ship, get over here. You've got to see this."

He pushed me into the dim kitchen where Brian was sitting, staring at his lap, fingering the white tissue paper wrapped around his present, which was Mossy. Behind him on the counter was a box full of Gooey Bars. There must have been over a hundred in there. Mr. Dodd saw me eyeing them and said, "We're saving them, aren't we, Bri?"

"Yes, sir."

"Go ahead, open it!" his father shouted, breathing heavy, snorting. An awful smell like sour milk hung in the air.

I didn't notice Mrs. Dodd until she snatched up the tissue paper as it fell to the ground. Her mouth was clamped shut, but she was making the slightest scraping sound like Teresa makes, grinding her teeth, only quieter. Standing in front of me, she was more pale than when I'd seen her behind the kitchen window, as pale as the cream-colored wall she was leaning against. Her skirt went all the way to the ground so I couldn't see her broken legs.

Brian ran his hand along the barrel to the muzzle, where he poked the tip of his finger inside and out, then down along the polished wood, over the trigger to the butt. Mr. Dodd wobbled and drummed his finger on the table, then snatched the gun out of Brian's hands. "You have to be real careful with her," he said, winking at Brian. "Look, son, dual-action bars, steel-to-steel lockup, twin extractors. She's yours."

Mrs. Dodd slid a chocolate Pepperidge Farm cake from its box and began cutting it into squares and putting the pieces on plates. Then she turned and looked out the window over the sink. She was small and wiry and her hair was pulled straight back into a tight ponytail. She was so quiet, I wondered if I would have heard anything if I didn't see her right there in front of me. I asked Brian once if his mother talked.

"Of course," he said.

"I've never heard her."

"She's shy."

"What does she do all day?"

"She watches soap operas and knits," he said. "And she's making photo albums."

I couldn't tell which part of the house it was coming from— this low buzzing like a radio in between stations, playing static. I stepped into the living room. The room smelled of anchovies and Old Spice. The couch and chairs shone. They were covered in plastic, slick with a greasy coating. In the far corner of the room there was a photo on top of the TV.

"Where do you think you're going?" Next thing I knew, Mr. Dodd was pushing me back into the kitchen.

"Nowhere."

"That's right, nowhere. Brian, did you tell Ship she could wander around our house?"

"No, sir."

"All right, then. The party's right here, wise guy. Do you understand English?"

Mrs. Dodd's eyes followed me the whole time—except when I looked at her. They glinted like they had pieces of flint in them. When I got closer, I saw they were the same gray-blue as Brian's, but they were darting all over the room.

"Come on, let's go try her out, partner. You can look at that later. Right now, I'm your owner's manual. Let's see, here's the ammo. Safety's on." Mr. Dodd put his arm around Brian. He shook the cardboard box of shells. Brian smiled at his dad.

Mr. Dodd handed the gun back to Brian and stepped over to Mrs. Dodd with the plate of birthday cake. "For God's sake, we didn't even sing 'Happy Birthday'! What's the matter with you? Put these back on here." He fit the cut pieces back into the square shape of the cake on its Styrofoam tray.

"Get over here, Ship. Help us sing 'Happy Birthday.' Come on, let's light these candles now." He picked up the cake with the lit candles and began singing.

Mrs. Dodd and I followed him, lighting a path to Brian.

"Blow them out, son!"

Brian slid back in his chair and took aim at the candles with his gun, pretending to blast them. *Phoo, pew, phoo pew."*

His father leaned back and howled. After the candles were blown out, Mr. Dodd picked up a piece of cake from the tray and popped it into his mouth. Mrs. Dodd followed and then Brian. They chewed in quick squirrelly bites. "Better have a piece before it's gone, Ship," Mr. Dodd said, taking another piece for himself.

Teresa said she would never eat cake out of a box or made from a mix and I usually wouldn't either, but I ate two pieces of Brian's birthday cake because I didn't know what else to do. Brian sat at the kitchen table and Mr. and Mrs. Dodd stood on either side of him, eating a second, then a third piece of cake. Who would guess anyone could make so much noise chewing one little piece of cake? He sounded just like a pig. As we chewed, our eyes rested on the new shotgun spread across Brian's lap.

"Okay, let's go, son." He grabbed Brian by the back of his collar, then shuffled toward the back door. Before Brian stepped out the door, Mrs. Dodd pressed her hand into his. "Please be careful, Brian." I had heard her crying all these nights, but these were the first words I heard her say. Her voice was like a girl's. When he went out the door, her eyes were watery. I didn't know if I was supposed to go with them or not. When I looked over at Mrs. Dodd, goose bumps rose on my arms and my nose prickled as if the air had just gone cold. She was telling me to go.

Next to the lilac tree, Mr. Dodd was crouched down with the shotgun propped up on his right shoulder, taking aim at the back woods, his finger on the trigger. "Now, remember the rules, son. Don't pull the gun to you by the muzzle and never touch the trigger until you're good and ready. That way you don't waste any shells." Then the gun went *pop!* like a very loud cap gun. The shot was so sudden and loud, I lost my breath. I almost fainted. A brown thing flew toward us, pivoting through the air, and landed in the brush. "You got it, Dad!" They both hollered and ran toward it. I held on to my ears.

When Mr. Dodd grabbed the squirrel around the neck, blood streamed out of its mouth, down its belly onto its fluffy tail, dripping into the dirt. He dropped the squirrel to the ground. "Nailed the son of a gun! Here, your turn." Carefully, he handed the gun to Brian, one hand on the butt, the other on the barrel. Brian licked his dry lips, smiling crooked.

"Okay, ready there, son?"

"I think I ate too much cake." He held his stomach.

"Pay attention now! She's loaded, so turn on the safety till you're ready to fire." Mr. Dodd licked his finger and stuck it in the air. "Almost no wind. Perfect. Take your time, pal. Wait for your target. Another one of these runts is gonna pop outta the woods any second. Turn your safety off now and keep your eyes peeled. That's it. Show her who's boss."

The more Mr. Dodd yapped on about how to use the gun, taking turns scratching and gesturing, the more Brian bounced up and down in his crouched position, stopping to tilt his gun to the sky, then yanking the polished butt of Mossy back onto his lap. Seeing a single robin flying overhead, Brian lurched forward. The gun exploded. The bird's wings fluttered as it gained speed, then swooped down, floating for a moment in silence before it flapped out of view. At the same time, blackbirds screeched and lifted like a dark cloud from the branches of a maple tree. The gun fired two times fast into the blue. I rocked back and forth like the sky was going to fall on me, but nothing fell except a single leaf from the lilac tree, which swayed back and forth, down to Mr. Dodd and Brian. The blackbirds beat their wings and disappeared in one swooshing mass.

"Missed," his father yelled after him.

Brian swung around, Mossy's muzzle swinging with him. "I'll get the next one."

"What are you trying to do, kill your own father?" Mr. Dodd dipped down. "Swing her right back around, for crying out loud! Take it easy, son. Birds are tricky."

A squirrel shot up a tree trunk. Brian pulled the trigger. The squirrel climbed higher, out of sight. Shaking his head side to side, Mr. Dodd hooked his thumbs into the pockets of his jeans and said, "Nothing. No more bullets in there. I hit one. You missed four—that's five. That's all. Enough for today. Give it here." Mr. Dodd threw the dead squirrel, thumping onto the lawn by Brian's feet like one of the *Boston Herald*s landing on their porch. He snatched the gun out of Brian's hands and trudged into the house.

Grasping the squirrel's tail, Brian stood facing the sun, his mouth hanging open. The grass was buzzing around him. He muttered something like "I wish he was here."

"Who?" I asked.

"Who what?" His voice cracked through the hot still air.

"Who do you wish was here?"

"No one."

"Come on," I told him. "Let's go. Who cares about a stupid gun?"

"Yeah, he can have it if he likes it so much." His right ear wiggled. He tossed the squirrel back onto the lawn and we took off into the woods.

I REMEMBER every single thing about Brian now that he's gone. I see him like he's right in front of me—the fifty-four freckles that I counted across his nose, the white scar along his jaw, his wide mouth, and his gray-blue eyes, where I see specks of myself floating.

Shadows bloom over the Dodds' white lawn. Mr. Dodd is crossing the yard, his right hand clutching Rabbit's frozen neck.

I want to stop him to find out what he did to Brian, but I'm afraid of him and Rabbit and someone's eyes are on me. The hair on the back of my neck stands straight up. I step out of the woods. Mrs. Dodd is staring out the kitchen window. Her eyes, glassy and cracked like an antique doll's, are going straight through me. It's as if I'm pressed up to the window, eye to eye with her.

I step back into the trees and wait for Mr. Dodd to come out of the garage, but he stays in there, breathing deep and grunting. So I walk around front. There is a grating sound like ice being chipped off a car window. I steam the glass on the garage door with my breath until I can see Mr. Dodd standing at his worktable. He is bent over Rabbit, cutting frozen white clumps from her.

She's an eating rabbit—is he going to eat her? Why doesn't he wait until she is thawed? Mr. Dodd has cut right through her dark pink flesh. The silver blade of his knife turns red with frozen blood. My bandaged hand, white with flecks of my own blood, accidentally bangs against the garage window, and Mr. Dodd swings his head in my direction. I take off, holding my hand straight up in the air.

After this, the only sign that the Dodds still live next door is the American flag Mr. Dodd hung from their front porch on the day of Ronald Reagan's inauguration. Other than that, I see Mr. Dodd when he is pulling in or out of his driveway to go to work or when he and Mrs. Dodd go for their Sunday drive. They don't answer my telephone calls or the notes I leave on their door. I stand outside their house in the afternoons before I go to Jimmy Joe's, but all I hear is the ticking of a clock, water running, slippered footsteps, the clanking of pots and pans, the refrigerator opening and closing, the heat breathing through the pipes, the droning of soap operas. And there is an endless *tit tit tit* sound, which must be Mrs. Dodd knitting. At night, Mr. Dodd keeps the TV blaring, clomps around, chews like a pig, and then burps. As far as I can tell, they never talk at all.

The next week, though, I hear Mr. Dodd say, "It's too damn quiet around here. I've got to get Brian back home." I start to think he has trapped Brian somewhere like the boiler room at the Gooey factory. I decide to follow him to work at five in the morning. I must walk around the factory a hundred times before I realize it's impossible to see anything through the small cubed windows. Then Mr. Dodd starts working doubles and it's too hard to keep up with his schedule. I see him in the think tank of his garage where he and Brian came up with ideas for the next great candy bar. He is slumped in his chair with his head in his hands. I think he misses Brian as much as I do.

If I follow the Dodds on Sunday, I bet I'll find out where Brian is. I call Classy Cab. "Would you be able to follow a car?"

"Follow a car?"

"Yes, I want to find out where someone's going."

"Do they know you're following them?"

"No."

"I don't know about that. Depends on the driver, I guess. You sound like a kid."

"I'm not," I say.

"Do you have the money?"

"Yes."

He doesn't say anything.

"I'll call back."

THE NEXT day I ask for a Classy Cab to be at our house on Sunday at ten in the morning. I give the man my last name and address and tell him to have the cab wait at the bottom of the driveway. When he asks where I'm going, I say Logan Airport.

On Sunday morning the Dodds leave early, right before Classy Cab pulls all the way to the top of our driveway and beeps. "What on earth is that?" Teresa asks. She puts on her high heels and goes out to talk to the driver. I slip into the shower just in time to hear her say, "There's a cab here. The guy said someone ordered a cab."

"A cab?" Helen answers.

"He said he's supposed to take someone to Logan Airport."

After a minute she says, "Does anyone know anything about this? I don't know what to tell him."

"It must be the wrong house," Helen says.

"That's what I said, but he said it was the Sooners."

"It wasn't me."

"Ship?"

"She's in the shower."

"That's weird." Later she tells Trudy, "I gave him a couple of dollars for his trouble."

I can't call Classy Cab for a while in case they recognize my voice. I figure I could hide in the back of the Dodds' pickup if the bed is filled with trash like it usually is. It wouldn't cost anything and it'd get me right to wherever they go on Sundays. Otherwise how am I ever going to find out anything?

A week after the Classy Cab came to our house, I go over to the Dodds' around 9:00 A.M. with an old blanket to cover myself when I get in the bed of the pickup. The house is dark and quiet as usual and the pickup's parked in the driveway. Trash bags and barrels, a broken fishing pole, Gooey wrappers, beer cans, coffee cups, and dirty snow fill the back. It's January and cold, but I climb in there.

As soon as I ball up underneath the old blanket, I feel Mrs. Dodd's eyes burning into me. I was sure all the shades were down. How could she have seen me? My skin is crawling. I can't stay here. A beer bottle rolls out of a loose trash bag, over the grooves of the bed, and smashes against the tailgate. I leap over the side of the truck with the blanket and run. When I am far enough away, I turn back and feel her eyes on me again. I don't know where they are coming from and I don't wait to find out.

Trudy said Brian would have said good-bye if it weren't for the snowstorm. Teresa thinks Mrs. Dodd is having a nervous breakdown and that's why they had to send Brian away. "Don't worry, he'll be back," they say. But they don't know anything.

One thing I'm trying to do is stop thinking about him. I don't go to Mr. Gray's or Mrs. Hayes's or anywhere we used to except Jimmy Joe's to help Teresa. No one seems to know why Brian went away. At first I hear people say—not to me, but I hear them—that Mrs. Dodd was put in Englewood State. Others say that Brian went on a shooting spree over Christmas, that he got kicked out of school, that the Department of Social Services took him away, and so on and so on.

In the locker room after gym class, Susie Long says to me, "I have some information you might be interested in." Her

Wolverines gym shorts hang from her fist and her T-shirt is slung over her shoulder. She thrusts her chest out, showing off her matching bra and underwear, black with lacy trim. Her stomach is flabby. "I'll whisper it to Lauren and you tell me if you can hear it." Her voice is sweet-sounding, but all her words end in a hiss.

She giggles as she walks back to her changing stall. "Think she'll hear?" she asks Lauren.

"Who knows? Maybe if you bark she'll hear you." They laugh. They're talking about the article in the *Herringtown Weekly* that quoted Dr. Gould saying I could hear sounds only dogs could hear. It didn't say I could hear sounds dogs *made*, but that doesn't stop her from barking at me whenever she walks by.

Susie clears her throat. "Here goes. My dad said that your so-called friend Brian is in military school in Virginia. I'm not sure why you don't know this when he's your *boyfriend*."

I stop untying the laces of my sneakers, glad she can't see my face burning. Even if she does know where Brian is, I don't want to hear about him from Susie Long. Anyway, there's a good chance she's lying. When Helen started dating Owen, Susie told her friends that Helen dyed her hair, when Helen doesn't. She said that Helen liked Owen just because his family is rich and a whole pack of other lies. "Don't pay any attention to her," Teresa told Helen. "She's a silly girl. She just wants attention."

"I also heard about what you two do in the woods behind the Gooey factory. Your ears must have gotten in the way." She bursts out giggling, then continues, "I guess he's not supposed to have anything to do with the *Sooner* girls anymore." She says our name like there's something wrong with us.

"How can he when he's not even here?" I ask out loud, but she can't hear me.

She hisses, then giggles some more. I wonder what she is going to say about me next.

"Did you hear me?" Susie says louder. "Ship Sooner, did you hear me?"

In a minute she's standing beside my stall, combing her long brown hair. "Well?" she says. "Did you hear what I said?"

"No." I'm waiting for her to leave before I change into my school clothes. I straighten my caps. "Anyway, Dr. Gould said my hearing would get worse as I got older. Pretty soon I'll have normal hearing."

"Normal?" she repeats, tossing her hair back. Her lips curl. "Right."

People finally get tired of talking about Brian and about why he left. *Brian.* I write him a letter, telling him I'll forget about what happened with him and Helen if he comes back, but I don't know where to send it.

As soon as she went back to Hair Camp, Trudy started smoking. She said she might as well die happy. Teresa told her she was going to have another heart attack and Trudy did. This one was worse than the last one. She had to spend two weeks in the hospital and the doctor said she couldn't go back to work for six months. Most nights Teresa spends at Trudy's. She doesn't have time to cook, so she brings Styrofoam boxes of leftover pasta from Jimmy Joe's. A lot of times I have pie for dinner—chocolate, blueberry, or Boston cream. On Fridays during Lent, Teresa makes egg salad or tuna sandwiches so we don't forget and eat meat.

Helen usually stays in her room. She waits until I'm finished in the kitchen, then fixes herself something and takes it upstairs to eat. I never actually see her eat, but I check the refrigerator to see what's missing and watch for her empty plate when she comes back downstairs. Some nights she takes only a few pieces of pasta, and other nights she takes a whole to-go box of ziti bolognese or fettuccine Alfredo.

On these nights, when it's just me and Helen, I'll start to do my homework, but then I'll hear Helen in her room and I can't concentrate on anything else. I listen to her cross her room to turn up the radio, open her window, and strike a match. This is followed by long, slow inhalations. I bet Owen smokes, too. I keep hearing her breathing and not breathing and those awful sounds Brian made. Some nights she takes Teresa's whiskey and drinks it in her room. I haven't seen her, but I smell it when she cleans out her glass in the bathroom. Also she bought a long cord so she could drag Teresa's phone into her room. Except for Teresa, Margie, and salespeople who she hangs up on, no one calls—not Brian and not Owen. Sometimes she calls WAAF if they're giving away free concert tickets, records, or T-shirts, and once she was the fifth caller instead of the sixth, the winning caller. I was glad she wasn't the sixth.

Of course she's been waiting for Owen to call since Christmas Eve. If he promised her something that afternoon, I'm pretty sure she didn't get it. If Helen and I talked, I'd tell her what Trudy told me—that men are overrated. But maybe she knows that, because three separate times I heard her crying. I wasn't sure the first time, but I am now. She was trying to be quiet by stuffing her head under a pillow, but I heard her through the pillow and through the walls. Just a murmur of crying—I couldn't believe it was hers.

Tonight Teresa doesn't go to Trudy's. "It's about time we had a family dinner," she says and makes French fries and hamburgers. Helen comes downstairs wearing an old Herringtown sweatshirt and sweatpants. Lately she wears any old thing. I bet if she were still dating Owen, she'd be wearing her Sassoon jeans. I pour the milk, Teresa sets the hamburgers in the center of the table, and Helen gets herself a Tab. Teresa asks, "So, how's school?"

"Okay," I say.

"Boring," Helen says.

"Why's that?"

"Just is."

"Well, there must be some news," Teresa says.

"Nope."

"Not a thing?" Teresa looks from me to Helen. "Why aren't you eating your hamburger?"

Helen shrugs.

I miss the sound of Trudy laughing and coughing and mixing drinks and the way she combed my hair with her fingers. "How's Trudy?" I ask.

"Oh, pretty much the same. Yesterday was another T-Day. That's why I stayed so late." Teresa calls the days Trudy thinks she's going to die T-Days. "It sure is quiet without her around, isn't it?"

Helen's eyes flash at Teresa. "*Why* did my dad leave?"

Teresa sets her hamburger down. Her hands slip off the table. "I don't know, Helen. He left one morning to go to work and never came back. He didn't leave a note and didn't say anything to anyone as far as I know. There's nothing to tell." We know this, but each time she says it, it makes less sense.

"There must be some reason."

At first Teresa doesn't answer. Then she says, "I don't know, I don't know. We were too young when we fell in love."

"How young?"

"Too young." Her eyes glaze over.

"Tell us something," Helen begs. "You never tell us anything."

As we wait for her to tell us something, I listen for the usual hum of the refrigerator, the ticking of the kitchen clock, and the heat moving through the walls, but all I hear is Teresa swallowing her breath. Finally she says, "The four of us used to sleep in the same bed."

"The same bed?" Helen asks.

Teresa nods, then laughs. "The bed took up most of the garage."

"What else? What else, Teresa?"

Teresa stares out the window, dark with night, as she says quietly, "I wanted you to think he was someone better. I wanted you to think I was someone better. We were young and stupid. He never wanted to get married."

"Why did he, then?" Helen squints across the table. "Why?"

Teresa pinches her lips shut.

"What if he came back after we left?" Helen asks, hitting her fork against her plate.

"I thought he was going to. He left everything behind. All

the money we saved up. We stayed until I couldn't stand it any longer."

I know what happened after that. We took our dad's truck and everything we owned and drove to Herringtown so Teresa could apply for the job at Jimmy Joe's that she read about in the *Globe*. She was twenty-five, Helen was almost four, and I was two.

"What if he's there now?" Helen asks.

That's what I'm thinking.

"Oh, no," Teresa says, "I don't think so. Don't forget, he left us."

The phone rings.

"I think it's for me," Helen says, jumping up. Smiling, she twists the cord around her finger. "Okay, I'll let you know." After she hangs up, Helen tosses her hair over her shoulder and says, "I want to take singing lessons."

"Oh?"

"Yes," Helen says. "No one takes my singing seriously."

Teresa bites into her hamburger.

"There's a place in Andover."

"Andover? That's a little far, isn't it?"

"It's thirty-five minutes."

"They're not at Andover Academy, are they?"

"No, they're not," she snaps.

"Helen, you know I have to work in the afternoons. How do you expect me to drive you there? And how much do they cost?"

"Twenty-five an hour, and Margie's brother said he could drive me. If I pay him."

"Good Lord. Do you have any money saved up?"

"I could pay for the first one."

"Are you sure about all this, Helen? This is what you really want to do?"

"Yes, I'm sure."

"Let me think about it. Are they once a week?"

Helen nods.

"That's a hundred a month."

"I know. Do you think I shouldn't do it, then?" She folds her arms across her chest.

"I didn't say that. It's a matter of whether we can afford it or not."

"I need to do this, Teresa."

"Why's it so important all of a sudden?" Teresa sets her hamburger back on her plate.

"It's not all of a sudden. Music transcends—"

"Transcends? Does it transcend all the bills and the mortgage, too?"

Helen's chair scrapes against the floor. "Can I be excused? I bet if Ship wanted lessons for her stupid hearing, she'd get them."

We listen to her running up the stairs, slamming her door. Teresa sighs. Silence settles around the table, thick and heavy— comfortable. Glad not to say anything, we finish our hamburgers. Helen's footsteps cross her bedroom floor and she turns her radio on to Simon and Garfunkel singing "Bridge Over Troubled Water." She sings along, carrying the notes too long and too high. Teresa and I look at each other, trying not to laugh. I eat Helen's hamburger.

"A hundred a month. She must think I'm a millionaire." Teresa shakes her head. "Thankfully one of you is sensible."

"Sometimes," I say, "I think Brian's never going to come home."

Staring out the window, Teresa says, "He'll be back, Ship, don't worry. People don't just disappear."

"What about Dad?"

She coughs and spits up a piece of hamburger. She starts laughing and can't stop until tears are pouring down her face. "That's true," she finally says, wiping her face. "He did disappear. You're right."

"Teresa, it's been almost six weeks and the Dodds don't return any of my messages."

"He'll be back, Ship." Teresa's eyes are glazed. "You know what I'd like to know? How she got stuck on this idea of singing."

I am about to remind her that Owen is in a band when I remember the guitar pick that I found between the pages of Teresa's dictionary.

"Maybe you could talk to her," she says.

"Me?"

"Well, she doesn't say anything to me."

"She doesn't even look at me."

"It wouldn't hurt to try. I wish you two were closer."

The phone rings. "I bet that's Trudy." Teresa rises. It's Jack. She grimaces then carries the phone into her bathroom. "Thanks anyway, Jack, but things are too busy here with Trudy being sick."

She turns on the faucet. "If that's what you want to think about us, that's just fine."

After that she has to call Trudy to tell her about Jack. After twenty minutes of waiting for her to stop talking, I can't wait any longer. "Teresa," I whisper. She pushes the mouthpiece to the side and leans toward me. "If I talk to Helen, will you talk to the Dodds?"

"Deal." She shifts the phone back to her mouth.

I go upstairs to wait for Helen to come out of her room so I can ask her about her singing. Then Teresa will go to the Dodds' to find out where Brian is. How could they not talk to her? Maybe she can ask about Johnny, too. I have to press my ear caps to my ears because Helen is singing like she's in an opera. Why can't she just sing regular? I'm embarrassed for her, but I keep listening from behind the closed door—just like I did at confession.

Helen was on one side of the confession box and I was on the other. She went first. When I heard her heavy breathing, I slipped my ear caps off. She said, "I read books I wasn't supposed to."

"Go on," Father Hannah said.

"I used fake covers, like *Moby-Dick* and *Jane Eyre*."

"*Moby-Dick* and *Jane Eyre*?" He coughed.

"Yes, Father."

"What were you reading?"

"Romances. Well"—she hesitated—"trash novels. My friend Margie got them from her mother."

"God gave you your eyesight to read good things. When you go home today, read something good."

"Yes, Father."

There was silence.

"Is there something else?" he asked.

"It's not fair that I don't have a father and everyone else does.

I don't even remember him. And I can't stand my sister," she whispered. "She listens to everything I say. And she thinks she's so great because she can hear everything."

"God has a plan for everyone, Helen. He is your father. Listen to Him." He paused. "He gave Ship exceptional hearing. That is His gift. He gave you special gifts, too."

"I can sing?"

"Well, then, that's His gift to you. We must accept the Lord's gifts as they are. I want you to do something extra nice for Ship today. And remember your gift. Go now, and say two Hail Marys and three Our Fathers."

She never did anything nice for me that day or ever since that I can remember. And I didn't think I was great, either. Father Hannah's feet scraped the floor as he turned to slide the screen between us open. His dark head was bent over his praying hands. I slipped my ear caps back on and felt myself plunging through the darkness. It was like a cold snake was crawling up my back. I had to confess.

"Shhh," he whispered.

I had rehearsed what I was going to say a hundred times, but I couldn't remember it now. He smelled like tuna fish. My tongue itched, my mouth watered. "I hear everything and I know I'm not supposed to." I couldn't stop the words from rushing out. "I heard everything Helen said."

"What did you hear?" he asked.

I repeated everything she said word for word, including that she was supposed to do something nice for me.

He gasped. "She was barely whispering. Did you take your ear caps off?" He lifted his eyes to meet mine.

"Yes."

"Ship Sooner," he said, "God blessed you with exceptional hearing, but you can't listen to other people's confessions. They're between each person and God. I'm simply the mediator. I want that to be very clear. And that means everything you tell me is just between us, too. Do we have a deal?"

"Yes, Father," I answered, thinking, *blessed*. He had written that I was blessed in the bulletin, but hearing him say it was different.

"Ship," he said, "God is the light shining through everything around you. All you have to do is look and you'll find Him. He already found you."

I never listened to another confession after Helen's. I had to say three Hail Marys, then I started looking for Him right away—in the spiderweb in the ashtray of the Continental, in the leaves of the pear tree, in Teresa's eyes, especially after a few whiskey sours, in the rain streaming down the kitchen window, and in the sea glass we'd been collecting in a jar. All afternoon I thought, *I am blessed*.

I remember thinking that I had a special role to play, though I didn't know what it was. The last thing Father Hannah said to me that day was "Let anyone with ears hear. Ship Sooner, use your gift wisely."

I haven't used my gift wisely.

"HELEN," I call, leaning against her door. "Helen?"

She doesn't reply.

"Helen, did you hear me? Are you deaf?"

She turns down the radio.

"I want to ask you about your singing. Why don't you answer me?"

After a long silence, she says, "Why should I when you listen to everything I say anyway?" She turns the radio back up.

I decide not to ask Helen about her singing tonight. Or the next day or the day after that either, and as far as I know, Teresa never reaches the Dodds to ask about Brian. She telephones and goes over there three times, but they don't answer her, and she finally gives up.

If Helen and I were talking, I'd tell her that Owen has a new girlfriend. I was in front of Jimmy Joe's when he pulled up in his father's BMW with a girl in the car. At first I thought it was Helen in the front seat, but this girl was wearing a fur coat. She stroked Owen's hair before she got out, then hurried past me without a glance. Owen slid his sunglasses up on his forehead and turned toward Jimmy Joe's. His leather seat squeaked when he shifted away from me, looking straight ahead again. I stared at him, trying hard to burn two holes through the back of his head. His girlfriend brushed by me as she passed, carrying a paper bag. Her blond ponytail swung across her back as she slid into the passenger seat, dropping the takeout on the backseat. I lifted my ear caps.

"Don't look now, but there's the sister of that crazy girl I was telling you about," he whispered to her.

Crazy? I could say what I wanted about Helen, but he couldn't. As the girl reached for the door of the car to pull it shut, I called out, "If she's so crazy, then why'd you give her a gold chain behind the Gooey factory?"

The girl's blank look of surprise quickly turned dark. "You gave her a gold chain?"

"Shut the door," Owen told her.

"When?"

"Shut the door first."

"What were you doing behind the Gooey factory?"

Owen's hands gripped the steering wheel. "Shut the door—she can hear everything we're saying. She has some kind of freaky hearing thing." He peeled away.

ONE AFTERNOON I call Classy Cab. "How long would it take to drive to Virginia?" I ask.

"Are you kidding me?"

"No."

"From where to where?"

"Herringtown to Virginia."

"A long time. We wouldn't be able to drive you there."

"How long?"

"I don't know, twelve hours."

"How much would it cost?"

"In a Classy Cab?" He laughed. "I don't know, six hundred dollars maybe—if we did it, which we don't."

I don't know if Brian is ever coming home. He hasn't written or called. I can't figure it out. All the days start to feel the same. I don't care what I hear or don't hear. I don't care about going to Waterfalls anymore. I don't care that Helen stays in her room all night and that Teresa spends all her time with Trudy. I don't care about the Dodds, the Gooey factory, school, or anything. Instead of going to the cafeteria, I eat my lunch in the library. One warm day I take off my ear caps and run through the woods, listening for whatever might be calling me.

I feel my blood pulsing and my skin growing warm like it used to, but that's all. Most of the time I feel sort of numb, like I'm in a trance, just waiting.

And the days pass one after another until winter finally turns to spring.

Part Two

A CALLING

S i x

IT'S GOOD FRIDAY OF Easter weekend, which is followed by April vacation, and I'm waiting outside Jimmy Joe's for Teresa. No one asks why I stand out here like this every afternoon. Teresa says if you do anything long enough people just get used to it. The Sinatra tape cracks and pops more than ever. *I know it's strictly*—pop—*taboo*—*need in me*—pop—*heart says, "—indeed," in*—pop—*me*.

Brian has been gone almost four months now. I wonder what I'd do if he just came walking down the street. *Those fingers*—pop, pop—*in my*—pop—*hair*. The tape stops short, garbling. I take my ear caps off and turn around to see if something is the matter inside Jimmy Joe's.

What I hear is the wind rushing through the tops of the trees, carrying the smell of rain. Blackbirds screech like a rusty hinge, the cars swoosh by, a glass clinks, a match strikes, someone inhales, the cash register door clangs, Laura's foot scrapes along the floor, then a police siren blasts and all of Main Street goes blurry in front of me—the noise is too much. My head snaps back like it has just been filled with hot water. But there was something else. I heard something else under all of this, or over it.

After the police car passes, I hear it again—the high pitch of something crying. The sound goes straight through the center of me. The wind keeps blowing and the blackbirds keep screeching and clucking as if nothing unusual has happened, but I hear something crying. It might be a hurt animal. Once when Mr. Dodd shot a raccoon going through their trash, it made desperate cries like this.

I run behind Jimmy Joe's parking lot, past the Dumpster, into the thick woods. In the stillness, the light falls onto puddles of last night's rain, so the overgrown trail shines and it's like I'm walking over water, right over the floating pine needles. The high screeches sound more like a baby's. I wait for it to stop, to be muffled by a blanket, by the walls cornering a crib, or by a mother's breast, but this crying is all I hear. I race, tripping through the brush.

My ear caps fall off and the crying becomes louder and clearer—I'll come back for my caps. The sun shifts through the pines, sending a fleeting path of light between me and a mound of dirt ahead; the cry is coming from the earth. The soil collapses on all sides of the sound rising from the ground. I stop, cool air sucking up my legs, and smell blood.

Something is breaking up through the dirt—two tiny fists punch the air. The soil crumbles around them. The hole is shallow and in it, wrapped in a hand towel stained with blood, half covered with earth, leaves, and ferns, is a baby, *a real baby*. My hands are huge around its tiny rib cage. When I lift it up, it pushes into my chest. Its dark sweaty head flops backward and its open mouth screams and spits. I almost drop it. Someone tried to bury a baby back here.

I hold its head, lopsided and squishy, in my hands. Its eyes are swollen, and even though it's crying, not a tear comes out, just a little yellow pus. It's so ugly, I want to put it back in the dirt where I found it. Then it stops crying just like that and reaches out to me. It lifts a fist toward me. When I put out a finger, it clutches onto it. I gasp at the strength of this tiny thing, tinged blue, especially its hands and feet.

The hoop of trees around us bends closer, letting a flash of sunlight through. The towel wrapped around its middle falls away. I try to brush off the dirt on its belly, holding back the clenched arms, keeping its kicking feet from me. The umbilical cord, cut and knotted with a shoelace, is stubby and caked with brown blood. I don't want to touch it.

It must have just happened. It must have just been born. Did I hear someone in labor? What does it sound like? I can't remember what I heard. Then I see the crack between the legs and the bluish-red flaps on each side—a girl. I squat down with her in my arms and begin to rub my fingers in small circles over her skin to warm her. She must belong to someone.

A bolt of fear licks through me. I jump up, holding her close to me, and search wildly around for whoever left her here. This must be some kind of trap. The birds have quit their shrieking, the squirrels are no longer scampering, and the wind has stopped blowing. The air is thick and still. In the open spaces between the treetops, a single plane hums across the sky. The sun shifts again, lighting a path in front of me as if showing me a way out.

No one is here. Just me and this baby. I close my eyes and think, when I look again, she'll be gone, but there she is in my arms, her tiny mottled body like that raccoon Mr. Dodd skinned and hung in their garage. I have to keep her warm. As soon as I put her down and start to unzip my jacket, she starts wailing again. I hold my hands over my ears and rock back and forth. I have to find my ear caps, but I can't leave her. She balls herself up even more, then kicks out, boxing the air. Her head is too big and her skin is slick and blue. She spits mucus and her arms and legs flail. She's so strange, I don't know what to do with her. I pick her up and she quiets, reaching out for my finger again when I put it close to her.

I close my eyes. I was in the woods a long time ago. I remember the smell of a dog, the warmth of its body wrapped around me and the sound of its heart beating. Also the dark and the light, the trees, the wind, the stars overhead—the whole world became this. I remember being curled up in a ball with the dog around me.

I open my eyes and she turns her head slightly toward me. Her ears stick straight out like Brian's. The ground slips beneath me. My head goes light and numb. She couldn't be Brian's. I laugh out loud. I'm breathing too quick. I rock side to side, then lean toward her and touch her earlobe with my finger. I scoop her up with my other hand. She stops breathing. Then she throws up on my neck and is better. She's so puny.

I try to clean her with the towel, but it's wet and filthy dirty, so I bend closer and try to wipe off a bloody clump with a leaf. The leaf crumbles, smearing the blood and goop and bits of leaf across her. I spit on my fingers and try to clean her that way.

When I lick my fingers, I taste her blood and salt like the blood from my own cuts and the salt from my own skin. I lick my fingers again, sweeping them across her again and again, until I am putting my tongue to her skin and licking the dirt and blood off her cheeks, her chin, up around her eyes.

I spit all the goop out and keep going over her neck, her shoulders, her underarms, her pulsing ribs, her bowlegs, and the littlest curled toes—my tongue rough on her skin. I spit out the dirt and blood and white stuff, bitter and salty, and then I do it again. When I stop, prickles run across the back of my neck and my mouth goes dry. I want to take her somewhere—away from here. Her silver-blue eyes flicker open. I lean closer. *Thump thump shhh, thump thump shhh.* Her heart beats so much faster than Brian's. I take off my bomber jacket and wrap her inside it. She could fit in the opening of one sleeve.

There is a birthmark on her heel, a deep red circle. I stare at it until it becomes bigger than she is, threatening to blot her out. Then it becomes smaller than a pinpoint. I can't take her to the police, they'd take her away.

Where did she come from, who left her here, is her mother going to come back for her? Her eyes are the color of Brian's. Did Helen get pregnant that time in the shed? But I saw her and she wasn't pregnant. Where did the baby come from? Could she be Laura's? Or a Gooey factory worker's or Joy Tucker's? Or someone driving through Herringtown?

The sky has become dark. I step back from the hole, not knowing what to do with her. She must know—her red face pinches as she screams a cry that seems to uncurl on her tongue, rattling its way out. I almost drop her again. I could have killed her. As I hold her out in front of me, my pulse races and my face flushes and breaks out in a sweat. She has almost no eyebrows or eyelashes and her puffy eyelids flicker. Her crying tunnels right through me. The ground swells up around us and the trees bend closer still. I want her to disappear. I want to disappear with her.

A branch snaps. The soft padding of footsteps and whispering voices float through the trees. They are coming back for her—they could be here in seconds. I am going to be caught. What have I done? I don't even know whose she is and I licked the blood and dirt and goop from her skin. I set her down inside my bomber jacket, and then throw up, spitting and gagging like she did.

A breeze sends some dead leaves skittering across the ground. A squirrel hurries up an oak tree, stopping midway to stare at us with dark twinkling eyes. I have to put her back. She weighs almost nothing. It's warm for April, but I can't take my bomber jacket off her. I zip it up around her and place her screaming, writhing body back into the hole where I found her. When she kicks through the jacket, the top layer of dirt caves in around her. Her screaming circles around me as I back away from her.

I'll leave now, and when I come back, she'll be gone and it'll be over as if I never found her, as if it never happened at all. Whoever is coming for her now will take her somewhere safe. If Teresa asks, I'll tell her I left my jacket in the woods, which I did. I can't take care of a baby. The footsteps and whispering sweep closer and I cover her with leaves, brush, and ferns the way I found her. Were they burying her or hiding her? She kicks and punches and keeps fighting this new covering until I can't stand it anymore. I have to turn away.

Once I went fishing with Brian and Mr. Dodd on Silver

River and found a fish stranded on shore, flopping side to side. With my big toe, I nudged its slippery body back into the water. With a wave of its tail, it swam away. I don't look back now.

The tree branches dip in the wind, sway, and whistle. One snaps. The sky is a dark haze of clouds. Her crying fades like the sound of the blackbirds flying away, their beating wings becoming softer and softer. My eyes blur so I can't see where I'm going. A branch slaps against my face and thorns scratch my skin, but I don't stop until I get to Main Street, where, shocked by the passing headlights, I freeze for a moment, then keep running until I am back at Jimmy Joe's. I stand there in the doorway, panting, my mouth thick with saliva, my skin coated in sweat.

" 'Cause it's witchcraft, wicked witchcraft.' " Laura sings as she lifts the salt and pepper shakers from an empty table to wipe underneath before setting them back down. " 'I know it's strictly taboo—' " Moving quickly around the tables, she doesn't drag her leg as much now that she's busy. Her hair is pulled back and her lips are painted red. Is the baby hers? Brian said she brought her customers upstairs after work.

An older couple sits down and Laura fills their glasses with water, then hands them menus. The woman smiles at Laura, shakes out her napkin, and spreads it over her knee. For a moment, everything is like it always is. The next second everyone looks suspicious. It could have been any of them.

"Teresa was looking for you. Did you see her?" Laura calls.

"No," I answer.

"Well, come in or out, don't just stand there with the door open. Are you hungry? I'll fix you something to eat if you want. Helen's over there." She points to the corner table.

What's Helen doing here? She never comes here anymore. As soon as I take a step forward, I want to be back outside where I can hear the wind and the baby. I whip around to run back out at the same time as a man and boy are coming in. The man's hand grazes my chest. Blood rushes to my face and I am suddenly aware of the roundness of my breasts and the curves of my hips. I am embarrassed, as if I have done something wrong.

"Oh, excuse me. I thought you were going in." Holding his son's hand, he smiles.

"Sorry." In the reflection on the front window we are all going to dinner together. Inside, silverware clinks against the plates, the music plays, voices circle around the room. I can't even tell who's talking. I've lost the baby—I can't hear her anymore. What do I do now? Before anything else happens, I clamp my hands over my ears.

"Come on," the man says to the boy.

I bet Brian's forgotten all about taking a taxi to Waterfalls to track down my dad. I follow the father and son to the bar, where Laura is clasping two menus under her arm, motioning the new customers to a table. I walk fast through the rush of noise pressing through my hands into my skull. I have to focus on something, I can't even hear Frank Sinatra. I follow Laura. She seats them, hands them menus, then places two glasses of water on their table. "I'll be right back to tell you the specials," she says. She puts her arm around my shoulders and pulls me back.

"Tonight you can get whatever you want. Anything," the man says to the boy. "Are you hungry? Get whatever you want. What do you feel like? What sounds good?"

I taste and smell her—her blood and spit in my mouth and on my clothes.

Laura returns to their table with a basket of bread and a dish of butter. "What do you say?" the man says to the boy as he reaches for a roll.

"Thank you," the boy says to Laura.

"Ship," Laura calls, pointing to Helen and Margie, "they're right over there. Where are your ear caps?"

Lifting her eyes from her soda glass, Helen leans across the table, whispering to Margie. I take a step toward them. When they see me, they lean back against the red cushions of the booth.

"Gross, what's that from?" Margie points to the front of my stained shirt.

Something wet is on my neck. I pull out a thorn, the pointy tip sticky with blood. I stare at my finger, remembering how she grabbed onto it. I have to go back.

"Ugh." Margie winces. "That's disgusting. Here. Why don't you use this." She passes me a napkin, but that makes it worse.

"Where were you?" Helen asks. "Aren't you usually home by now?" She pulls the straw to her mouth and draws on it. Her eyes half closed, her lids sparkle with blue eye shadow. She's wearing too much makeup. Still, her face is pale and puffy.

"Nowhere," I say. I can't hear the baby. She'll die if I don't go back.

"How could you be nowhere?" She taps the outside of her glass. "Teresa was just here looking for you, you know. What were you doing?"

"What are *you* doing?" I ask her. "You never come here anymore."

"What's it to you? Why shouldn't I be here?"

"Just asking."

"Maybe I'm eating here tonight if that's all right with you. At least I'm not standing there with stuff all over my shirt like an idiot."

I wobble and have to hold on to the table to catch myself. The noise is making me nauseous. I need fresh air. Should I just run?

Officer Robinson walks in with a large Styrofoam cup of coffee. He lifts his cap and runs a hand through the dark waves of hair as he takes in the room like he's memorizing it. He throws a leg over a bar stool, and half smiling, waves his hand in a sweeping arc around the room. Helen and Margie wave back. I start to wave but see the red tips of my fingers and shove my hands into my pockets. I can't let him see me. He turns his cap upside down, fingering the rim. I know I should tell him I found a baby, but I'm not going to. I'm not telling anyone.

"It'll just be a couple more minutes." With a plate of pasta in either hand, Laura hurries past Officer Robinson.

"Sure thing, Laura," he says, reaching for his wallet.

"Anything happening tonight?" she calls back.

"This is it."

Helen glances from me to Officer Robinson. Then she slides out of the booth, saying she'll be right back. When Officer Robinson sees Helen approaching, he swings around to face her, straddling the bar stool. He's around Teresa's age, but he looks like he's in high school when he smiles at Helen. He taps the floor with his shiny black boots and spins his hat on his first finger. I try to listen to what they're saying, but Margie, tugging my arm, yells in my ear, "Why don't you sit down so I can fix your shirt, Ship? You can sit here until Helen gets back."

Everyone seems to be talking at once. All the noise rises, bouncing back and forth inside my head. I have to get out before it's too late, before I'm trapped in here—I have to save her. How could I have left her there?

Margie stands to lean closer to my ear. Though she is two years older than I am, I'm taller. Her arm is fleshy against my skin and she wears a sickeningly sweet perfume. "Hello? Did you hear me? Earth to Ship," she yells, giggling, sending a sharp pain straight through my skull. When she leans toward me again and opens her mouth, I snap at her, biting the air, catching a few strands of her hair between my teeth.

"Oh, my God!" she cries out in a hurt voice, pulling her arms close to her chest. Backing up, she turns in Helen's direction and yells, "She bit me!"

People at the other tables look over. I pull a wisp of Margie's hair from my mouth and walk past her, past the father with his son, past Officer Robinson and Helen, and past Laura. "Ship Sooner, where are you going? Did you eat any supper?" Laura calls behind me. "And where's your jacket?"

"I'm going to get it." I walk faster.

"Put on your ear caps, too."

I run down the sidewalk alongside a Bonanza bus spewing a thick trail of exhaust. The passengers in the window seats stare at me. I wish I were on that bus, leaving Herringtown, going somewhere—anywhere. I'd sit back in a cushioned seat, watching the highway and fields and towns pass by one by one until I got to the very end. That's where I'd get out.

Mr. Gray steps off the bus and flips his straggly ponytail over his shoulder onto his back. Every few steps he sucks spit up from the back of his throat, as if there is a small pool of drool there. I'm so sick of it all. I stop at the edge of the woods, paralyzed, disgusted, letting this thought sink in: I could leave.

I see the angry red face screaming up at me from the dirt and feel her tiny hand clutching my finger and I take off fast into the dark woods. I'm leaving Herringtown. I'm careful not to get caught in the thornbushes or whacked by a branch. The moon shines through the hazy sky, making the ground glow briefly before the light disappears again.

I don't hear the baby crying, and then I do. She's calling me. I follow the sound of her until I see my bomber jacket, her shape moving inside it, and the dirt cupping her on either side.

Seven

SHE LETS OUT A wail when I step near her. "I'm sorry." When I pick her up this time, I know I'm not going to put her back down. Her head flops backward, too heavy for the rest of her. I catch it in my palm, afraid at first if I move it'll fall off. Then slowly I brush off everything sticking to her—dirt, leaves, white specks of wool from the inside of the bomber jacket—and set her head on my shoulder, spreading my hand over the center of her back, up along her neck. I walk her around and around the hole.

The year I was seven, the Willgohs, who lived in the Dodds' house, had their baby. That first summer after Mr. Willgohs left for work, I'd stand outside their living room window. "Come in, Ship," Mrs. Willgohs would sing out when she saw me. She was from the South, so all her words stretched and distorted like when you talk through a tube. She had me sit on the end of the couch with my elbow propped up on a cushion. Then she placed baby Rosie in my arms and gave me a warm bottle to feed her until she fell asleep. While I did this, Mrs. Willgohs cleaned her house, talked on the phone, painted her toenails, or flipped through her mail-order catalogs. She even left me there a few times while she went to get her hair done. That baby smelled like melted butter and cream, and while she was sleeping she made noises like she was whispering to me.

Her mouth opened and closed, puckering and purring, whimpering, and then smiling briefly. Sometimes she'd wake up and I knew enough to burp her, but I never left the end of the couch until Mrs. Willgohs came home, even if my arm ached so bad I thought it would fall off. Mrs. Willgohs didn't care that I wore ear caps, and sometimes she sent me home with a dollar. That winter the Willgohs moved. I ran down Hawthorn Street after their car as they drove away, but they didn't stop. I haven't held a baby since then, and I've never walked around with one.

The clouds rumble in the dark sky and the wind blows through the trees. She must be hungry because I am starving. I trace the outline of her body, holding my finger just above her. Her breath goes in and out. She twitches, and then a jolt runs through her like electricity, making her eyelids flutter. Then, as quickly as it came, it leaves her quiet and still. Clouds cover the moon.

It could have been anyone, but I keep seeing Helen's puffy, pale face. Now that I think of it, her breasts have gotten bigger and she's been wearing such bulky clothes. But not even Helen would leave a baby in the woods. The wind hisses through old leaves.

I am going to save her—we have to leave now.

My stomach cramps and gurgles. Her head rests between my shoulder and neck, her heart beating into mine. As soon as I take a step, I hear voices behind me, to the side, and all around. The muffled voices, the wind against my ear, and her sounds blur together. A white light flashes through the trees. I stop. They are following us. Is it Helen? Officer Robinson?

A single raindrop splats on my cheek and without thinking anymore, I turn around and start toward home. It's hard enough to walk fast and impossible to run. She rests her cheek on my neck. She needs milk. I tuck her under my T-shirt and drape my bomber jacket over the front of me, covering her. I used to bring home turtles, snakes, salamanders, birds, bugs, and everything else tucked in my shirt—until Teresa found the hurt sparrow in my sock drawer. And then one of the snakes got loose in the house. We never did find it. Teresa was sure that she was going to wake up in the middle of the night and find it coiled up beside her in bed. It was only a little garter, but Teresa said, "Ship Sooner, I don't want you bringing another animal into this house. You don't know what germs they're carrying."

I almost trip over a root twisting out of the ground. Fog has settled between the trees. Usually from here I can see the back of Brian's house, but not now, and even if I could, it'd be quiet and the shades would be drawn. Sometimes when I pass by, I think I'm going to see Brian standing back here where I saw him the first time, hitting stones. It was May and the lilacs had just blossomed and I swear that's what I smell now, though they haven't bloomed yet. "We're almost there," I tell her.

The sky shakes above and the air is heavy and wet. I hunch over, making a shell around her as I walk through the sheets of darkness. For a minute, it seems I have lost track of everything. Then the pear tree rises up before me and I know I am home. I go in the back way, through the kitchen. Beads of sweat and rain drip off me onto the black and white squares of linoleum. "Helen," I call, trembling. Could she be Helen's? "Helen, are you here?" The echo of my voice comes back to me.

As soon as I turn on the lights, I see Teresa has been baking sweet rolls, Easter bread, raspberry danish, cinnamon raisin buns, meringues, and of course, pies. Trays of cookies and rolls, loaves and rings of bread are set on top of the refrigerator, the stove, the tabletop, the toaster oven, the seats of the chairs. I hear a soft plop of blueberry or lemon pie filling settling, then the tiniest crack of meringue crust, then nothing. The room smells of chocolate, cream, butter, vanilla, and fruit. Flour dust rises around my feet. The pipes breathe and rattle, the floors creak, and the wind whistles around the house.

On the stool in the center of the kitchen, there are two sandwiches on a plate covered in Saran Wrap with a note that reads: "Helene and Ship, tuna sandwiches. Be good girls. Love, T." A year ago, when Helen started taking French, she decided to spell her name the French way. Plain "Helen" was too boring. I never spell it like that.

With my right arm, I hold the baby like a small bundle, resting her body on my side, her head on my chest. She looks even stranger in the light. She has red spots with yellow-white centers and her hands and feet are blue. I don't know what's worse—her crying or her not crying. She's so quiet now, I wonder if there is something wrong with her. Is that why they left her in the woods? My insides ache.

The baby slowly opens her puffy eyes, rolling side to side, blinking, as if she's trying to focus on something. Dull gray in the dark, her eyes circle around until they finally seem to land on the back window, through which I see the glare of the insect zapper. It has been turned on ever since Trudy gave it to Teresa last Christmas to get rid of any early bugs. It isn't zapping now, just burning fluorescent purple. The baby's eyes close again. I turn the oven to broil and open the door, letting its heat spread through the kitchen.

I eye the sweet pastries and baked goods, rows and rows of them, as if I'm looking into a pastry case without the glass. I pick the one with the most confectionery sugar drizzled over the top. The dough is perfectly brown, soft and chewy. I pick up a cinnamon raisin bun, turn out the kitchen light, and concentrate on the sweet moist dough. Then I eat another danish, rocking the baby on my hip. When I close my eyes, I see Silver River, a streak of blue on our map, running through Herringtown, down into Rhode Island. If we follow Silver River, it'll take us to Waterfalls. That's what we have to do.

I listen for Margie's brother's car or the Continental. The baby shivers into me and then we both shiver into the heat of the oven. Small drops of rain hit the roof and the gutters. Without warning, she starts gasping, spitting up yellow stuff. I use my finger like a spoon to scoop the spit from her mouth.

Luckily, last summer Teresa decided we should all learn CPR after we started going to the beach every week so Trudy could exercise. Teresa bought the biggest doll she could find to practice on and taught us how to sweep the doll's mouth, push a fist in his gut, and breathe and pump and breathe and pump. One of us practiced CPR while the others watched, timing with a stopwatch. We named the doll Mr. Gray, Mr. Dodd, Father Hannah, Brian, or one of Teresa's boyfriends while whoever's turn it was put her lips on the doll's. One of us was giving CPR to a giant doll and the rest of us were laughing and cheering her on. After a few weeks, Teresa decided we were all good enough and put the doll back in its box and into the basement.

The baby brings her hand to her mouth, and in another second, she is breathing fine again. I turn off the oven and close the door, take her upstairs and lay her in the middle of my bed. Her screaming body kicks out at me. In the mirror, my hair is plastered to my head and has bits of leaves and twigs in it. Dirt streaks one side of my face. My neck, the collar of my shirt, and my fingers are stained dark with blood. I roll my dirty shirt into a ball and shove it under the bed, then put on my Superman shirt. Teresa says the S is for Ship.

I cocoon her in my sweatshirt to carry her into the bathroom. I let the sweatshirt fall to the floor and run the sink water until it's lukewarm. Afraid she'll slip through my fingers, she's wriggling so much, I squeeze her too tight and she starts crying again. Being in the bathroom is like being in the doctor's office, with every sound bouncing off the shiny hard surfaces, breaking my ears—but I can't let her go.

Helen's Big Red gum wrappers are in the trash can. I kick through the rest of the trash to see if there are any tampon wrappers. Wouldn't I have noticed if she were pregnant?

When I hold the baby under the faucet running a warm trickle, she swallows her wailing, gasps, and pinches her face. I try to prop her up with my arm, my hand cupping her head, but she is too slippery and I think I'm going to lose her in the sink. I hold her against me, but this doesn't work either, so I drop a towel in the sink and put her on top of it. My hand covers her entire chest, shoulders, and neck. I run a warm washcloth over her face, neck, and belly, around the umbilical cord, between her frog legs and tiny toes. My fingers work like a brush, cleaning her face, under her eyes, around her open mouth. I don't want to break her.

I can't stop staring at her big ears. I keep seeing the way Brian looked at Helen. And her mouth was there, I saw it. That's what happened. That's why he had to leave. I think my legs are going to give out beneath me. My stomach hurts. A metal flavor lines the back of my mouth. I push the thought away. Her ears flap when I wash behind them. I have to take care of her. I have to take her away from here.

When I finish rinsing her, I hear a car. It could be Helen or Teresa coming home or even Officer Robinson coming for her. I drop the washcloth and cover her in my sweatshirt again. I press her against me and creep to the window in the front hall. Everything is still and dark. There is no car. Am I hearing things?

I set her squirming body on my bed so I can think straight for a minute. I slip on dry socks and sneakers. In the top drawer of my bureau, I have eighty-eight dollars, which I tuck deep into the front pocket of my straight blue jeans. I've never stayed in a hotel before, but we could do that, the two of us.

Now I have to dress her and fast, but it's impossible. I need something to wrap around her. In the linen closet where Teresa keeps the medical supplies, I find the Ace bandages she bought for Helen when she sprained her ankle cheerleading. I start at the middle and wrap the bandage around her belly, right up to her chest, not too tight around the tops of her legs. After this, I slip a long-sleeved Wolverines T-shirt over her head, folding it over and tying the loose arms around her.

Brian used to carry Rabbit tucked inside his shirt. I need a little pouch to carry her in or a big Ace bandage to wrap her around my waist—the blanket our dad gave Helen that she uses for a shawl. She's going to kill me when she finds out I took the only thing he left her, but I don't care. I march into her room and grab it from where it's draped over her bed-post. Now Helen doesn't have anything from our father except the name Pineapple Princess. I'm taking this blanket, but his guitar pick, buttons, and sweater stained with paint will have to stay in the back of my closet hidden inside a shoe box. When I find him, I won't need all the things of his that I've collected.

There is only one picture on my wall: a photo of me, Teresa, and Helen that Trudy took at Singing Beach last July. Brian was there, too, but Teresa wanted a picture of the three of us. Helen, wearing a silver string bikini, stands in the front of the photo with her arms crossed over her flat, tanned stomach. A few weeks before, her skin was red and bubbling from lying out slathered in baby oil. The day we all went to the beach was one of the only days of the summer she spent with us. A half step behind Helen, Teresa wears a bathing cap and makes a face at Trudy. I am just to the left behind Teresa, and behind me is the blue line of sea. In a red Speedo, I am long and straight.

Looking at the photograph now, I can practically smell the salt and seaweed. I loved that day. I didn't have to wear my ear caps at all because I was swimming most of the time. I could hear underwater, but all the sounds were muffled like they are after it snows. My wet hair that Teresa says is the color of a new penny hangs to my waist. My fingers are stuck in my ears because of the seagulls. Trudy must have told us to smile or say cheese because our mouths are open, showing our teeth bright against our tanned, freckled faces.

I remember two things that happened that day. First, Helen sat on the beach towel with her legs spread far enough apart that anyone could see the dark hair curling out the edge of her silver bikini bottoms. Brian saw. Then on the way home, Helen, Brian, and I fell asleep in the backseat of the car, and when I woke up, Brian's knee had slid up against Helen's leg. I should have known. My skin went hot at once—I should have known it then.

That night Helen stayed out until six in the morning. She could have been with Brian. Teresa, who was waiting in the living room, must have been too tired to take Helen to the end of the driveway for one of their chats. "You can't do this, Helen. You can't just stay out all night. I didn't even know where you were. You said you were going to the movies," Teresa said. "I feel like half the people in my life have disappeared—and I don't want you to be next. Do you understand?"

"I'm sitting right here."

"Well, you weren't for the last seven hours. I was worried. Do you understand that?"

"Sorry. I fell asleep at Margie's."

"Were her parents home?"

"Not really."

"Not really?" Teresa sighed. "Were you drinking?"

"A little."

"I can smell it. What about Owen—was he there?"

"His family's on vacation."

"Was he there, I asked."

"For a little while. Lots of people were there."

"I just don't want anything to happen to you, all right?"

Brian could have been there. Was she meeting Brian at the shed then? I keep seeing them together and hearing the sounds they made and I know I have to take the baby far, far away. The baby looks at me with a wrinkled-up, red face like she's think-ing the same thing.

Outside, lightning cracks so loud I go numb. As the light enters the window at a slant, exposing us, I rock from my heels to my toes. My body seems hollow and the baby looks strange, wrapped in a bundle on my bed. She screams and the rain pelts against the glass. I don't have time to think. Sweat runs down my back as I plug my ears with toilet paper. I stuff a couple of T-shirts into my knapsack, then scoop her up. "Shhh." I shut my bedroom door behind me.

The crates Teresa uses to carry her pies are stacked by the kitchen door. They are deep and padded so the pies won't slide around when we drive them to Jimmy Joe's. I set the baby inside one of them. The pear tree scrapes against the window and its top branches reach into the stormy sky.

Last summer a couple driving through Herringtown who had heard about our giant pear tree stopped to photograph it. "Don't get too close," Teresa warned them as she waved from the kitchen and pointed to the signs. "If one of those pears falls, it could kill you!" Afterward the couple came to our door despite Teresa's warnings. They wanted to know how the pear tree got that way. Trudy said the soil had been blessed.

Teresa said, "Come on, Trudy, whoever used to live here overfertilized the soil."

"With *what*?" Helen asked.

"I don't know, fish and seaweed. That's what it smells like when it rains. A fisherman must have lived here before us."

"That's ridiculous," Trudy answered. "The ocean is twenty-five minutes away."

"Maybe it's just weird like some other things around here," Helen said, turning to me. The couple stared at me.

"Helen," Teresa said.

"It's got to be the tallest pear tree in the world," the man said. "You should report it to the *Guinness Book of World Records*."

"I will," Teresa said, sighing. "One of these days."

I TURN back to the baby in the pie crate. Her eyes wander, then she starts crying again. She screams out for breaths, her face bright red. I fall back against the wall, holding on to my head. I don't know what to do. The toilet paper falls out of my ears and this time I use balls of dough from an Easter roll to plug them up.

She must be hungry. I haven't even tried to feed her yet. I fill a jar with milk and put it in my knapsack along with some Easter rolls, raspberry danish, and cinnamon buns.

It takes a long time to hold her in place with one hand and to pull the long blanket like a scarf around my back and loop it around my waist with the other. I bend over, losing the blanket a few times before I get it wrapped around my chest like a huge belt, holding her against me. When I lift my hands in the air, she stays in place. She is so close we are like one thing. I put a V-neck sweater on, covering all of her but her head, which my bomber jacket zips over, leaving plenty of room for her to breathe. In the reflection on the kitchen door, I can't see her at all. No one would ever know I have a baby under here.

Last, I slip on my lucky hat, a blue-and-white knit with a pom-pom hanging off the end. Teresa named it my lucky hat because the first time I wore it I found five dollars, and every time after that, I found at least a nickel. Before that, I went without a hat because the cold never bothered me.

As soon as I step outside, the phone rings. I stop, but don't turn around to answer it. It's probably Teresa or it could be Laura calling about this weekend's orders. After eight rings, it stops. When I look up at the pear tree, I see Laura as a little girl falling through the air. Her braids fly up on either side of her screaming face and when she lands, her legs crumple beneath her. I close my eyes and walk away from the pear tree.

She is easier to carry now; her head doesn't flop from side to side. We cross our backyard and cut through the maple trees to the Dodds' backyard. The clouds drift apart, letting the moon through, lighting up the back of their house and wet lawn for a moment. Rabbit's water bottle dangles beside the window that Brian cut. I'd use Rabbit's bottle for the baby, but it'd be bad luck. Squatting, I find the jar of milk in my knapsack, then unzip my jacket. I loosen the blanket around her and lift her out. Wound in the Ace bandage, she is like a tiny mummy. I try to tilt the jar to pour a tiny stream of milk into her mouth, but it runs around the curve of her lips, down her chin, onto her neck. I dip my finger into the milk and put it in her mouth. By the time she sucks, there is almost nothing there. She doesn't seem hungry. Her breath is slow and even like purring, her heart thumps, and her eyes flutter open and shut.

Something flickers silver in the dark—Brian's jackknife. He must have dropped it after he cut the meshing. The edges of the blade are rusted. I snap the knife open, then shut, and let it slip through my fingers to the ground.

Drops of milk that have fallen from her face and seeped into the unraveled end of the Ace bandage drip to the dirt, where they dissolve in a second. If I soak a piece of cloth in the milk, I could drip it into her mouth the same way. I unwind the Ace bandage until it reaches her mouth, then soak the end. Touching her cheek with my finger, I lead her to the drops of milk that fall from the end of the bandage. She sucks a little. I dip the cloth into the milk again, dripping it between her lips. She pinches her mouth together, making the tiniest clicking sounds in the back of her throat. For a moment her body goes rigid; then her eyes close and she relaxes.

I reach for the jackknife. Cold in my palm, I snap it shut and slip it into my pocket. When a squirrel running along the tree branch above us shakes the rain down from the leaves, I think how lucky that squirrel is, having nothing in the whole world to worry about.

Margie's brother's Volkswagen bug, which sounds like our lawn mower, pulls up our driveway, a door slams, and footsteps cross the grass. Every day he picks up Helen and drives her and Margie to school, but he never took Helen to those twenty-five-dollar-an-hour singing lessons in Andover. I never heard Helen or Teresa bring them up again either. As soon as Helen opens the front door, Margie's brother drives away. The lights in our house go on, then off as Helen moves through the rooms, calling me. "Ship! Are you home, Ship?" I knock the jar of milk over, leaving only about a teaspoon. The white liquid forms a puddle on the ground, then is gone. Where do I get more milk now? "She's not going to find us," I whisper into the baby's big ear. "I'm not going to leave you either, don't worry."

I remember what Helen said to me after my checkup with Dr. Gould. Teresa said she wanted to talk to Dr. Gould alone and for me and Helen to wait in the car. I didn't hear what they said in his office, but I heard what Helen said from the front seat of the Continental. She whipped around to face me in the back and said, "No wonder my dad left."

"He was my dad, too," I said.

She flung herself back around. "Just shut up."

The baby's hand closes around my finger in that fierce grip. Where knuckles should be, she has tiny dimples. What would she do without me? She needs me.

When I rise, I realize my legs have fallen asleep and my arms are sore from holding her. I put her underneath my sweater and wind the blanket around and around, wrapping her tight against me. She can't weigh more than Rabbit or a five-pound bag of Domino Sugar.

Helen's voice trails after me as I walk away. Could she have had the baby, then gone home to shower and fix herself up before she met Margie at Jimmy Joe's? How could she? How could we have not noticed? Trudy has been too sick and Teresa's been too busy, and me—I don't know. Have I been walking around like a sleepwalker, waiting for Brian to come back?

The sweat has dried on top of the baby's head, and now her light wispy hair blows straight up. I don't know how long I walk before I'm right back where I found her. Torn or kicked apart, the hole is spread across the clearing in clumps. Closer, I see that the ground has been dug into, the sides are wider, and it is half filled with the loose dirt. It could have been a dog or it could have been whoever was following me. The clouds push fast across the sky, covering the light of the moon. This is the longest I've ever gone without my caps.

With the dough in my ears, it's like I'm swimming underwater, but I miss the pressure of the caps on my ears. I could go back for them now, but I don't. I want to hear everything. That way I'll lose my hearing faster, like Dr. Gould said, and I'll become *normal*. It's happening, I know it is. After I leave Herringtown, no one will know about my ear caps anyway. They won't know anything about me. I clasp her closer so she can't see where she was buried. Does anyone know I have found a baby? Has someone come back for her?

Something blows up into my face, fluttering like the wings of a bat. I step back, spitting, slapping at it until I realize it's only a Gooey Bar wrapper, the red letters on gold paper shiny with rain. Brian and Mr. Dodd were always eating the Gooey Bars Mr. Dodd brought home from work. The day Brian got Rabbit, Mr. Dodd came outside eating one. He was wearing thin gray boxer shorts and that was all, and when he walked, I could see his thing swinging. I was wearing cutoffs and his eyes were running up and down me. I crouched on all fours on the lawn like Rabbit to hide from him.

Mr. Dodd gripped his belly, shaking from laughing so hard. He bent over me and whispered, "Pretty." Then he crumpled the Gooey Bar wrapper in his fist and pressed his hand to the split of his crotch, scratching a dark tangle of hair through the light cotton shorts.

"Ship, how about we go sailing sometime. You and me on your ship. How's that?" he chuckled, tossing his wrapper in the wind. Then he turned to Brian. "We could invent a candy bar better than this. It's good, but not that good. What do you say, son?"

"Sure, Dad."

Mr. Dodd started back to the kitchen. As he opened the door, he yelled to Brian, "Are you going to take good care of that rabbit, son?"

"Yes, sir," Brian answered and the door slapped shut.

I kick the wrapper away. Anybody could have been eating a Gooey Bar, not just Mr. Dodd. Anyway, what would he be doing back here? What if it was Brian? But I've been saying that since he left.

She spits up a small stream of white goop, which slides down the inside of my jacket. Her skin is warm and her heart is beating fast. I lean back against a maple tree, resting my head against the bark, but after a short while, I know we can't stay here—it's too cold for a baby. We have to find somewhere to stay tonight. I'm going to take care of her. If I gave her up now, I wouldn't get in trouble, but I can't. I found her—I saved her. She's more mine than anyone else's.

The best thing to do to keep warm is to walk, so I pace around the clearing. The church bells ring for Good Friday mass and I remember the church basement. It's warm in there and Father Hannah never locks the door. He hasn't locked any of his doors since he's been in Herringtown. Trudy said Sister Julia, who lives in the rectory with him, locks his doors. "She's always hovering over him like he's some kind of baby." Teresa says Trudy's jealous.

I head off the back way behind the neighbors' houses, where the lights are on in the kitchens and the living rooms, where families are eating supper or watching television. I creep along the edge of the woods. A dark-haired woman picks up the telephone and dials. A man throws a baby boy in the air and catches him. A dog scratches, a glass breaks, a toilet flushes, a blow-dryer whirs, a girl cries, and someone is chopping vegetables on a cutting board.

Everything is different from the outside—sharper, more focused, as if I've never really noticed what was inside before. It makes me miss home when I haven't even really left yet. It makes me want to be home, where Teresa is baking her pies and talking to Trudy on the telephone about who came into Hair Camp and told her this or that. It makes me want to hear Helen sing so loud Teresa has to ask her to quiet down because she can't think straight, which really means she can't hear Trudy's gossip. I decide to walk by Trudy's to see Teresa one more time before I leave Herringtown for good.

From Trudy's driveway, where the Continental is parked, I hear her coughing, a long cough that seems to pull at her insides and make her choke on them. She and Teresa are in the bedroom at the far end of the house on the first and only floor. Right after we came to Herringtown, Teresa went to Hair Camp and told Trudy she wanted a new look. She was starting over. Trudy cut and dyed her hair to look exactly like her own, which Teresa told us later was an awful Marilyn Monroe imitation. Teresa was so shocked she couldn't speak. I saw her like that once when Mr. Grant sent back his half-eaten pie. No one had ever sent her pie back. Helen burst out crying when she saw Teresa with her new hair. I was only two and don't remember what I thought of it or Trudy, who took us to her house, where she and Teresa made their first whiskey sours. Trudy still cuts Teresa's hair, but now it's chestnut brown and hangs in loose waves to her shoulders.

Crouching outside the bedroom window, I hear Teresa saying to Trudy, "How about a cream-cheese-and-olive sandwich?"

"I know I'm supposed to be on this stupid diet, but I've been eating all day. I can't help it," Trudy says.

"Oh, that's all right," Teresa says. "It's different if you're sick."

"It is, isn't it? But I'm so fat. I might as well just tape the cream cheese and olive to my thigh." Trudy's voice is hoarse and tired. The rocking chair squeaks on the floor beside Trudy's bed. "What would you have if it was your very last meal?"

"If it was my execution meal," Teresa answers, "I'd start off with a baked potato with lots of butter and sour cream. Then I'd have a nice juicy steak, red in the middle. For dessert—"

"That's all you'd have for supper?" She sounds amazed. "I mean, if you were about to die?" Her voice scrapes inside my ears. Then it goes quiet.

"Shhh," Teresa says, setting her glass down.

The bed shakes and the floorboards creak and I know Trudy is crying. "Let's not talk about dying." Teresa's voice cracks. After a minute she asks, "Do you regret anything?"

"I regret the fact that Father Hannah is a priest," Trudy says, sniffling. "He's the only man I've ever been in love with."

Teresa laughs.

"What about you?"

"I wish I'd said good-bye to my grandparents. They were so good to me," Teresa says. "Not a day goes by that I don't think about them."

"Every time I see Dad I think it's going to be the last," Trudy says. "He's so old now. I hate leaving him there, not that he knows the difference. I can't bear the idea of ending up like that."

"Let's not talk about getting old."

"Good idea."

"Promise?"

Trudy nods. "Did you call home?"

"I talked to Helen. They're both home."

"Good."

"I'll go soon. But first I'll make you a sandwich."

Why did Helen say I was home?

When the baby stirs in my arms, I tiptoe around to the dining room, where there are three new wigs, different lengths of white-blond hair set on Styrofoam heads lined up on the table. Teresa passes through the living room to the kitchen. The fork hits the side of the dish, squishing the cream cheese, olives, and olive juice. Next she'll spread it across the bread and cut it into quarters. I've seen her make sandwiches so many times, it's like I'm standing beside her. But I'm not. I'm leaving.

.   .   .

I TAKE the long way to town, winding along the edge of woods around the Gooey factory. The smokestacks on the looming brick building pump white puffs into the dark haze of night. The familiar whirring hum like a low fan comes from the factory, followed by a clunk-clunk, then the whirring again. I stop to breathe in the lingering smells of butter, creamy nougat, caramel, chocolate, peanut butter, and marshmallow. And the oil and smoke rising out of the stacks. If the wind's blowing just right, I can smell the factory from our house.

Sometimes we'd wait for Mr. Dodd to give us a ride home from Gooey. For someone who says the Gooey Bar isn't that great, he eats more of them than anyone I know. There is a basket of them on the receptionist's desk in the front lobby and I bet he never leaves without grabbing at least one or two of them. One time I saw him stuff his pockets with them. That was the day he invited us in for a tour when we knew no one besides the workers was allowed past the front lobby.

Mr. Dodd said, "How about a quick tour around the place?"

"Are we allowed?" Brian asked.

"Did you forget who you're talking to? I'm security and your uncle owns this place. If I say so, then you are. Now, do you want to see it or not?"

It was after 6:00 P.M. and the lobby and hallway were dark and the receptionist's desk empty. "Shhh," Mr. Dodd told us. "This way. I don't want Hurley to see us. He's always minding everyone else's business."

Down the hallway a door slammed shut. Before we knew

what was happening, Mr. Dodd flung himself around, grabbing our sleeves, and pushed us into a closet that smelled of old water, bug spray, and disinfectant. "Get down and don't make a sound," he told us. Mr. Dodd breathed heavy and Brian's heart thumped, louder than the hum and whir and occasional clank of the candy machines. The floors and walls vibrated around us.

After a while, Mr. Dodd lifted his head and said, "Okay, I think we can move now." He opened the closet door, looked both ways, and motioned us forward with a wave of his hand.

As we followed him down a long hallway, the humming and whirring became more of a churning and clacking. I needed to tell Mr. Dodd that the noise might be too much for me, but he kept pushing us forward, telling us to be quiet. "Shhh," he whispered, creeping along, peeking around the corners before he turned. "We're going to the blending room where all the chocolate is mixed. There are these cylinders that can mix a thousand pounds of chocolate at a time. You've got to see the size of the paddles in there. Want to know a secret?"

Brian said, "Yes, sir."

"Promise you won't say a word?"

We nodded.

"I put my hand in there—right into the chocolate. It's as smooth as cream.

"Oh, come here a minute. You have to see this." He unlocked a windowless metal door. "This is the boiler room. See those? They could supply enough power to keep the entire town of Herringtown going. No joke. Look here."

"Brian," I whispered, pointing to my ears, "I have to go back."

"Dad," Brain said. "Dad?"

The boilers sounded like the train coming into Herring-town. "See, when you make candy, you need lots of steam. Lots—"

The door closed shut behind us. "Joe? That you?"

Mr. Dodd hunkered down, but there was nothing to hide behind except us.

"Joe?"

"I had to check the boilers." Mr. Dodd stood up. "They were making such a racket, I thought something was wrong. We're leaving right now. You're not going to say anything, are you, Lee?"

"You better get on out of here with those kids now." Lee stood there holding on to his mop handle and shaking his head as we passed him. My head was just starting to throb. I pressed my caps close to my head, relieved that this was the end of our tour. On the way out of the factory was when Mr. Dodd grabbed as many Gooey Bars as he could stuff in his pockets.

THE DOOR of the shed is open. I slow down and listen for him breathing, but it's quiet, except for a soft murmur. "Brian?" Something stirs, rustling in a blanket in the corner of the room. I walk through the dark, kicking over a candle. A sharp meow rises from the blanket. In the bit of moonlight, I make out four wet balls of fur sucking on the white belly of a mother cat. She meows again, circling her tail around them. The kittens' mouths release their mother's teats with tiny pops before they ball up and sleep, and she licks their fur until it is slick. I lick the top of the baby's head, cool and salty, and the ridge of her ears. *Brian.*

There is one more thing to do before I go to the rectory. Outside, the air whistles and whines through the leaves. Steam from the factory dissolves in the night sky. The baby's eyes open and shut and the pom-pom on my lucky hat swishes as I walk. Up until now, I've spent most of my time blocking sounds out.

Music from Jimmy Joe's floats by: *I can make the rain go—* pop—*any time I move my finger. Lucky*—pop—*me, can't you see.* Tripping in the tall grass, I almost fall to the ground, which is covered in broken glass. What if I hurt her? Then what would I do? What if she starts crying and someone hears? I slide my back along the underside of the bridge, dragging my palm along the cement wall until my finger slips into the hole. I place my thumb on the baby's forehead for good luck and then put my thumb inside the hole and, closing my eyes tight, turn. *I wish, I wish, I wish. I wish she was mine.*

A car sputters down Main Street, a bat dips down, *phit phit phit,* and Father Hannah's voice rises in a singsong melody. I can't make out what he's saying, only the sound of the words like a stream of notes. "Use your gift wisely, Ship," he said, and I know that this is why I found the baby, this is why he called me blessed. A cold wind blows under the bridge—it's time to move on.

When I see the light shining from the church, an urge comes over me to tell Father Hannah everything. Maybe he'd write about me in the church bulletin again, this time saying that because of my exceptional hearing, I found a baby in the woods. Last time he wrote, "After confession last Saturday, a miracle happened in St. Peter's parking lot. Ship Sooner heard the back tire of the family car making an odd sound and refused to get in. It turns out the tire was just about to fall off the axle. This could have caused a fatal accident. Thank the Lord, Ship Sooner has been blessed with exceptional hearing."

People in Herringtown knew about me after I started wearing the ear caps, but it wasn't until Father Hannah wrote I was blessed and the *Herringtown Weekly* published a photo of me standing in front of the pear tree with the headline SHIP SOONER SAVES FAMILY FROM CAR ACCIDENT that they really believed it. They looked at me different, wide-eyed and sideways. I was ten years old and they started lowering their voices when I was around. Sometimes in Jimmy Joe's or the school cafeteria they'd move their seats. When I told Teresa, she said, "You can't really blame them, Ship." She started taking her phone calls in the basement. The kids at school said I had bionic hearing and started calling me Bionic Girl.

For a while some people, like Trudy and Laura, were waiting for the next miracle to happen. Teresa said the *Herringtown Weekly* made me seem like some kind of interpreter of signs or fortune-teller and that they must be hard up for news. She was furious with Trudy for talking to the reporter. In the paper, it said, "A very close friend of the Sooners, Trudy Lovell, said, 'I knew all along about Ship's extraordinary hearing. I knew when I cut her hair and she wouldn't let the scissors near her ears. This is no coincidence.'"

Helen didn't know why everyone made such a big deal about my hearing. But like everyone else, she'd lower her voice when I was there. Not that she spent much time with me since I started wearing the ear caps, but after this she didn't spend any.

I watch the church empty out. Normally, we would all be at Good Friday mass, but not this year. A bird feeder made from a half-gallon milk carton swings from the oak tree at the end of the parking lot. I wouldn't be surprised if Father Hannah already knew about this baby. His robes swish as he heads to the rectory, past the church. In the upstairs light, his dark shape crosses the window. The baby is quiet as we make our way to the church basement.

Inside, it is warm, dark, and musty, and smells of holy water. Brian and I came down here one Saturday and found a bag of Eucharist wafers on the kitchen counter. First we let them melt nice and slow on our tongues like at mass, then we stuffed five or six in our mouths at a time until half the bag was gone. I thought we sinned, but Brian said we didn't because it was just like eating crackers. That's one thing I never confessed to Father Hannah. Another thing is what I saw Helen doing with Owen and Brian.

I put my hand close to her mouth to feel her breath. Her eyes flitter open and her mouth pinches up and goes *tchh, tchh, tchh*. I am the only one she has. Her lips are rimmed white with spit. I kiss her and taste her, salty and hot.

"Here we are," I say, taking my jacket off, lining the kitchen sink with it. I unwrap the blanket and set her gently down in the sink. The skin on the top of her head is all dried out and peeling. She scrunches her face into a red ball and takes turns crying and catching her breath as I unwrap the Ace bandage. I must have wrapped her too tightly. "Please be quiet," I say, "before Father Hannah hears you."

Red bumps have spread over the skin around the crack between her legs. All I can do is stare at it, as if I put it there. I run a kitchen cloth under the water until it is warm and use the dishwashing soap to clean her. Then I open all the cabinets, searching for something to put over the rash. There are cups, plates, a tea set, napkins, boxes of candles, vanilla extract, baking soda, Domino Sugar, a tin of Crisco, and a box of prunes. When Teresa makes pecan pie crust, she works the extra Crisco into her hands. She says it's better than any skin cream. I dig my fingers in, through the top of the thick, gray fat to where it is creamy and light, and spread the Crisco all over the baby, including her peeling head, turning her red skin whitish pink. Everywhere except the stubby umbilical cord, covered with dried blood. She stops crying. Her lips suck the air and her limbs relax.

I roll the wet Ace bandage into a ball and toss it in the garbage can. In the drawer beneath the counter, there is an apron decorated with red gladiolas. I wrap this around her, one flower covering her from chin to toe like a giant diaper. Then I put the Wolverines shirt back on her, over the apron.

The small refrigerator purrs. There must be something for her—she needs to drink something. When I open the door, a rotten smell seeps out. There is a pint container of half-and-half gone bad, a corner piece of a vanilla cake with pink roses, cracked and dry, and a bottle of Sprite. I empty the old soda and fill the bottle with water, then add sugar. She'll drink it if it's sweet. Sitting at the kitchen table, I soak a cloth with the sugar water and, holding up her head, let the water drip between her lips, my fingers pressing gently against her cheek. She sucks at it a little and I watch her swallow and breathe, her body pulling in and out.

I stare at her flat baby nose, her puckered mouth, the bit of silky hair, her large round ears, and tiny red body, and I stop seeing her as anyone else's. Each time she breathes, I do, too. After a while her eyes close and her mouth goes slack.

I carry her through the carpeted room with the folded metal chairs stacked against the wall, where I had CCD class with Miss Hayes in second and third grades. Every class, Miss Hayes would tell us to draw pictures, then she'd go into the coatroom, where she'd pace back and forth, puffing on her cigarette, the smoke drifting through the rows of chairs. Then she'd roll more lipstick on, puckering and smacking her lips as she did. When she returned, she'd walk around our desks, saying in her breathy voice, "Oh, nice. Very good. We'll hang that up for Father Hannah to see." Once she stopped at my desk. "Oh, Ship, you're too much. Jesus never wore earmuffs!"

"They're ear *caps*."

"All right, Jesus never wore ear caps." She laughed, holding up my picture for the class to see. A few of the other kids laughed, too. Someone said, "He could fix Ship's hearing."

"Yes, that's right, if Jesus were here today, He could give Ship normal hearing."

That was before Father Hannah said I was blessed.

Inside the closet are drawing supplies, old CCD books, bags of donated clothes, coats hung on a rod, and the cradle Miss Hayes used to make the nativity scene for our Christmas photo. I glance up to see if there is a green suit jacket that smells like olives. The sleeves would be too long, one would have a tear, and the edges of the pockets would be frayed. There's no green coat like Brian's, but there is a fake black fur coat, which I spread over the dusty wooden bottom of the cradle. When I put her down, her head lolls side to side. "When we leave Herringtown, you'll never have to go to CCD," I tell her, "or school or church or Hair Camp or the dentist or anywhere."

Her eyes close, her arms go limp, and she drools a string of spit from the corner of her mouth. Through the window on the far side of the room, the shadows of the trees bend in the wind and the branches brush against the glass. Above us, the jackets hang like still clouds. I take a snorkel coat to rest my head on.

I listen for her heart beating, and when I hear its steady thumping, I curl up beside her. The last thing I hear before I fall asleep is a faint clicking from the back of her mouth. I pick out the balls of dough I have plugged in my ears and shove them into my pocket in case she's trying to tell me something.

Eight

EXCEPT FOR THE GLOW of the moonlight through the window across the room, it is still dark. She blinks, opens her swollen gray eyes, and bursts out crying. The noise splits my head open, and my body feels bruised, my neck broken. I stand up, my head in the coats. Father Hannah is going to hear her if I don't do something fast. I listen for footsteps, but I can't hear anything over her crying. I lift her out of the cradle. What am I supposed to do with her? Her head falls backward, her dry lips make sucking noises as she catches her breath. All the while her heart beats soft and steady. I rock her like I rock myself, back and forth, watching her cry. Not a single tear falls from her eyes. Finally she stops.

When I undress her, I find a grayish white load inside the apron. I roll the whole thing up into a ball and stuff it into the pocket of a plaid raincoat. I clean her again. Her mother could have left her at the church or a hospital or anywhere. But then she may have been caught. And I wouldn't have found her. I smooth her wisps of white hair. Her forehead wrinkles up, her lips purse. She takes the sugar water, her face turning pink. "Good baby," I say. "That's a good baby." I peer into her eyes and promise her I'll take care of her, I won't leave her.

A wood owl's *hoo-hoo* carries through the trees, along with the other birds singing their early morning songs. In the kitchen, water drips slowly from the faucet and the pipes gurgle. Each sound is clear and distinct. My head doesn't throb and go numb like it usually does when I'm not wearing my ear caps.

I carry her into the kitchen, setting her inside the sink again. It's hard to believe I was ever this small. I see the gleam of the silver teakettle in her eyes. It's just like the one in our kitchen, and for a second, I wish I could take her home and keep her there with Teresa and Trudy—but we have to leave Herringtown if I'm going to keep her. We'll follow Silver River south to Waterfalls. I fill the soda bottle with water and sugar to take with me.

As soon as we get outside in the cool air, I forget all about the kettle, the basement, and home and I head for the woods before anyone sees me. The air is so clean after the rain, I breathe it in gulps. Lining the walkway, yellow daffodils open wide like mouths. The sun is beginning to edge up into the sky. A spider slips down from a dogwood branch on an invisible thread and flails over the air, searching for something to wrap its web around. A fly buzzes nearby.

The sweet scent of sugar and the creamy buttery smells of her fill my nostrils. I put my hand on her thumping chest. Off in the woods, there is a gentle thud of something falling to the ground. All at once I am pulled forward, all my senses fixed in a straight line, pushing us ahead. My pom-pom bounces as I walk, my feet in step with the beating of my heart.

A baby bird has fallen out of its nest. It lies between the roots of a maple tree, blood oozing up between its brown feathers with white tips. The pure smell grips me. I bend too close and the tip of my nose touches the warm red pool welled up on its breast. Blood drips to my lip, dissolving there. I hear my pulse beating through the skin of my wrist—a softer beating than my heart.

The baby starts crying. I am squishing her as I bend over the bird. She has to realize I am doing this for her. Everything I do is for her. It's because of her that I'm here now with the taste of bird's blood in my mouth. I lift the bird up in my palm. Then suddenly repulsed, I jerk back, dropping the bird to the ground. I am afraid. Lost.

A pine needle swishes slowly to the ground, carving the air. I stop and watch it, pulling her closer. A little explosion goes off in my chest. She is telling me to go on. Her body is like a weight centering me, a sixth sense leading all the others. We have to go before the sun rises any higher. My stomach growls, barks up at me.

Today is Holy Saturday, which means Teresa will bring all the rolls, bread, pies, and pastries to Jimmy Joe's and then go to Trudy's, and Helen will spend most of the day in her room, singing, waiting for Owen to call, and doing whatever else she does in there. I wonder where they think I am. I wonder if Teresa still thinks I'm home when I'm not. I cut through the woods to South Street, which will take us to Route 6, where Silver River is.

At South Street, I hear a truck and I know I should get out of sight, but the purring of the engine is familiar and I wait right where I am as the pickup floats toward me. We see each other at the same time. Mr. Dodd jams on the brakes and stops smack in the middle of the road. Trash cans roll, crashing into each other and against the sides of the bed of the truck.

"Ship Sooner, is that you?" he asks through the half-open window. "What are you doing out so early?" Without my ear caps on, his voice is rougher, like sandpaper scraping inside my ears.

As he idles the engine, she stirs—her small knees bend, her toes pinch, and her fists jab into me. She's so small underneath my bomber, he couldn't possibly see her there, but I fold my arms across my chest anyway. This is how Helen stands. Was it because she was hiding something, too? I hunch over slightly because Mr. Dodd is eyeballing me. Except for the times he's left the Gooey factory or pulled in or out of his driveway, I haven't seen him since Brian left.

"What's the matter with you, Ship? You get over here and let me see you," Mr. Dodd yells from his truck window.

I step closer. I want to ask him why he didn't answer my notes or phone calls. I let it ring twenty, thirty, sometimes forty times. Once, forty-three—I counted.

Sliding his elbow forward, he leans farther out the window and hollers, "Ship Sooner, I'm not going anywhere until you come over here, do you hear me?" He's wearing Brian's green suit jacket. The sleeves are even longer on Mr. Dodd than they were on Brian. "Now, get in," he orders.

"Where did Brian go?" I ask. "Why didn't he say anything before he left?"

He must not hear me because he just chuckles, squinting, his eyes red and sagging. He looks funny, like he's drunk, but I don't smell beer or anything. Then his face turns serious. "You're bleeding, Ship."

I wipe my nose with my sleeve. "Oh, I guess I got a bloody nose."

He sighs. "Get in, I'll give you a ride."

As he stares at me, she moves beneath my clothes. I remember the way he and Brian were looking down Helen's open shirt on my birthday night. The idea of taking off at full speed flashes through my mind, but I can't take my eyes off the green jacket. I'm scared as I walk toward the passenger side of the car, but I remind myself it's just Mr. Dodd. I've ridden in his truck tons of times. If I don't go, he might get suspicious. Underneath the green jacket he wears his uniform of light brown pants and a matching button-down shirt with GOOEY BAR written across the top left. I lift myself onto the black vinyl seat littered with Styrofoam cups, paper bags, Budweiser cans, peanut shells, and Gooey Bar wrappers, praying that she doesn't start crying now. With a sweep of his hand, he slides everything off the seat, onto the floor.

Once I'm sitting next to Mr. Dodd, this fierce need to protect her comes over me, so strong I almost lose my breath. I feel myself get bigger, puff up. At the same time, part of me seems to be leaking into her.

"When are we going sailing, Ship?" Mr. Dodd howls and slaps his thigh and gives me a sidelong glance, shaking his head. Then he starts dancing his fingers across the top of the steering wheel. Sweat lines his forehead, dripping down around his ears, where his hair has started to gray.

I don't see what's so funny. If he wanted to see me so much, then why hasn't he answered his doorbell or telephone in the last four months? "Where's Brian?" I ask again.

His mouth twitches strangely as he shakes his head. "I sure didn't expect to see you on my way home this morning."

Luckily she hasn't started coughing or spitting. I keep one arm crossed over her tiny body and the other on the dashboard. He has no idea. When I look at him now, I see him hunched over Rabbit, hacking at her frozen fur.

"Look behind the seat, Ship!" he shouts, tiny flecks of spit flying onto the dashboard.

I gasp. It's jammed with Gooey Bars. "Can I have one?"

"I'm saving them," he squeals, letting out a little grunt.

"For what?"

"I got almost four hundred total, but it's a surprise." He frowns, then his face goes blank.

"For what?"

"If I told you," he yells, "it wouldn't be a surprise!"

I'm sure he stole them. I wonder if he's still trying to invent a new candy bar in the think tank. The first time they went into their think tank, Mr. Dodd said to Brian, "Who couldn't invent a candy bar? The Gooey Bar is so simple. Anybody could think of that. I'm going to come up with something with a little zing. What do kids love, Brian? Tell me."

"Chocolate?"

"Sure, sure, but what else? What about sandwiches? What's your favorite sandwich?"

"Pickles and cheese."

"Besides that?"

"Banana and cheese."

"Forget the cheese. I'm talking about the most popular sandwich there is. What would you have with peanut butter?"

"Marshmallow."

"Come on, son, what about peanut butter and jelly? Kids love them. Now, what if it were covered in chocolate?" His voice rose. Then there was a slapping sound which must have been him hitting Brian on the back.

"What do you say we try to whip it up in the testing room?"

In his Gooey uniform, Mr. Dodd walked ahead of Brian into the kitchen. I moved closer, sidling up to their kitchen window. The pots and pans clanked against each other until Mr. Dodd said, "Here's the testing pan."

"Isn't that for Jiffy muffins?"

"Not anymore. Okay, first the peanut butter. Then the Smucker's. Make it nice, just like that. A little bar. Leave enough room for the chocolate to cover the whole thing.

"Good, just like that. And I just so happen to have some of Gooey's special hardening chocolate."

"Are you allowed to use that, Dad?"

"Sure, they'll never know. Don't forget it's your uncle's chocolate. This is just for the test anyway. Pat that down and smooth it out. Good.

"Now, let's cover it. As soon as it hardens, we'll have a bite. You're about to witness the invention of the next greatest candy bar in the universe. Step back, please."

"What will we call it?" Brian asked.

"The Dodd Bar, no question about it. One more minute."

"Yes, sir."

"One day we'll have our own candy factory. You know that, don't you, Bri? Okay, let's have a taste now."

"That was only forty seconds."

"Close enough."

After a little while, Mr. Dodd said, "What do you think?"

"Let me have another taste."

"See, you can't stop eating it! Is it better than the Gooey Bar?"

"It's a little mushy or something."

"Too much jelly?"

"I don't know, sir. Maybe it needs something crunchy."

"That's it, son. Like those crispy things. What do we have? How about cornflakes? Frosted Flakes? Even better.

"Come on, help me crush them up. We'll put a layer of those between the peanut butter and jelly. This is great."

Brian gulped and stared at his father.

"What's the matter with you, son? Put a little elbow grease into it." After a minute he said, "Much better than the Gooey Bar, isn't it, Brian?"

"Something's not right. I think it needs nougat or something to make it all stick together," Brian answered.

"I knew there was a reason I asked you to be my partner. I know, let's add some Karo syrup to the Frosted Flakes so it all sticks together. Go get it, Brian. Chop, chop."

"There's only maple syrup."

"Good enough." After a few minutes, Mr. Dodd shouted, "Perfecto! Get your mother down here, Brian. She can take a picture."

The next time it was banana and peanut butter cups. After

that, it was balls of Wonder bread rolled in chocolate, and then melted marshmallows, Cheerios, and pineapple.

WHEN MR. DODD comes to a sudden stop, I hold her in place and brace us against the dashboard. The trash barrels go crashing around in the back again. I bet he dumps his trash into the Gooey Dumpster when no one's there. Is he going to surprise Brian? Is Brian coming home?

"Where's Brian?"

He speeds up, leaning on the steering wheel. "I'm beat. I had to work a double." He flicks on the radio and starts humming. His digital watch reads 6:10 A.M. "I love driving at this time of the morning. Sometimes I don't even stop at the stop signs."

His head seems to have sunk into his neck, and his eyes are bloodshot, bruised looking. I just don't know if I can believe anything Mr. Dodd says. Maybe if I ask about Johnny, he'll answer me. "Where's . . ." I start, but I promised Brian I wouldn't say anything about Johnny. And Mr. Dodd's being so strange, I don't want to make him mad. "Where are we going? Because I should go home soon."

"Home?" he repeats. "What were you doing walking around back there if you wanted to go home?"

"Nothing. I was going home."

He looks sideways at me. "You're not running away, are you?"

"No."

He turns to me. "Anything the matter? Are you cold or something?"

"No."

"I could turn the heat on."

I shake my head.

"Where are your ear things?"

"Caps," I say. "My ear *caps*."

"Where are they?"

I shrug. "I forgot them."

"You should be wearing them." He shakes his head. "You weren't spying on anyone this morning, were you? You weren't up at the Gooey factory, were you?"

"No," I say, "I just forgot them. Where are we going?"

After a minute, he answers, "Harry's. We're going to Harry's, the only place open this early." He taps his fingers on the cracked vinyl seat cover, then on his thigh, spread across the seat. I scrunch myself up against the door.

It's just Mr. Dodd, Brian's dad, who lives next door and who used to take us fishing. I say, "Remember when we went to Silver River to fish and there were so many fish, one of them jumped onto shore?"

His head twists toward me. He nods, then clamps his mouth shut and frowns. He turns up the radio and speeds ahead. One hand grips the wheel and the other picks at the loose threads of Brian's pocket. I stare at the jacket like if I stare at it long enough, Brian will be sitting here wearing it instead of Mr. Dodd. One by one Mr. Dodd's fingers disappear into the frayed wool. I wonder if he has discovered the slit in the right sleeve.

"Here we are," he says. "Harry's Doughnuts. And there's Harry's new pickup." He points to a shiny red Ford in the back lot. "How many doughnuts do you think he had to sell to buy that baby?" The screen door flaps open and Harry steps onto the top stair. He knocks a cigarette out of his pack and lights it. Leaning to the side, careful to keep one arm around her, I pretend to pick something up off the floor so Harry doesn't see me. Mr. Dodd waves, drives into the front lot, and cuts the engine. We both listen to it going *clink clink* as it settles. "Harry's got half a dozen doughnuts waiting for me right now," he says proudly. "I come here every day."

"You eat six doughnuts a day?"

"Mrs. Dodd has a couple, too."

"A doughnut takes three days to digest." That's why Helen never eats them.

"So?" he asks. "What difference does that make? I've got three days."

"I guess it only matters if you're on a diet."

"I'm on the seafood diet." He pauses. "I see food and I eat it."

When he breaks out laughing, the baby half coughs and half cries, so I start to laugh loudly and cough, too. Mr. Dodd looks pleased. Opening the door, he asks, "Coffee, Ship?"

"Sure," I tell him, though I've never had coffee in my life. I follow the bald spot on the back of his head up the stairs, inside to the doughnut counter. I slowly open the passenger door, reach back behind the seat, and grab as many Gooey Bars as I can. I slide out of the pickup and trot through Harry's parking lot into the woods, where I hide behind a tree to watch for Mr. Dodd. "We're safe," I tell her.

After a couple minutes, he steps out, balancing two large coffees and a white bag. "Crap!" he cries, nearly dropping the coffees. He puts them on the porch railing and shakes out his hand. "Pisser." Then he picks up the Styrofoam cups again. When he gets to the truck, he sets the coffees and bag on the hood and turns to open his door.

"Ship?" He turns around. "Where'd you go now, Ship? Are you hiding on me? Ship Sooner!" He peers in the bed of the pickup, then underneath the truck. "Goddamn it all. What am I supposed to do with two coffees?"

Harry steps out the front door. He wipes his hands on his white apron, his eyes panning the empty lot. "Who you talking to, Joe?"

Mr. Dodd shrugs and throws out both his arms.

"Huh? You okay, Joe?"

"Of course I'm okay." Mr. Dodd mumbles something, snatches the coffees and doughnuts, gets into his pickup, and barrels away.

Harry leans against the railing, lights another cigarette, and takes a long drag, blowing a stream of smoke into the crisp morning air. I wait until Mr. Dodd's truck has gone quiet and Harry has stabbed out his cigarette and gone back inside. The screen door slams and bounces, slaps and slams again.

I eat two of the Gooey Bars straightaway, concentrating first on the chocolate and then on the nougat, letting it melt slowly in my mouth. Mr. Dodd must be collecting them for Brian. Who else would they be for? But he was being so strange. *What if Brian died?* The thought almost knocks me over. Was that why Mr. Dodd didn't answer me? He can't be dead.

The sky goes from gray to pink to blue as I go deeper into the woods. I walk until I can't hear the traffic anymore—only the birds, the wind, my footsteps, her breathing, her heart beating. Unzipping my jacket, I trace the shape of her head, more of an oval now, her big ears, and the tiny arc of her chin. Her skin is as soft as powder. We walk through a beam of pink-yellow light. Her fingers reach toward me. She doesn't care about my hearing. I'm all she has.

We are free. Free from Mr. Dodd, free from Helen, Margie, Laura, Officer Robinson, Trudy, Teresa, and everyone else in Herringtown. No one can stop us from going to Silver River. I slide my knapsack off and swing it around with my left arm, then inch down, leaning my back against a tree, spreading my legs out in front of me. I find Teresa's danishes. The frosting has started to melt. I eat two slowly, then a roll. I lay her down beside me on my jacket and curl myself around her like the mother cat wrapped herself around her kittens. I could stay here with her forever, just like this, eating Teresa's sweet rolls, smelling the pine needles and earth, and listening to her breathing.

I wonder who her mother is and if she got pregnant in the shed behind the Gooey factory. I wonder who else was in there. I think of Owen thrusting himself into Helen's face, Brian touching the top of Helen's head, Mr. Gray making his dirty phone calls, Mrs. Hayes bicycling in her bra, Trudy collecting Father Hannah's hair in a plastic bag, Teresa telling Jack she's still a married woman. And I think of my father and I wonder if he's like Hud at the end of the movie, standing alone. The thing is, *she* came out of all that—she wouldn't be here if *that* hadn't happened.

In the distance, I hear the sound of Silver River, where we'll be soon. I've never been there without Brian and Mr. Dodd. The sun melts my limbs. My eyes close and the trees swirl around above me, disappearing into black.

. . . .

WHEN I wake, the trees are still spinning. She is spread out on my bomber jacket beside me. Half of her face is red and the other half is pale. When I pick her up, she stops crying. A thread of spittle hangs from her mouth. I reach into my bag for the sugar water, but it must have spilled because the bottle is empty.

As soon as I place her on her back to change her, she starts crying again. Inside the Wolverines shirt I've wrapped around her is a sticky, greenish-black lump. I clean her with the ends of the shirt, then toss it to the side, kicking some leaves over it. I take off my S shirt underneath my sweater and put that on her. When I get her milk and diapers, everything will be better. Slits of blue sky are visible through the tops of the trees. I walk around and around with her, but her crying only becomes louder and more desperate.

I pull my lucky hat down over my ears and slip her under my sweater against my skin to soften her crying. Her velvety head slides up over my belly and my chest. She brushes her open mouth over my breast. I don't know if I prop her into it or if she just finds it, but her mouth clamps onto my nipple. When she sucks, it pinches and tickles, sending goose bumps up and down me. She lets go and begins to cry for a minute, then starts suck-ing again.

I close my eyes and sit down, leaning against an oak tree. I let her suck because at least she's quiet. Two squirrels stop chasing each other to cock their heads at us. Birds flutter from branch to branch and a red fox darts into the hollow of a log. The top of her head has a ring of sweat around it. She sucks like that's the only thing in the whole world—until her head tilts back and she falls asleep again, spittle trickling over my breast, down my side. A white drop like a perfect pearl hangs from the tip of my breast. She has spit up last night's milk. I watch the droplet fall.

The flapping of wings rises around us as blackbirds lift out of the trees. They screech and cluck and beat their wings as if they are trying to tell us something. I wonder if we have done something wrong. We better go. The birds follow us, painting the sky black as they fly from one tree to the next. She doesn't stir. The light falls through the trees on the birds' oily purple-black feathers. Their shadows edge closer and I walk faster. The swish of wings flutters through my hair. What do they want? They dip so close I can see into their shrieking mouths, their cries like razors in my ears. I cover her and run toward the opening in the woods. The cloud of blackbirds hovers at the edge of the woods. Some settle in the trees and others fly back in the direction they came from.

Keeping out of sight of the few cars streaming by, I walk just inside the trees along Route 6 until I see the Mobil gas station and Mike's Mini-Mart. On the other side of the road is Sammy's, which from here looks like a shoe box strung with flashing neon lights. We stopped there on our way home from fishing once so Mr. Dodd could use the bathroom. Brian and I stayed in the car and watched the neon Budweiser bottle flaring on, then off. Brian said they had strippers inside and that's why everyone went there.

"Do they take everything off?" I asked.

"Except for the little ribbons that hang from their tits."

"How do you know?"

"Everybody knows."

"Did your dad tell you?"

"No. He doesn't even know I know."

"Why didn't you tell me before?"

"Dunno. Never thought about it."

"Well, what do they look like?"

He cupped his two hands way out in front of his chest. "Big."

I drew my hands up to my breasts, and thought, would he like me more if mine were big?

I don't know what time of the afternoon it is, but there are already about a dozen cars in Sammy's parking lot. I zip my jacket all the way to the top, then walk into Mike's. The bells on the door ring out and the fluorescent lights hum and buzz. Luckily the cashier doesn't look at me. I slide open the dairy door and grab a quart of whole milk. My face burns as I take the smallest box of Pampers I can find from the shelf, holding it close to my chest. I'm tempted to slip it under my shirt with the baby, but I carry it up to the register with the milk.

Once I heard Mr. Dodd say, "Don't you understand? He has to wear Pampers." Then he added, "Whatever they're called. He's an adult and he wears diapers."

Later when I asked Brian if he knew any adults who wore diapers, he asked, "Why?"

"I was just wondering."

"Oh." Then he said, "Sometimes sick people wear them."

"Do you know any?"

"Why would I?" He turned away, so I didn't ask him anything else about it.

The cashier is tall and skinny, with a pointy chin propped in the palm of his hand. His name tag says Steve. Beside the register is a half-eaten Snickers bar. He stops staring out the window to pick up my things and punch the prices into the register. The bells over the door ring as someone enters. I don't turn around. I pull the folded bills out of my pocket. The boy looks at the wad, then at my purchases, and finally at me.

"Six-forty," he says. His breath smells like hot dog.

Without looking at him, I slide seven ones across the counter. The register chings, the cash drawer opens and shuts. When I turn around, the lights glare and bounce off everything. Ice clanks into a tall cup, soda gurgles, and the soda machine buzzes. My head is beginning to pound. I have to go back outside. "Thanks," I say when he gives me my change, and I bolt.

The highway breeze whips against my hot face as an eighteen-wheeler cruises by. No one is looking for me. No one knows I have a baby under my jacket. I am in disguise—I am someone else. I breathe in the open air, clearing the clutter of the store from my head; then I quickly walk around the back, noticing myself in the reflection of the glass. My eyes are a sharp electric blue, drawing me closer. I stare at myself. I look older, taller. When I touch the front of my bomber jacket where she is, I feel her and the ends of my fingers tingle. That's why my eyes are this strange blue in the store glass. I comb my wild hair back with my fingers like Trudy does.

A long low *grrrr* rises from behind the Dumpster. A dirty white dog tied by a short rope around the trunk of a tree snarls from the back of its mouth. It leaps up from a dirt hole and lunges toward us, snapping its yellow teeth. We stand there without moving until he quiets, then step closer, letting the dog sniff us. He shakes a cloud of dirt and dust around himself. His collar clinks and a bird flutters out of the bush behind us and flies through the light above the trees and disappears. *Hope is the thing with feathers—*

I set the bag down and stroke under the dog's chin and behind its ears. "Good dog," I say. "That's a good dog." He pulls to the end of the leash, stretching on his hind legs, his front paws dangling as he strains with the rest of his body. His ears flicker back and forth. His tongue hangs out; then he licks around his mouth. I unhook him.

He ducks into the sunlight and lopes toward the woods, sniffing after the bird or squirrel. When he turns back to us, we follow him, dodging trees, listening for his panting. A rabbit zips out from under the brush, a brown flash zigzagging across our path. The white dog races after it. My heart leaps. For a second I want to chase after them. But the baby's eye catches on a triangle of light cutting through the trees. Her lips are dry and puckered—I have to feed her.

When I drip the milk into her mouth, it runs from the corners of her lips on to her neck and she chokes a little, but after a while, a tiny stream of it goes down. I drink some, too, right from the quart container. She spreads her tiny bluish fingers across the air. "Don't worry," I tell her, "I won't leave you." Her puffy eyes flicker open and wander over me, the trees, the light beyond us. If I hadn't found her, she might have died.

I spread her out on my jacket to change her. The crack between her legs is pinkish and swollen and still shiny from the

Crisco. She sneezes, her whole face crumpling, her arms and legs thrusting forward. I laugh and she begins to cry again, softly at first. "Don't cry. Shhh, that's all right. That's my good baby." I want to sing something to her. What song did my dad sing to me? *It can happen*—all I hear is Frank Sinatra—*young at heart*. I hum along as I change her diaper.

I watched Mrs. Willgohs change Rosie plenty of times, but she made it look so easy. I lift up my baby's tiny legs and slide the diaper under her bum. The diaper's so big, it seems like it'll swallow her up, and I forget if the sticky tags go in the front or back. The closed diaper covers her entire belly and chest. Just as I pull my S shirt down over her legs, the white dog trots back with the brown rabbit in its mouth.

The rabbit's head dangles, flip-flopping side to side, jerking a beat behind the dog's trot. First Rabbit disappeared last Christmas Eve and then Brian. What is going to happen now? The brown rabbit is still warm when the dog drops it at my feet and sits, panting beside it. Under the bright afternoon sky, the white dog's mouth twitches, his ears prick forward, listening and waiting, and his tail smacks the ground. His dark eyes stare into mine.

I cover my baby in the bomber jacket. The wind brushes over us, rustling the leaves around us. I wait there in the quiet of the woods, wanting to believe the brown rabbit is going to breathe again. I listen to the soft clicking in the back of the baby's throat and try to figure out what she is telling me. What matters is that she lives—that I save her. Then things will be better. Things will be right. The baby whistles through her mouth in a silvery hum. Everything has led me to her.

The white dog lies beside us, guarding us. The trees make a

sheltering dome overhead as the shadows grow longer in the late afternoon. I remember being curled inside a dog and hearing the clink of his collar when he shifted positions or shook his head. I was lost and the night was cold and it was warm there with the dog. He licked the skin of my neck, up under my chin. I could feel my blood pumping, the heat working its way through my body. With my fingers pressed to my neck, I check my pulse now, then I check hers.

Fairy tales can come—or...I miss Laura singing along to Sinatra and I miss Trudy and Teresa talking in the kitchen as they make their whiskey sours. I miss Teresa humming and patting around the kitchen, baking and laughing, her greenest eyes, her hair, the clack of her high heels. *It can happen*...I miss Brian, but I've missed him for months. I don't miss Helen one bit. Half the reason we're leaving is because of her. *If you're young*... We're going to follow Silver River to Waterfalls.

It suddenly seems strange I'm going all the way to Waterfalls to find my dad when I don't even know who he is. What if he's not there like Teresa said? What if he doesn't want to see me? Up until now he was what my life was missing.

Thick dark clumps of blood dot the rabbit's neck where the dog's teeth sank. I trace the smooth handle of Brian's jackknife inside my pocket, then pull it out and flip it open. I hold the bend of the rabbit's leg against the ground and set the blade on its front paw. Then I remember Mr. Dodd cutting Rabbit's fur in the garage and I can't make myself push the blade down— not even for good luck. I let the jackknife slip out of my hand, then kick it away.

The white dog leaps up and paws the ground around the

rabbit. He sniffs its bloody neck, smearing the tip of his nose red. The sky darkens and the wind picks up. The baby sleeps. A trickle of sweat runs down my back. The white dog lifts his nose, sniffing the air, then starts forward, running fast. I listen to the rhythm of his four paws thumping and, without thinking, I charge after the dog, galloping like he is, one-two, three-four. But I can't leave her—I go back to get her. Then we follow the white dog.

The dog's head thrashes around inside a trash bag. He stops when a can of tuna rolls out. The fish and oil smells make my mouth water. The dog shoves his nose into the can and licks the oily bottom.

From out of nowhere, a voice calls my name. My face flushes and my legs go weak. *Helen.* What is she doing out here? A shudder runs through me, rattling us both. Clutching the baby, I step back from the open trash bag and the dog. I freeze. She could have died behind Jimmy Joe's. The tuna can drops from the dog's mouth, landing with a *ping*. Helen can't find us. She'll ruin everything.

"Ship," Helen calls again from far away. "Ship, if you hear me, say something. Please answer me. I need to talk to you—it's really important. Ship!" She's begging, but I don't care. She can't have the baby. She's mine. I close my eyes and hear Helen laughing. I remember the wind carrying her laughter like it was following me.

The day my ear caps arrived, it was warm and we were eating lunch outside. When I put them on, I could hear each sound, separate and distinct. A fly buzzed over my sandwich, a leaf fell, Teresa hummed. The thing was, the sounds didn't hurt anymore; they didn't pile up and press against the back of my head. The air stopped hissing through my brain, my fingers stopped trembling, and the bright colors didn't hurt my eyes.

"How do they feel, Ship?" Teresa asked.

"Good," I said, touching the plastic covering of the caps. "I feel brand new."

"Look at them," Helen snorted. "Everyone's going to laugh when they see them."

"They will not," Teresa said. "Dr. Gould ordered those special. It's like wearing braces."

"Except everyone has braces and no one has ear plugs," Helen said, her lips curling up.

"They're ear *caps*."

"If anyone does laugh, we won't pay any attention to them, will we, Ship?" Teresa said.

Then Helen laughed. She threw back her head and laughed high and mean. I flung the caps off my head to the ground, which made her laugh even harder.

"Helen," Teresa said, "stop that. There's not one single thing wrong with those ear caps. Come back here, Ship! "Ship, come back here right now. Ship!"

Even when I was deep in the woods, I could hear Teresa calling and Helen laughing and saying that was why our dad left—because of me—and I kept running until I didn't know where I was anymore. All the trees looked the same, only darker. It was the end of summer, just before first grade started. Herringtown didn't have kindergarten then, so I never went. Near the end of the day, I spotted a dog curled into a saucer of dirt on the edge of the woods. All I wanted to do was rest, so I stopped beside the dog, watching him sleep until something made me crawl into the bed of dirt around him. He woke, his heart beat, and his tail thumped as he circled me. Then he settled back down around me.

Somebody, probably the dog's owner, must have found me there in the morning and brought me home. I remember Teresa and Trudy were crying in the kitchen and I didn't know why, because nothing was the matter with me. Helen was there, too. She was supposed to say she was sorry.

"Go ahead, Helen. Say you're sorry," Teresa said. "Tell Ship you're sorry. Go on."

But she wouldn't. Teresa told her to, but she never did.

THE WHITE dog is panting and looking up at me. No matter what, Helen can't find us. Nothing can happen to my baby. I rock her tiny swaddled body away from the dog sniffing the bloody brown rabbit, already starting to stiffen. The light falls through the trees in slices. I wonder if Teresa knows I've left. Where does she think I am? What has Helen told her? What will I do if she calls me? Who else is looking for me? Anybody? Why are people always looking for what isn't there and never see what's right in front of them? I did the same thing all that time, waiting for Brian to come back. Now here I am doing it again with my dad, when I might never find him. I don't even know who I'm looking for. I just know I have to find him. First, we have to get to Silver River.

The white dog's ears perk up at the same time as I hear a high whistle through the trees. His eyes dart over us; then he lunges through the woods. My eyes follow his path. I wrap her in my jacket and feed her. Between letting small drops of milk fall into her mouth, I rock her back and forth until I can't hear the echo of Helen's voice any longer.

One by one the stars appear on the black sky. I should bury the brown rabbit so bad luck doesn't follow us around, but I don't. Its little pink tongue sticks out the side of its mouth like a cartoon bunny's, but when I look again, I see glassy stillness in its eyes. The blood on its neck has thickened and its flesh has turned hard. I stare at the night sky until I see a star fall in a dizzying streak. Then I pack everything except the jackknife, wrap her close to me with the blanket, and go the same way the dog went.

Nine

WHEN I CIRCLE BACK to Route 6, headlights gleam, then fade, the globes of the parking lot lamps in Mike's Mini-Mart glow, and the red neon SAM Y's sign, which is missing an M flashes. At first I don't notice the Herringtown police car pulled up in front of Sammy's. I can't let them see me. I crouch behind a trash barrel on the edge of Mike's parking lot until there is a lull in the traffic.

The white dog is tied to the bumper of a lemon yellow pickup whose door reads LUMBER LIQUIDATORS. The dog stirs up the dirt, red in the neon glow. The neon buzzes like the bug zapper. He tugs on the end of his rope, choking and barking until I am there, rubbing between his ears and under his chin, telling him to be quiet before anyone finds us. But the music is playing so loud inside, I'm sure they can't hear. I wonder if ladies are stripping and how they do it. I wonder if their breasts are as big as Brian said they were.

I walk around the back of Sammy's. The stairs, the floor, and the posts of the porch sag under the weight of the roof. Some shingles have slipped and hang like Halloween teeth. The planks on the staircase have splintered, with holes big enough to step through, the railing has separated from the stairs, and the posts are cracked or missing. Both windows have flower boxes, filled with a few inches of dirt. When I shake the sides, the boxes seem sturdy and deep enough to make a little crib, so I wrap her in my jacket and set her carefully in the one on my right. Though the porch shakes from the music playing inside, she doesn't even blink. I look through the window.

Smoke hangs in thin clouds over the men hollering and whistling. With cigarettes and beer in their hands, they stand around the stage. A few of them push a man wearing a cowboy hat forward. The man thrusts a bill in the air. Then I see her legs, in black stockings and knee-high boots, spread out in front of him. Her hips are doing the hula around and around, and when she leans forward, I see her breasts with little sparkling gold tassels hanging on the ends, which she shakes in front of the cowboy's face. They're like two huge hanging sacks. The cowboy folds a bill into her lacy black underwear and then grabs at one of the swinging breasts. She pulls back, out of my sight, before I can see who she is. The men around the cowboy laugh and shove him side to side.

After I stopped here that time with Brian and Mr. Dodd, I asked Teresa whether she knew Sammy's was a strip joint. Helen answered, "Everybody knows about it, Ship. For someone who can hear everything, you sure are clueless."

"I think a lot of people we know go there, including Jack. Those poor ladies. It can be a messy business." Teresa took a deep breath. "But that's how I got you two!"

"Teresa," Helen said, rolling her eyes.

The song ends, and a few of the men swing their heads toward Officer Robinson, who walks through the middle of the room. The crowd parts around him. I tug on the window until it lifts a few inches. Smoke and noise seep out around me. I think Officer Robinson is going to arrest the man who grabbed the stripper's breast or maybe the stripper herself, but he slaps another man on the back. I hear, "I'm still a guy."

The man laughs and slaps him back. I can't hear him. I can't hear anything. Officer Robinson holds up what looks like a photo. Is he looking for me? I hear, "Missing," then "Sure haven't." Does he know about the baby? The man shakes his head. "How long...anything...I sure will." He nods and takes a long swig of beer. "Don't know...before..." Officer Robinson shows another man the photo.

Blessed. You have been blessed, Father Hannah told me. Now I can't hear them. Isn't this what I wanted?

We have to leave right now. The white dog barks short and sharp, then growls. Someone is pulling into the parking lot. I flatten myself against the rotting clapboards.

"Shut up," a voice calls.

"Why's that dumb asshole dog always barking at us?"

"Why don't you find out?" A silver car door opens. Laughter mixes with kicking and scuffling. Someone grunts, another groans. "Bastards!" The car jerks forward, then stops. Someone thumps to the ground and the passenger door slams closed. "Come on, you assholes. We can't stay."

I tiptoe to where she is sleeping in the flower box. I want to bark, too, to keep them away from her. When I peek around the corner of the shed again, their headlights shine on the white dog, pulling and barking at the end of his short rope. A few yards away, the boy they pushed out of the car rolls over. His head hanging, he starts to lift his upper body into a push-up, then collapses in the dirt.

"Toss him a couple of beers at least." I know that voice. *How about giving Brian a turn?* Owen Hart is driving. *Pretend it's me.*

Someone unrolls the back window and hurls out a couple of cans to the boy. The boy jumps up and runs after Owen's car, yelling, "Stupid assholes!" The silver BMW veers backward. Owen and two others inside the car laugh. The moon briefly lights the sagging porch. Someone thumps against the dashboard or roof of the car and sings along, " 'Cuz I'm as free as a bird now—yeah, and this bird you cannot cha-a-ange—' "

The boy stumbles toward his friends. The white dog snaps in his direction. Owen revs the car and flashes his headlights on the boy, who freezes except for his head darting from the car to the dog and back again. His shirt, dirty and torn, hangs out of his pants. A strange smile spreads over his face then he charges the dog full-on. For a moment, the dog seems confused and yelps, but then he leaps forward, twisting in the air. The cloth of the boy's pants tears and there is a quick crunch.

"Son of a bitch," the boy cries and folds over. The rope around the white dog has come loose, but he doesn't run. Clutching his leg, the boy limps toward Owen's car. "Help me, you guys."

"Open the door," Owen shouts. "Let him in!" *Cuz I'm as free as a bird...*

"Dumb asshole dog," someone says. *And this bird you cannot....* The boy gets into the BMW.

Owen lets the engine idle, then revs the car, jolting forward, heading straight for the white dog. The dog runs along the front tire on the driver's side. The car swerves into him. There is a single thump, then the BMW tears out of the parking lot, leaving a trail of dust. Something terrible has happened. Scrambling with his front legs, the dog drags his crushed back legs in jerking motions until he is under the bed of the yellow pickup.

Our Continental with the crushed-up front floats slowly down Route 6. They're looking for me, too. I want to run after them and tell them about the white dog. They could help. I want to go home, but no one can find out about the baby. No one. I put my hand above her mouth to feel her breath. It's warm. Luckily, she slept through it all, but I wonder if she knows what happened. I wonder if somehow we always know what happens right beside us even while we're sleeping, even when we're two days old.

I crawl my way over to the dog, breathing hard, licking himself. He's curled up against the inside of the left tire. One of his front legs sticks out at a right angle. He lifts his head, whimpers, then turns back to his wounds. Crouching under the tailgate, the air presses around me. I hear a clicking. This time, it's coming from the back of my own throat. I close my eyes and listen until the dog's breathing is thick and raspy and I feel like I'm being poured out of a dream. The baby made that clicking sound and Brian, too, and now me.

The first time I heard it was last summer when Trudy first told Teresa that she was dying. "I'm not supposed to eat chocolate pie," Trudy said about the piece she had just finished, dropping her face into her hands over the empty plate. Her shoulders started shaking and her breath came out all choked up. I remember stopping outside the kitchen window. A spider was inching its way down a thread on the side of the house when Trudy told Teresa that the doctor told her she could have a heart attack if she didn't go on a diet and stop smoking and drinking. I heard her say this, then that click-clicking started.

Blood spills out of the dog's mouth like it spilled out of the mouth of the squirrel Mr. Dodd shot in their backyard. Just like that his mouth collapses and his breaths stop. He's not supposed to die. Just a couple of hours ago we were following him through the woods, and now he's dead. It could happen to the baby, too, and it would be my fault. *Click*. Could Brian be dead?

Crouching there, not sure what's worse, what's ahead or what's behind, I know we have to keep on going. We have to get to Silver River before we do anything else.

Mr. Dodd's engine thrums as he pulls into the parking lot. His headlights light the ground under my feet. He swings his pickup into a space at the far end of the parking lot. " 'My bonnie lies over the ocean,' " he sings, slamming the door, clanging his keys. " 'My bonnie lies over the sea.' " His workboots kick up the dust. " 'Oh, bring back, bring back—' "

As soon as he goes inside Sammy's, I go to her. In the dark, I kick one of the cans of beer Owen and his friends threw out of the BMW. I put the two cans in my knapsack and hurry on. She pinches her cheeks and makes sucking sounds. The softest little noises pull me closer. I push her up under my chin so she doesn't try to drink from my breast again. A spasm rushes through her tiny stomach up through her chest, making the muscles tighten along my shoulders and neck, pulling like a rope down my back. I hear her breathing and I breathe in. The cramped space inside my head loosens, undoes. Before anyone sees us, I walk away from the white dog folded in the dirt under the yellow pickup.

Like in a trance, I walk for a long time—until I hear the pull and wash of water pushing downstream. The sky has cleared and is white with stars. The Budweiser is warm and fizzes over the edge of the can when I open it. It tastes awful, like the yeast mixture before Teresa adds the flour to make her oatmeal bread, but I drink it anyway, then toss the can under a bush. Even after it has stopped, the can keeps rolling slowly and the ground does, too, and the trees and my sneakers. I burp like Mr. Dodd and she jumps a little.

I keep hearing the thud of Owen's car hitting the white dog and the dog's gruff breathing and then not breathing and I want it to stop. I add these to my list of sounds that I hope never to hear again, which includes sirens and whistles, Helen singing, driving through tunnels, firecrackers, Mossy, lightning, Trudy's racking cough, Brian breathing and moaning, Mr. Dodd cutting Rabbit's frozen fur, Helen laughing and saying she was our dad's favorite, and so on and so on.

I hope the white dog isn't going to be bad luck following us around. No one'd ever think of going to Silver River to look for me, not unless they had police dogs trailing us. But I'd hear them coming and I'd walk through the water like they do in the movies. As I finish the second beer, my head seems to reach the top of the trees, the sky. My face tingles. The only other time I drank beer was with Brian when we were fishing.

"You said you'd go to Waterfalls with me," I yell at the river.

The woods eat up my voice. The baby's head rolls backward. I laugh and my laughter fills the quiet around us. My hat slips off my head. When I put it back on I remember something that happened years ago, before I got the ear caps.

I was at Jordan Marsh, following Teresa and Trudy past the men's clothing, through the perfume and jewelry departments. The air was so crammed with music and voices and powerful smells that I had to stop. I walked back to the display of men's hats and found a great black fur hat with the softest earflaps and strings that tied under my chin. It slid over my ears like a cushion. Then I made my way through the men's dress shirts and pants, ties and boxers, crawled through an opening on a rack of tan, gray, and black slacks, and curled up on the carpet. With the fur hat on, I watched the empty pant legs swaying around me as the shoppers browsed, scraping the hangers on the racks around me until I fell asleep, sheltered in a circle of pants.

I dreamed my father was shopping here. He flipped through the pants on my rack, fingered the wool, and checked the tags. He knew I was there and he was working his way through the pants one pair at a time, getting closer to me. He was about to reach down to me when a saleslady tapped my shoulder. "What on earth are you doing down here?" she said, the wrinkles pinching up around her eyes and mouth.

"Where's my dad?"

She glanced around the store. "What's your name?"

"Ship."

"Ship?" She frowned at me, then lifted the hat off my head. "Hmph, this belongs to the store, young lady." She tucked it under her arm.

With her hand under my armpit, she pulled me back through the men's clothing. "Your father's not in the dressing room, is he?"

"No," I said, "he was right here."

"Come on, I'll take you to the information desk."

Maybe he was waiting for me there.

"What's your father's name?"

I drew a blank, then said, "Dad."

She squished up her nose and laughed to the receptionist. "Can you page 'Dad' to the information desk?"

WE'RE ALMOST at Silver River. I swallow the wind, which is blowing the leaves in circles, scattering them over the hard ground. It's too cold to stay here. Every few minutes I check her under my bomber jacket. Tomorrow I'll bring her somewhere with heat and hot water, a hotel. For now we have to keep going. When we get to Waterfalls everything will be better. How long will it take us to get there? A week? We can't take a bus. She couldn't go that long without crying. That's the thing about taxis. The drivers never ask questions. We've taken Classy Cabs home from Jimmy Joe's plenty of times after Teresa and Trudy have had too much to drink.

We walk through the empty dirt parking lot past the FRIEND-SHIP CAMP sign and arrow, past Silver River Restaurant, whose windows are boarded up until June, and down the narrow path that turns left to the river. Mr. Dodd never paid any attention to the sign that says PARKING FOR SILVER RIVER CUSTOMERS ONLY. He parked in the Friendship Camp lot every time we went fishing.

"What are they going to do? Call me unfriendly?" He would laugh to himself, holding his hand over his stomach.

From here, the river is a gray light flowing through the dark. I sit on a flat rock on the edge of the water where Mr. Dodd used to set his bait and tackle boxes. Then he'd set up a line of three or four poles along the shore. No one is here now.

A branch spirals past us down the river; a leaf follows, dipping in and out of the water before it disappears. Down the river something goes *plunk*. I take Brian's school photo out of my knapsack. His hair is sticking up and he is smiling because he had to turn his T-shirt inside out, the one with the finger pointing to the side that says, "I'm with stupid." That *was* Brian. I let the photo slip through my fingers. As soon as it hits the water, it flips over, makes a licking sound, and is swallowed up. My face burns and my ears hum as the current takes him away.

She opens her swollen gray eyes as if she knows what I have just done. I see Brian when I look at her. My skin goes cold and this buzzing starts up in my ears. I swat around my head, my heart races, and I can't see straight. Everything is at a slant. When I close my eyes and try to remember him, all I see is a black screen. I'm starting over now. Teresa always said coming to Herringtown was like starting over for her. She wanted to be someone else, not the person she was when our dad left. I'm leaving Herringtown to be someone else.

As I walk along the river's edge, I'm so busy peering into the water I don't notice someone is fishing until I am a few feet away from him. Tall and hunched over his line, he must have fallen asleep standing up. There he is. When I try to yell, my mouth is too dry and nothing comes out but a grunt.

"Holy shit!" The man whips around, facing me. Stepping back too fast, he kicks his tackle box with his heel. "You tryin' to gimme a heart attack or something? Christ, what the hell are you doing?"

"Sorry," I say, my arms around her. "I thought you were someone else."

He laughs; then clearing the back of his throat, he hacks up a wad of spit. His skin is pockmarked and red and his eyes are dark and watery like the white dog's. "If you don't mind me asking, who did you plan on meeting out here? I come out here about every Saturday night and I've never seen anyone."

He stops laughing and squints hard at me. His arm holding the fishing pole goes slack. "Hey, what do you got there underneath your coat?"

"Where?" I shift my weight.

"Right there under that jacket, that's where."

"Why?"

He looks long and hard at me and swallows his spit. "Because I don't know nothin' about babies, but I think you got one under there, that's why."

His fishing pole nearly snaps out of his hand. Struggling to hold on to it, he spins back around to the river. His flannel shirt flaps open, showing his bare stomach. When he reels in his line, nothing is on the hook. "You're running away, aren't you?"

Cold works its way up around my arms and legs, like I'm stepping into the walk-in at Jimmy Joe's on one of the hottest days of the summer. What if he tells the police? What if they find me? Then, more than the cold, something terrible grabs hold of me, like the time I almost ran smack into that huge pig, bleeding as it hung by the hooves from the ceiling of the walk-in. Teresa would kill me if she knew I was in the middle of the woods with a strange man.

He picks up a thermos, opens the lid, and pours the cup full. "Coffee? You look cold." He drinks down the steaming cup, refills it, and passes it to me.

"Thanks." I sip the coffee, thick and bitter, warming my hands. Then I hand it back to him.

After he gulps the rest, he says, "Now, are you going to tell me what you've got under there?"

"Why do you want to know?"

"It's a baby, isn't it?"

I don't answer him.

"Is it yours?"

I stare into his eyes. "Yes," I answer.

He wipes his mouth with the back of his hand and looks at me sideways. "It's okay, isn't it?"

"Yeah, she's okay."

"Can I see?"

Wrapping my arms around my waist, I start to back up. No one can see her.

"Where are you going?"

The blue pom-pom on my lucky hat bounces against my cheek as I walk backward, eyeing him.

"Okay, okay, come back here. You can't stay outside all night. You'll freeze. I'll make a fire."

He's right. I stop.

"I'm not going to do anything, I swear." He sets his pole down and walks over to the circle of rocks on the sandy part of the shore. He breaks small branches and crisscrosses them, then adds a layer of thicker branches over this. Then he crumples up a piece of paper, lights it, and holds it in a few places under the wood until the fire catches. "Damn," he says, shaking his fingers. Then, "There. The wood dried out pretty good today. Now, come over here and warm yourself up."

He sits hunched over on a rock a couple of feet from the fire. He gurgles, clearing the back of his throat again, and spits. I take a step closer. The light flickers over his skin, highlighting each pockmark. His ears are perfect and small, like petals fixed neatly on the sides of his head.

"What are you looking at?"

"Nothing."

"Well, quit staring. You're making me nervous. Why don't you sit down?"

I crouch by the crackling fire, trying not to look at his ears. "At first," I say, "I thought you were my dad."

"Your dad? Does he fish out here?"

I shrug. "No."

"Is he looking for you?"

I whip my head to face him. "I don't know."

"Do your parents know about—"

"No."

"They must be pretty worried about you."

What if the police have tracked down my dad and he's looking for me, too? Would he know who I am?

"Do you have a boyfriend?"

"Sort of." My head goes hot.

"Did you tell him?"

"No."

He pokes the fire with a stick, popping red, blue, and yellow streaks. His eyes rest on me, taking me in. He says, "You're real pretty."

I don't answer him. I don't believe him anyway.

"Where are you headed?"

"Down the river."

After a minute he says, "You know where I'd go if I were you?"

"Where?"

"Home, that's where. First thing in the morning." He pulls his flannel shirt tight around himself. "For tonight you can use my sleeping bag."

"Thanks."

What if I went home and Teresa wasn't there? What if Helen was the only one at home? What if Trudy died? What if Brian died? What if they took the baby away and I never saw her again? I can't go home.

After a while the man gets up and walks into the dark. He returns with a sleeping bag, which he unrolls at my feet. He says, "It'll keep you warm. And the baby. I know it's none of my damn business, but is it really yours?"

"Yeah, she's mine."

"Uh-huh." He nods. "How old are you anyway?"

"Thirteen."

"What are you going to do with her?"

"Keep her."

He nods. "Don't you need to take her to the hospital or something?"

"There's nothing the matter with her." As soon as I say it I start to think that there is. She makes a sound, something between a meow and a bleat. What if something happens to her? I can't hear her heart beating. I slip my hand inside my jacket. She is alive. I repeat, "There's nothing the matter with her. I have to feed her now."

"Okay, okay." The fire sparks and crackles when he adds a few more branches. Then, pointing to the river, he says, "I'll be right over there."

I squeeze milk drops into her mouth, letting her suck on the end of the cloth. His line whistles through the night, then the lure plunks into the water. I unzip the sleeping bag and work myself feet-first inside it.

The man reels his line in. How did he know I had a baby under here? No one else knew. From the back, he looks neck-less, hunched over his pole. Last summer Brian was standing just down the way, reeling in a largemouth bass. The fish leaped out of the water, flashing silver as it tried to wriggle off his line.

"You got him, Bri, nice and slow. It's a big one, I can tell," Mr. Dodd yelled.

"Look at that! Bring him all the way in. Thatta boy!" Mr. Dodd slapped his thigh and danced around Brian and the flop-ping fish. "Okay, hit him hard. Smack him against the ground."

Brian stared at the fish like he was hypnotized.

"Go ahead, nail him!"

Brian put his hands in his pockets.

"Are you listening to me, Brian? Huh?" He punched Brian lightly on the shoulder.

"Did you forget how to talk or something?" He nudged him again. "You some kind of dummy? Hit 'em, Bri. He's your fish.

He's gotta weigh a good three and a half pounds." He slapped the back of Brian's head.

Brian jumped back and flung his arms out to the sides, then turned to his father. "Want me to hit him?" Without waiting for his father to answer, he grabbed the fish by the tail and whacked it on the ground from one side to the other until it was splattering blood. It's a miracle that fish stayed in one piece. Red-faced, Brian finally stopped and looked at what he had done. The fish was barely breathing, blood bubbling from its gills.

"Looks like Johnny," Brian said under his breath.

"What'd you say?" Mr. Dodd asked. His mouth closed and his eyes went hard and narrow. "Son, what did you say?"

"I said," Brian stared at the fish, "looks like I won."

Mr. Dodd broke into a smile as Brian lifted the fish by the tail and dipped it in the water, streaming a triangle of red in the river, then dropped it back onto the shore. "Well, you showed him all right," Mr. Dodd said, smiling.

"Come on, Ship, have a beer with us," he yelled, cracking one open for Brian and then for himself. Mr. Dodd hit his can into Brian's and they threw their heads back and gulped. When he was done, Mr. Dodd turned the can upside down to show us it was empty, wiped his mouth with the back of his hand, then crushed the can in his fist and kicked it into the water.

"Go ahead. A little beer's not going to hurt you," Mr. Dodd said.

Brian laughed. He didn't sound like himself. I tried to gulp it like they did, but it went up my nose and I ended up spitting most of it out. They burst out laughing.

After two beers, I found myself laughing, too. The fish was funny, Brian and Mr. Dodd were funny, the river, the trees, and everything else in the whole wide world was funny, too.

That was almost a year ago—a long, long time ago.

I WAKE once in the night when the man leans over me and with a finger lifts the hair off my face. The earth tilts forward. I see into the black tunnel of his ear, then he is gone. I don't even know his name. How does he know what I should do? The treetops sway in the dark sky, and for a moment I think I am up there looking down on us.

Buffered by the trees, my hat, and the sleeping bag pulled up around my head, the air is gentle and balmy in my ears. The last of the fire's white embers smolder and smoke. A dead leaf falls off a branch, skidding to the ground with the faintest scrape. Her breathing becomes thicker, heavier.

Once, I don't remember when, the wind was blowing against the glass and Teresa was whispering. I miss her. She's the one I miss. She used to come into my room at night. I'd wait for the crack of light to spread across the floor. Then she'd be there. That's what I'm going to do for my baby.

When she shifts in her sleep, I shift to fit her.

Ten

WHEN THE SKY LIGHTENS to the dimmest gray, I wake. Her eyes crack open, then her mouth, but she doesn't cry. I sit up, wriggling out of the sleeping bag. A single bead of sweat rolls off my forehead onto the top of her head. Curled up, the man snores beside his fishing pole. I leave my last two Gooey Bars on top of the sleeping bag for him and walk away. Maybe I'm just tired, but I feel dead—everywhere except where she is on my chest. I keep on, following the river from a distance in case the man comes after us.

As the sun edges up, a trail of light leads us to the crossroads. A smoky fry smell floats up from down the road, where there is the dim blue shape of a restaurant we have passed in the car but never eaten at. If we go out to eat, we go to Jimmy Joe's, unless we're at the beach. Then we stop at the Seafood Shack for fried clams and calamari and French fries.

My stomach muscles jump every which way, rumbling and groaning like Silver River. I better feed her before we go in. "You have to eat something," I tell her. "You have to." But she won't take any drops of milk. Because I don't know what else to do, I hold her under my sweater, rocking her, trying to make her better. She mouths my chest until her lips find the tip of my breast. Please let there be some milk for her. She sucks a little and cries, then sucks a little more, and finally falls back asleep. I wrap her around me with the blanket and zip up my bomber jacket.

Blue with white trim looping and swirling like script along the slope of the roof, Kay's Diner looks like a gingerbread house. Inside, all the tables are set with checkered cloths and white vases are filled with daffodils. It is warm and smells of greasy bacon and sausage, eggs and toast, and muffins and sweet things like Teresa makes. Whistling and the clanking of pans comes from the back of the diner. Before anyone sees me, I duck through the door with the silhouette of a lady wearing a bell-shaped dress, locking us in. No one will see us in here.

Her tiny head presses against the center of my chest. I lift my sweater and examine my breasts, cupping the palms of my hands over them one at a time, pinching my nipples. Not a drop of milk comes out. I look at us in the pink, heart-shaped mirror. My hair is a tangled mess with bits of leaves in it and the sides of my face are streaked with dirt. Blood has dried over a scratch that runs under my chin to my neck.

Using paper towels soaked in warm water and soap, I wash my face and hands, then her face, hands, and head, which is still peeling but doesn't seem gross like it did before. I run my hand over her soft scalp. "Now where do we go? Where do we go now?" I whisper to her. Her lips slightly parted, she keeps sleeping on my chest. She is part of me. Does she need to go to the hospital like that man at Silver River said?

Inside the mirror, I find a wooden brush with a thick handle on the glass shelves. Slowly I brush all the snarls out of my long tangle of hair. I lean closer to the glass. Either my neck is longer or I'm holding my head higher. My copper hair shimmers, drawing the light all around my face. My eyes are sharper blue and my face seems to have settled around them.

After I return the brush, I zip my bomber jacket and clean the sink. When I go out front an older man with runny eyes and a double chin greets me. "Good morning, young lady," he says, speaking through his nose, as if his mouth is too heavy. "You're early. Anyone joining you?"

"Um, yes," I say. Maybe that man by the river will find me here. "My father."

"All right, then. Sit wherever you like."

He follows me to a table to the right of the front window.

"How about some juice?"

"Yes, please. Orange juice and milk, and I'd like some sausage, bacon, and ham."

His eyebrows lift, but his runny eyes keep right on looking at me. He sets a menu on my plate and on the plate across from me. "Coming right up."

The front door opens as the waiter starts to shuffle away from my table. Two girls in Easter hats with pink and yellow ribbons and matching dresses barge through the door, followed by their dad, who waves. I wave back.

"Morning, Charlie," the old man says. "Don't you girls look pretty today."

I pick up my napkin. Of course they weren't waving to me.

"Morning, Henry. Thought we were going to be the first ones here."

"Looks like we have an early bird." He winks at me.

"Why is she sitting at our table, Dad?" the younger girl asks.

"Shh, there are plenty of tables." Charlie smiles at me.

"Here, Dad. Let's sit here," the older girl says.

He turns to his daughter. "All right."

The baby stirs, making a purring sound. I think she must be getting hungry now and decide to take the milk into the bathroom to feed her. But when I put my hand over her, she stops moving.

In a few minutes, Henry brings me my breakfast. I pop a whole sausage into my mouth, trying to count to thirty chews as Teresa says I should before I swallow. As seven chews, I stuff in a strip of hot bacon, then fold in a slice of ham. I take a drink of my juice, then reach for another piece of bacon when I notice Charlie and his older daughter staring at me. Henry shuffles toward me, his eyes on his thick-soled black shoes.

"How is everything?" he asks in his nasal voice.

I'm still hungry. "Could I have another order of everything? For my dad."

"Sure thing. Will he be here soon?"

"Yes."

"Where is he?" he asks softly.

"Herringtown. He had to go back there." I pause. "We were fishing last night."

"That's a good fifteen-minute drive. Did he drop you here first?"

"Yes, sir."

"Henry," he says. "Call me Henry. What's your name?"

"Sheila."

"That's a pretty name. Whereabouts are you from?"

"Waterfalls. Rhode Island."

"That's quite a ways."

His watery gaze lingers on me. I've said too much.

The front door opens with a ring and Henry shuffles off to greet the new customers. Next thing an older couple wearing matching sweatsuits sits beside me. Though they smile at me, I'm sure they're thinking that something is wrong with me, sitting here alone. I have the baby, but no one knows that. "My dad should be here any minute," I explain to them.

"Oh, that's good." They smile and nod and turn back to each other.

I wish I were back in the woods.

Charlie orders coffee, orange juice, and hot oatmeal for himself and blueberry pancakes for his daughters. The younger one, who is around four years old, asks, pointing out the window, "What's in there, Dad?" Through the window, a gold coffeepot hanging beside the KAY'S DINER sign spurts puffy clouds into the morning air.

"Just steam," he answers.

"Why?"

"For the fun of it. See, it looks like a real coffeepot."

"Why do you have to ask that every time we come here?" the older girl asks.

She ignores her sister. "Is it real, Dad?"

"The steam is real steam, but it's not really a coffeepot."

"It's pretend?"

"Well, it's not pretend, it's real, but it doesn't make coffee."

"Why, Dad?"

"Why what?"

"Why doesn't it make coffee?"

"Just because," he answers. "Now eat your pancakes. Aren't they good?"

Instead of eating the second order of bacon, sausage, and ham, I watch Charlie and his daughters eat, listening to them argue about who has more blueberries in her pancakes and who is hogging the maple syrup. I do this until it seems like the baby and I are sharing the table with them.

"Why is she eating alone?" the younger girl asks.

I hunch myself around the baby—I'm not alone.

"I think she's waiting for her dad."

"Where's her dad?"

"I don't know, he's coming. Let's not talk about it now."

"Why is she eating with her jacket on, Dad? You never let us do that."

"If she were my daughter, I wouldn't let her eat with a jacket on," he says. "Now don't stare."

My breath catches in my throat. I never thought my dad would be bald like Charlie.

Charlie pushes his cereal bowl forward, reaches around to pull his wallet from his back pocket, opens it, and places a twenty on the table. They can't just leave. We need somewhere to go, too. How can we go all the way to Waterfalls when I don't know who I'm looking for? I look for Henry so I can pay, too. He's carrying an empty tray back toward the swinging doors by the kitchen.

When he comes out, Charlie and his daughters are putting on their coats. "How much is my bill?"

"What about your father?"

"I'll wait outside for him."

He looks at me for what seems like a very long time. The leather of his shoes creaks as he stands there. "Five seventy-five," he says. "You can come back inside if you need to."

"Thank you."

From the open door, Charlie and his daughters wave to Henry. If we went home with them, she would get better, I know she would. As I count seven bills onto the table, Charlie races through the parking lot after his daughters, both holding their hats on, ribbons and hair flying back. "I won!" The older one smashes into the back of a silver station wagon, followed by the younger one, who shouts, "Dad's last!"

"One of these days, I'm going to beat you both," Charlie tells them. "Just you wait and see."

"Sure, Dad." They laugh at him as they pile into the front seat. "That's what you always say."

The sun prints my shadow on the pavement. Up ahead is the open blue sky. A gust of steam whooshes out of the cof-feepot like a full breath, followed by a lull. I wait for the next whoosh and the next. Church bells ring, a plane flies over-head, pots, pans, and dishes clank inside Kay's. Charlie's car pulls out of the parking lot. "Sure, Dad," I say out loud, "that's what you always say." I look around as if I have forgotten something, as if I have left something behind. What am I missing? She presses against my skin, reminding me that she is still here. Where do I take her now? All I want is to find a place for us.

When I look back, Henry is standing by the front register with his ear to the phone. I cut across the parking lot, walking blindly into the sun's glare in the same direction Charlie's silver car went. I've grown used to carrying her—the weight of her, the warmth and shape of her on my chest. I want her to tell me where we should go, but she is too quiet, hardly moving. Tiny green buds crinkle open on the ends of the branches. Blood rushes to the ends of my fingertips. My chest hurts and it's hard to breathe. We need somewhere to go.

I take the first street I come to, Cedar. A man is walking a golden retriever. He is balding like Charlie, but he isn't Charlie. I follow him anyway, watching him stop when his dog sniffs and pees, then continue when the dog does. "Good boy," he says.

All the houses look the same except one is white with black shutters, another gray with blue shutters, one has a fenced yard, another, Easter decorations. None has a giant pear tree. The man hums, a telephone rings, a child cries, an egg cracks, someone plays the piano, someone else sneezes. I wonder which house belongs to the man walking his dog. I wonder if we could go there.

The dog's collar clinks and the man whistles as he walks. Staying a good twenty yards behind him, I stop when he does. He turns once to me and smiles. Maybe my dad *is* balding. I smile back, then bend down and pretend to tie my shoelaces. He is still looking at me when I am done. Why doesn't he ask me if I need anything? Why doesn't he ask me if I need somewhere to go? He clucks to the dog and they walk quickly down the next driveway, through the front door. Just as I step into their driveway, a police car passes on the road where we just were, where Kay's is. Are they looking for me?

The leash drops, metal clanking against a hard floor. "Good boy," the man says again, patting the dog. "That's a good boy."

"What took you so long, Dad?" a boy yells.

"Dad?" he yells again.

Yellow, pink, and green plastic Easter eggs sway from the branches of a lilac tree in the middle of their lawn. One cracks and the wind blows the halves of the shell onto the grass. I cross their lawn to put the egg back together. When I am a few feet from the tree, a short woman with straight auburn hair opens the front door. "Excuse me, do you want something?" Her voice is so cold I stop in my tracks. She says it like I've done something wrong. I want to tell her that we need a place to go.

"I told you she was following me," the man says from somewhere behind the door.

"Who is it, Dad? Let me see."

"Are you looking for someone?" the woman asks. Her fingers grip the door, ready to close it.

My face burns with shame. What have I done? What did I expect? What did I think I'd find here? I turn at once, cutting back across the lawn, through the silvery morning air. The door shuts behind me.

The baby's breaths are thick and slow. "I'm sorry. We're going home now. We're going back." As soon as I say this, I breathe easier. Finally. We need to go home.

After we walk past Kay's, we go through the woods on the road that runs beside Silver River. I look to the sky. A blackbird lifts out of an oak tree, opening its wings, unrolling its feathers.

Spit has dried on the edges of her mouth. Her head rises and falls as I walk, but other than that, she doesn't stir. If I brought her to Father Hannah, he could bring her to the hospital to make sure she's all right. I've seen him baptize dozens of babies. After, he'd tell us to "welcome these new children of God," and we'd clap. Are we all children of God? Is she? Is Helen? How could she be now? Father Hannah would know what to do and he wouldn't tell anyone either. Then he'd give me my baby back.

The cries of the blackbirds wind in and out of the trees. I am hot and breathless, almost running. I listen to the sound of my heart beating fast and hard and follow it.

When I get to Sammy's, the parking lot is empty. There is no sign of the white dog, only tire tracks, cigarette stubs, and empty beer cans. Across the street, a Herringtown police car is parked in front of Mike's Mini-Mart. The store bells ring as Officer Robinson strolls out with a tall coffee in one hand and my ear caps in the other. They look so strange dangling from his hand, I want to take them away from him. But he tosses them onto the passenger seat, sits in the cruiser, spills the top of his coffee in the parking lot, then shuts the door. If they found my ear caps, do they know about the baby, too? Did they find the hole where she was buried? Is he going to arrest me for kidnapping her? If I give her to Father Hannah, they won't know I had her.

I wait until there is no traffic in sight, then cross the road and wind behind Mike's to where the white dog was yesterday. The same old, bearded man I saw behind Jimmy Joe's twice reaches into the Dumpster. About three weeks ago, I was standing in front of Jimmy Joe's just as it was getting dark when I heard a rustling out back. This man pulled half a loaf of bread out of the Dumpster, sat down at the edge of the woods, and ate it. The next day at the same time he ate pasta with his fingers. The day after that I left a to-go box of linguine carbonara Teresa brought home beside the Dumpster with a fork. She calls it a heart attack on a plate and won't touch it, but I love it. He took the box and fork, but I haven't seen him since.

Now he pulls out a package of hamburger buns from Mike's Dumpster and starts eating one. He slumps against the side of the building beside a worn knapsack and a paper bag and eats two more buns quickly, then drinks from the paper bag. Bits of chewed bun stick to his thick gray beard. He takes off his baseball cap and places it upside down on his lap. Long fingers run through his straggly hair, down to his chest, brushing crumbs off his dirty brown sweater. Then one at a time, his fingers creep into the cap, prying under the seams, scratching the nylon. *Scritch, scritch,* he goes, like a mouse working its way through wood.

The sun pushes higher. The cooing of morning birds calls out and cars pass on Route 6 like waves from far away. The ground swells up around my feet, pushing me forward. We are getting closer. Hurry, I tell myself, faster—we are almost there.

Part Three

LET ANYONE
WITH EARS
HEAR

Eleven

THE SHALLOW HOLE HAS been filled and covered with
leaves as if she had never been buried there. I stare at
the spot where I found her, circling around and around
it. The wind sweeps the ground, showing the prints of whoever
trampled over the dirt. The ground carries the *thump thump* of
footsteps and the air carries the *shhh* of someone breathing—
like a heartbeat outside someone. A sharp light angles through
the trees, catching the corner of a black trash bag fluttering out
the end of a hollow tree. Something inside the plastic bag keeps
it from blowing away. Someone is running toward us. The footsteps and breathing become louder. I pull the trash bag out of
the tree.

We're going to be caught here. I could run, but instead I
open the bag. A hissing fills my ears—a steady hissing that rises
into a buzzing. My mouth goes dry. In the back of my throat I
taste the bitter coffee I drank last night. The zipper of Helen's
Sassoon jeans is broken, the crotch is stained with dark blood,
and the sides have been cut down to the thighs. I close my eyes,
waiting for her to find me.

"Ship, Ship," she calls. "Ship, is that you? Wait for me. I've been looking everywhere for you." There she is, out of breath, standing in front of me. Her flushed face is wet. She gasps, a stab of breath, then gulps air.

The trash bag slips through my fingers to the ground. I want to kill her. My blood rises and flows too fast through my veins. I think I can hear it streaming to the top of my head like water moving through a hose. If the baby wasn't wrapped around me, I'd throw myself at Helen and gouge out her ice eyes.

But her eyes are glassy and wide-open, like they've melted into pools. She whispers, "Where have you been? I've been looking for you."

She inches closer. "I can't believe I finally found you. Where is she? What did you do with her?"

"You left her here," I say through my teeth. I can't look at her. The baby is so warm, like a hot water bottle on my chest. How could she be Helen's? "Why didn't you finish burying her?"

"I wasn't burying her. I was trying to keep her warm. All this water came pouring out of me in the bathroom in the middle of math. I didn't know where to go. It hurt so much I could hardly walk." The words come out too fast.

"You could have gone home. You could have gone to Trudy's or Father Hannah's."

"I WAS walking home, but I didn't make it. Do you think I planned it that way? As soon as it got dark, I went back to get her. I wasn't going to leave her. I came back right after I saw you and she was gone. YOU TOOK HER."

"You left her here."

"You took her. SHE'S MINE. I didn't want anyone to know. Why did you take her? What did you do with her?"

"She could have died." I can't let Helen see her. She's more mine than hers. "You went home—took a shower—went to Jimmy Joe's?"

"I couldn't take her anywhere in the middle of the afternoon. I went back to get her, Ship. You have to believe me," she whispers. "I knew you found her. Is she all right? TELL ME SHE'S ALL RIGHT." When Helen's voice rises, the baby lifts her head. I want to cover her ears. My arms circle her, guarding her.

"What about my ear caps? I just saw Officer Robinson with them. Did he find them here?"

"No, I did. I told him I found them behind the Gooey factory. They were trying to figure out when you left them there."

"Does anyone know? Officer Robinson or Margie?"

"No, I didn't tell anyone. No one. Except Owen."

"Owen?" Not Brian, not Brian, not Brian.

"I had to tell him."

"You didn't even put her in a blanket." I step back from her.

"All I had was a towel from my gym locker. Is she all right? Where is she? Where'd you put her? What did you do with her? She's my baby, Ship."

She's mine, I want to tell her, but I'm scared of Helen, of what she might do. The baby's going to cry. "I'm taking her to Father Hannah."

"I was going to get her, Ship, I was. You don't even know what happened!" She grabs my arm, her fingernails pressing through the leather of my jacket. She's too close. I shake her hand loose. She squeezes her hand around her own wrist. We stare at each other. When she lets go, there are four fingernail marks, moon slivers pressed on her white skin.

"How could I have a baby?" She drops to her knees. Her uncombed hair falls on either side of her face as she rocks back and forth. "He wanted me to have an abortion, but I waited too long. Then I just wanted it to be over. I thought once it was over, he'd come back."

"Owen?"

She nods.

I put my palms on my chest where the baby's head is under my jacket. "No one knows except Owen?"

"No. What would they say?" She says it like it's my fault. Her eyes flash at me. "But I came back for her—I DID." Her eyes flash at me. "What if something happened to her when YOU HAD HER?"

"It didn't." Once when Teresa was telling the story of me being born in the car, she said, "Even if something happened to me, Ship could have lived for two days without being fed."

I stare at Helen. "Nothing happened to her," I say.

"Where is she?" she begs quietly. "I couldn't tell anyone." Mascara runs in black streaks down her cheeks. She wipes her nose with the back of her hand, smearing snot in a green line through the mascara. "He said it was my problem. He said—he said a lot of things." Using the bottom of her sweatshirt, she wipes off her face, then reties her ponytail, which is tangled with bits of leaves. "I kept thinking he was going to call, but—"

"Why'd you listen to him?" I ask. How could Helen think she could just hide the baby as if it never happened? But here I am, hiding her, too.

"I don't know. I couldn't help it, I wanted him to like me." Her teeth are clenched. "Tell me she's all right. That nothing happened to her."

Has she forgotten about what I saw? She acts like she hasn't done anything, like it all happened to her. "What about Brian?"

"What about him?"

"Why'd you do that?" She was on her knees like she is now with her face there and Brian breathing. That was four months ago. She was already pregnant.

"That? Do you think I wanted to? I didn't. Owen told me to—he said if I did it, then—then—I thought—I believed him, that's why. You have no idea. I'm sorry." Her chest caves in as sobs heave out of her. She covers her mouth with her hands, choking the sound of her cries. "I didn't know what I was going to do. I couldn't tell anyone."

I rest my hand on the top of her head. I can't remember the last time I touched Helen. When she looks up, her eyes are bright green and wet. Thawed. She says, "I feel like I'm going crazy. I still don't know what I'm going to do." Her chest moves in and out.

A trickle of blood runs down her cheek where she has scratched herself. "You're bleeding."

After a while, she repeats, "I'm sorry." She dries her face with her sweatshirt. "Where is she? Please tell me."

"Is there anything wrong with her?" I ask, wondering if that is why Helen left her.

She frowns. "What do you mean?"

"She's so small."

"I didn't know when it was going to happen. I think she was early. I just want to see her." Helen starts crying again. She whispers, "Let me see her, Ship. Please let me see her. You're the one with the miracle hearing."

I don't know what she means, and just because I hear everything, it doesn't mean I understand it. "I can't help it. Do you think I want to wear ear caps?" I lean toward her. "Besides, I'm losing my hearing," I whisper, though I hear the softest clicking in the back of the baby's throat and the thumping of her heart. I feel sorry for Helen—sorry that she left the baby in the woods. I unzip my bomber jacket.

The baby's so still when I unwrap the blanket around us, Helen sucks in her breath. When she sees the fuzzy top of the baby's head hanging to the side on my chest, she whispers, "Is she alive?" Her voice never sounded so soft in my ears.

"Yes," I say.

"My blanket," Helen says as it floats into a white heap at my feet. "Why's she so quiet? I mean, why isn't she doing anything?"

"She sleeps a lot," I say, cradling her.

"You sure she's all right?"

I nod.

The baby's fingers suddenly reach toward Helen, who sways back.

"She's just a baby," I whisper.

Helen wipes her nose on her sleeve and says sharply, "Did anyone see YOU?"

"No."

"No one? Are you sure?"

"Well, a guy fishing at Silver River saw me, but he didn't see her."

"You can't tell anyone about her or where you found her or

ANYTHING." She starts to grab hold of me and stops herself. "Promise," she whispers.

Milk must be spilling from Helen's breasts because she takes a napkin from her pocket, lifts her shirt, and pats the napkin underneath her bra. The baby's mouth puckers. I wonder if she smells it.

"Does Teresa know anything?" I ask.

"Nothing. She's worried to death about *you* right now."

"Where does she think I am?"

"She thinks you ran away. Maybe to find Brian."

"Did you tell her I was at home Friday night?" The baby's head rests against my neck and my shoulder. Her arms and legs spread out across my chest, gripping onto me.

"Yes," she says, staring at the baby. "I didn't want anyone to find you but me. She didn't find out until yesterday. And I washed the shirt you left under your bed."

"You better get rid of these jeans."

"I will. Now promise me you won't say anything." She picks up the end of the blanket, its faded moons and stars dull gold in the sunlight. It smells like the baby. "You can't tell anyone, Ship. Promise. Here, I want you to have this. Keep it."

"It's just a blanket," I say. "I don't care if he gave it to you."

"I know."

"Let's leave it with her."

Helen holds herself like she is freezing, her mouth a crack. Her fingers glide over the top of her baby's head. Her baby. The plastic bag with her ripped, stained jeans crinkles in the breeze.

"Take her to Father Hannah now. He won't say anything. He doesn't have to."

"You have to tell Teresa."

"No, I don't!" she cries. "We can't tell anyone."

"We don't have to say she's yours. I'd just say I found her in the woods."

"It's not that simple, Ship."

My chest swells. "We could keep her."

"You can't just find a baby in the woods and keep her. Anyway, they'd know. They'd figure it out. Do you know Teresa was pregnant when she got married?"

Why does Helen know this and not me? "With—you?"

"Of course with me."

"Is that why they got married?"

Helen nods.

"Oh." My mind goes blank. I clutch onto the baby. "Why didn't she tell me?"

Helen shrugs.

I must hold the baby too tight. She chokes and coughs. Her face turns an angry red with blue veins lining her forehead and eyelids.

"Hurry up," Helen says. "Go!"

When her eyes meet mine this time, a powerful, dazed look passes between us—one that comes only from sharing a secret like this. After wrapping the baby tight around with the blanket again, I leave, turning once to see Helen lifting her shirt. A white napkin floats to the ground. She didn't even nurse her baby.

Going the back way around the Gooey factory takes longer, but I have to take it. Silvery blue smoke slips out of the smokestack. There is a whining, then a thin whistling, followed by a *clunk, clunk,* before the smoke disappears in the blue sky. The air smells of chocolate and caramel. Even while hurrying, I breathe it in, holding it in as long as I can, like Trudy holds in her cigarette smoke. *That's why they got married.* My mouth stays puckered, ready for the next breath.

THE CHURCH bells ring and the cars pull out of the parking lot. After a few minutes, I step out from behind the oak tree. Mrs. Hayes stands halfway down the church steps, holding her hand like a visor over her eyes as she talks to Father Hannah. Her pink satin dress swells up around her knees when the wind blows. "I have some Easter rolls for you, Father. I'll bring them by later this afternoon," she calls.

I wonder if Teresa went to mass. Why didn't she tell me what she told Helen? Why didn't she want me to know? Was it because our dad never wanted us? Teresa did—she wanted us.

With my eyes closed, I trace the outline of the baby's face until I have memorized the curve of her big ears, her tiny nose, her smooth cheeks, her lips that part to let my finger slip through, then suck. A silk daisy fallen off someone's Easter hat blows down the stairs step by step after Father Hannah. I start to follow his long swishing black robes, then stop. My legs are like lead and my arms hang uselessly at my sides. Already I miss the smell of her skin and the touch of her puny elbows, knees, and toes on my chest. I miss the sound of her breathing and her shifting against me. I miss her weight pulling me forward, guiding me.

I dash up the stairs into the church vestibule, where it is cool and dark and smells of holy water. I'm going to keep her, I am. I need her. I find myself face-to-face with a Jesus statue I must have passed a million times before and never noticed. I stare into the pockets of shadow beneath His eyes. He is leaning toward me, lifting His sad dark eyes, trying to tell me something. He leans closer. His voice is a high murmur in my ear. *There's no love like a mother's love. There's no love like a mother's love.*

I am more her mother than Helen is. We're going home now.

Twelve

MAIN STREET IS DESERTED except for a couple of cars parked in front of Jimmy Joe's. The air smells of roasted garlic and fresh bread. *Something in your eyes*—pop—*was so inviting. Something*—pop—*in your smile*. From the alley next to Chuck's Hardware across the street from Jimmy Joe's, I watch Laura lift chairs off the tables and set them in their places. Her foot scrapes the ground behind her as she crosses the floor. Someone is already hunched over at the bar—Mr. Grant. Laura opens the front door, clamps it there with a wooden block, and sweeps the dust out of the restaurant. As she sweeps, she sings, " 'We were strangers in the night.' "

Propping the broom against the glass front of Jimmy Joe's, she pats around the wide pocket of her waitressing dress for her pack of Virginia Slims, slides one out, lights it, and takes a deep pull. The end of her cigarette crackles.

"Quiet out there, huh?" Mr. Grant calls out to Laura.

"Like a ghost town."

On a hubcap next to the trash can, something stares back at me—the shape of me, vague and distorted. There I am. When I look from a different angle, though, my reflection vanishes from the silver rim. The sun blots me into white. I close my eyes, then open them to see the whole of me there on the hubcap again. For the last two days the baby has been on my chest. I want to call out to everyone that I'm going to keep her, that she's mine. There is no place to go. I don't want to be on the outside, looking in. I want to be part of something. We belong here.

Little—pop—*did we know, love was just a glance*—pop—*away*. Does Frank Sinatra know anything about love?

Two days ago, I was right there where Laura is, waiting for Brian to come back. Since the day he left, I've been waiting for him as if nothing else in the world mattered—up until I found the baby, that is. Finally I don't feel like I'm missing something.

Laura stubs out her cigarette, flicking the butt onto the street. She takes the broom back inside, leaving the door wide open.

"Pies gone?" Mr. Grant asks.

"Every single one," Laura says. "Teresa couldn't bake a thing yesterday. Poor thing is worried sick. I stopped by there yesterday, you know."

"The Sooners? You did?"

"Yes, I did." She told me she'd never go there.

"Well, well. Any news?"

"I guess she's run away before, so that's what Teresa thinks. She was right in here on Friday, too. Wish I paid more attention now. But no matter how many times I say it, it won't change anything."

I have to tell Teresa I'm all right. I can't imagine the house without her rolling out her pie dough, trimming the edges, whipping up meringues, stirring lemon and chocolate filling, apple and cherry. I march out of the alley. Here I am in plain sight, walking right down Main Street. Look.

"I guess she was in the mini-mart across from Sammy's," Laura says.

"I'll have another," Mr. Grant says. A glass hits the bar. "It's strange that boy—what's his name, he was late for the bus every goddamn day—he's home."

"The Dodd boy?"

"He came in on the train last night. I was picking up Barbara's sister."

"He did?"

Brian.

"Guess he was in Virginia."

"Virginia? Does Teresa know?" Laura lowers the volume on the cassette player. "She thinks Ship might be looking for him."

"She knows all right. She was there, looking for Ship."

"It doesn't make sense."

I don't know if Laura or Mr. Grant or anyone else sees me. With both arms tight around my waist, holding her, I run as fast as I can, cutting through the white and green shards of light between the trees. I think I must be going faster than the speed of sound because I don't hear anything. *Nothing*. I head toward the crown of the giant pear tree, its tiny new leaves bursting into the blue sky, and I don't stop until I get to the front of the Dodds' house.

The American flag slaps against itself. Its shadow falls over me. I've been waiting so long. I listen for the usual sounds of the Dodds' TV blasting, water running, needles clicking, Mr. Dodd chewing or burping, Brian breathing, his heart racing like mine is. What I hear over the flapping of the flag is something I've never heard before—a slow hollow grinding like a broken washing machine.

I barge up to the front door with my hand in a fist, ready to knock, when a face smashes up against the plate of glass beside the door. It pinches and twists and a string of drool hangs from the howling mouth. The nose flattens and distorts, blue eyes bulge at me, and the mouth opens and shuts again and again. Brian? I stumble backward down the stairs, barely keeping my balance, then sidestep behind the short pine trees.

"Get off the goddamn window." Mr. Dodd grunts. "Just knock it off, did you hear me? What are you looking at now? I don't see anything, do you? Now close your trap. Shut it up. Do you want everyone in Herringtown to hear you?"

That can't be Brian, I say to myself. How could it be? What happened to him? My back against the clapboards, I try to catch my breath without making any noise.

"Come on, pipe down now. No one's out there. We don't want Mrs. Sooner or the police coming back here either," Mr. Dodd says. Then he mutters, "I knew this wasn't a good idea."

"It's okay." That's Brian—he's inside. Was that his face on the window?

"It's a good thing they saw you get off that train last night, Brian. I told them you were in Virginia and didn't know anything about Ship, but I don't think they believed me until you stepped off the train. You looked real sharp, too. I'm proud of you, son."

"Where do you think Ship is?" Brian asks.

"I don't know, I don't know."

"I need to find her."

I stop breathing.

"What? What for? The police will find her. That's their job."

"No, please, I need to find her, sir. I know where she goes." His voice is deeper.

"Well, let's talk about it after our Easter dinner, how's that?" Then he says in a loud, flat voice, "I told you this wasn't a good idea."

"I just asked for one day, that's all," Mrs. Dodd says.

Howls turn into long uneven vowel sounds.

"There will be no crying today. Understand?"

"We're going to have a good time," Mr. Dodd says. "Aren't we going to have a good time, Brian?"

"Yes, sir."

"A nice, quiet family dinner, that's right. That ham must be ready by now. Is the ham ready yet?"

"Come on," Brian says in a softer voice now, "let's go back. That's it. Pretty soon you'll be doing everything like you used to."

Who's he talking to? "I just have to see him once," I whisper to the baby, "then we'll go home."

"Brian Dodd, sit at the head of the table. Go ahead. You look real sharp with your new haircut."

Feet scuffle and chairs scrape against the floor. The oven door scrapes open, a rack slides out, dishes clank, a beer can cracks open and sprays.

Hearing is not enough—I have to get in there. With my back pressed to the house, I make my way around the side, inching toward the kitchen window. I trail my finger over the metal doors of the bulkhead, hot in the sun. The doors are slightly ajar, the padlock unlocked. I might not be able to see him from the kitchen window, and anyway that face might press against the glass again. The hinges creak when I lift the door enough to step under, then I gently let it back down, closing out the light.

I let my breath out as my eyes get used to the dark. Boxes are piled high into stacks, making walls around me. In black marker, they are labeled Johnny's Clothes, Johnny's Bedroom, Johnny's Baseball Cards, Johnny's Books, Johnny's Schoolwork, and everything else about Johnny. What's his stuff doing down here?

Mr. Dodd's voice drones through the basement floor. "I said we're not going to talk about it now. We're going to have a nice family dinner."

"Why can't we talk about it, Joe?"

"Because I said so, that's why."

The voice says something I can't understand. The sounds twist up in his mouth.

I tiptoe across the cement floor to the stairs. The door leading to the kitchen is cracked open about an inch, framing it in light. As I creep up step by step, Mr. Dodd's voice gets louder. One thing I didn't notice last time I was in their house is this tinny hum coming through the walls like the buzzing at the hospital.

"Don't be ridiculous, I'm not upsetting him," he says. "We're all together, now let's enjoy our meal. Ham's good. Isn't it good?"

I wonder if Mr. and Mrs. Dodd ate Rabbit. I wonder if he said, "Rabbit's good. Isn't she good?"

"If you hold it like this, it's easier," Brian says.

Someone's breathing thick and raspy like a needle stuck at the end of a record.

"Thatta boy. Pass me that mustard now. That's it."

When I get to the top stair, I should be able to see something through the crack.

"Now are you going to tell us about school?" Mr. Dodd asks.

There is a grunt, then a gurgling, followed by a stream of nonsense sounds flying loud and furious. The noise twists and blasts through my head like the baby's crying did at first. He is saying something, but I can't tell what—a chair is rocking too hard, slamming back and forth on the floor.

"What's he doing now?" Mr. Dodd calls out. "What? What's he pointing at? The basement? Nothing's down there but a bunch of your boxes, you big dummy." He laughs.

"Shhh. Stop now. Please stop. Leave him alone," Mrs. Dodd says.

"Don't shush me, for crissake. Somebody's got to discipline him." He sounds disgusted.

"He doesn't understand, Dad."

"Sure he does."

"No, he doesn't."

"How do you know?"

Mrs. Dodd says, "It's all right, Johnny."

"He's not a baby." Then Mr. Dodd yells, "Something's burning!"

Mrs. Dodd lets out a yelp, followed by light footsteps. In the middle of all this, I rush to the last stair before the door. Through the crack, I see Mrs. Dodd's back bent over as she holds the oven door open, letting the smoke pour out, and pulls out a tray of burned rolls.

Over the blabbering in the other room, Brian's voice rises. "You're going to make him sick if you keep doing that, Dad."

Next thing, there is an explosive burp and the retching sound of vomit. Mr. Dodd yells, "For God's sake!"

Mrs. Dodd drops the tray to the floor and runs back to the dining room. Mr. Dodd huffs through the kitchen and out the back door, letting it slap shut. Mrs. Dodd starts crying. "I'm sorry. It's my fault, I'm sorry." Mr. Dodd's truck peels out of the driveway.

"Come on now, let's go upstairs and clean you up. I'm sorry, Johnny, I'm sorry."

"It's not your fault, Ma!" Brian screams. His voice cracks and rises, then goes deep again. "He knows it isn't your fault. Don't you, Johnny?"

"I want my sons at home, Brian."

"I know you do. Don't cry, Ma."

There is a shuffling of footsteps. "Help me get him upstairs now. That's it," Mrs. Dodd says. "Up you go. Don't worry, I'm going to clean you up. Everything's going to be all right, you'll see."

The Dodds' kitchen is cloudy with smoke and stinks of vomit. The last time I was here, I stood right there eating Brian's birthday cake, while Mr. Dodd was chewing louder than a pig. This time I'm going to find out what's really going on.

My hands reach around the baby. Her forehead is hot and her cheeks are flushed. I unzip my bomber jacket. She doesn't stir—she doesn't reach out to me. Her head hangs limp, her eyes are closed, and her mouth is dry. What is the matter with her?

One of the plates on the table set for four is full of throw-up, and there is a pool of it on the platter around the ham. Upstairs, Johnny is swallowing breaths and spitting them out again. Water runs and footsteps cross back and forth. Brian is so close. The chairs around the table where they were eating their Easter supper are pushed back out of place. One is knocked over. Three beer cans lay on their sides underneath the table. I pull the shade and lift the window to let the terrible smells out. Brian's Mossberg stands propped in the corner of the room. The wall-paper is gray with dark pink swirling roses. The only thing on the wall is a plaque engraved with the words TODAY IS THE TOMORROW YOU WORRIED ABOUT YESTERDAY.

I just want to see him, then we'll go. In the living room, all the chairs and the sofa are covered in thick plastic. I sit in the place where I used to feed the Willgohs baby. The chair crinkles and I slide across the slippery seat. The arms of the chair are coated in grease and bits of old food are stuck in the crevices. Not until I look up at a photograph propped up on top of the TV in front of me do I remember what Brian looks like. It's of him, Mr. and Mrs. Dodd, and someone who must be Johnny. In front of a scene of a painted lake, they don't even look like the Dodds. The lake is Magic Marker blue and the leaves on the trees beside the lake are like palm fronds, they're so big and green with yellow light falling between them. On the shore, a Sunfish rests with its sail rolled up beside it. Smiling, they stand side by side in a line, seeming almost happy.

In an orange Hawaiian shirt, Mr. Dodd is tan and his teeth

look too white. He stands there like a cardboard cutout next to Mrs. Dodd, much younger and plumper in a purple sundress. I've never seen her smiling before. Though someone seems to have made an attempt to comb Brian's hair behind his ears, clumps of it stick straight up. His nose is peeling and he is smiling as wide as his father. In order of height, Johnny, if that's who it is, is last. He doesn't look like the person I saw before, except for his eyes, which are the color of the lake in the picture behind them.

From upstairs comes a low rumbling. Why couldn't Brian tell me about Johnny? I set the framed photo back on top of the TV. The only other photo in the room is of Ronald Reagan sitting in a big leather chair with Nancy standing at his side. They pose with camera-smiles like the Dodds in their photo. Next to the TV in a basket are Mrs. Dodd's knitting needles and yarn. A ball of yellow yarn has unrolled on the orange and green carpet, which covers the whole floor and continues up the stairs where Brian and his mother are.

My baby is drooping in my arms. Some is wrong with her. "I'm going to take you home," I tell her, running my hand over her tiny back. Her eyes don't open. Her fingers don't budge. She doesn't hold on to me. I can't hear her at all.

Outside, a cloud passes, and a shadow falls across the room. Alone in this silence, this mess, I look at the bowl of boiled potatoes, hardened with butter and yellow marshmallow chicks floating on a plateful of spilled soda. I set a cracked glass upright.

Then I hear him whistling. He is dragging his fingers along the wall. Each step knocks inside my head, telling me he is closer, until he is standing in front of me. *Brian.*

"Ship." He stops short, blushing.

My heart stops—that's how I know.

"What are you doing?"

The room tilts back. "Hi," I say.

He has a crew cut, which makes his ears stick out even more and makes him look bigger. Maybe he is bigger. His voice is bigger. I miss him even though he's standing right in front of me. He still seems like a stranger. He says, "I thought something happened to you."

"I thought something happened to *you*," I say. "What'd you do to your hair?"

He laughs and runs his hand over his spiked hair. "Everyone has them. Regulations," he says.

"At military school?"

He nods.

"Why didn't you write or call?"

"I couldn't. I wanted to."

Water runs upstairs, followed by garbled sounds, then a cooing, a murmuring like the baby makes right before she sleeps, but louder. She stirs a little, her motion vibrating through me.

"How long have you been here?" he whispers, glancing at the spoiled dinner.

"Who's that upstairs?"

"Upstairs?" He takes a deep breath. "My little brother."

"Johnny?"

"Yeah, but you can't tell anyone, Ship. No one's supposed to know. My dad would kill me. He'd kill you, too. He made us swear on the Bible. That's why I couldn't tell you."

"What happened to him?"

"You know, the accident."

"The one with your mother?"

"Yeah." He nods. "We didn't think he was going to live. He doesn't even know what's going on. Ma was driving. He was in the front seat. I told him to sit there so I could have the back." He breathes fast.

"I'm glad it wasn't me." I barely hear him. He doesn't look at me.

"Why are you hiding him?" I keep my arms around her underneath my bomber jacket.

"My dad—he'd kill me if he knew I told you all this. No one's supposed to know anything about him." He leans closer. I try to hear his heart.

"Where does he stay?"

"Englewood State."

Englewood is a half-hour drive north, close to New Hampshire. "That's where you go on Sundays?"

Brian nods. "It's close to my uncle's. He pays for it."

"Your mother wants him to come back home, doesn't she?"

Brian glances upstairs. "Yeah."

"Are you going to move back?"

"I hope so." The scar running under his chin turns blue. "My dad keeps saying that I have to carry the family name."

"Is that why you have to go to military school?"

"Pretty much." He closes his eyes and clenches his mouth.

"You shouldn't have left without telling me." I stare into his shut eyes.

"I wasn't planning on it. My dad"—he pauses—"made me."

"Why?"

"He said I was wasting my time here. He wants me to be somebody. I don't know who." He laughs.

The sun flashes through the window. Upstairs, Mrs. Dodd is murmuring to Johnny.

"I saw."

"You saw?"

"You and Helen."

He closes his eyes and runs a hand over his short hair.

"Why did you do that?" I ask.

"I don't know. I couldn't help it." He looks down, pulling on his ear. "I didn't know what else to do. I wish it never happened."

"Is that all you did?"

"Yeah, that's all."

Neither of us says anything. My mouth goes dry. I think of Trudy crying over her execution meal, Owen Hart running over the white dog, the man sitting by the Dumpster, me following a stranger home, Helen's ripped, stained jeans. The whole world is a big, stupid, lonely place. I want to tell Brian about all the things that happened while he was gone. I want to show him the baby wrapped up inside my coat like Rabbit and the way she grabs hold of my finger. For two days I carried her, fed her, and kept her warm.

"Now it just seems stupid," I say about what happened.

"I wish I could take it back."

I want to tell him everything. I want him to hear me. I reach out and touch the tip of his ear. He doesn't move.

"Brian, who are you talking to down there?" Mrs. Dodd calls.

"I'm cleaning up, Ma." He looks frantically around. "You

have to go before they see you." He puts his hands on my shoulders, pushing me toward the kitchen. "You have to believe me. I'll tell you about everything, I promise."

Footsteps cross the upstairs. "Brian!" his mother calls again. "Is your father home?"

He clamps his hot hands over my ears. "Do you believe me?" His hands loosen.

I used to look for my reflection in his eyes, but now I see only him. I step back, letting the afternoon light fall between us. "Yes," I say.

"Brian, why aren't you answering me?"

Mr. Dodd's pickup pulls into the driveway. The radio and engine clink to a quick stop, then the door slams shut. "Hurry, go down here." Brian pushes me toward the open basement door.

When the kitchen door opens, I find myself again standing on the top basement stair.

"Hi, Dad," Brian says. "What'd you get?"

"Doughnuts from Harry's. How about one?"

"Is there a jelly?"

"Sure is."

"Thanks."

"You're a good kid, Brian. Come on in here with your father." He starts asking Brian about his school grades. In the kitchen, Mrs. Dodd's feet pit-pat across the floor and water rings against the sink. They're hiding Johnny at Englewood. Step by step I back down the stairs.

I open the box that says Johnny's Photos. On the first page of the top photo album, there is a picture of Johnny flying an eagle kite with wings so big they look like they'll lift him right up into the sky. Brian, who is running behind Johnny, focuses on the person with the camera while Johnny looks somewhere beyond the white clouds in the right corner of the picture. I feel Johnny staring down at me right now.

The basement door swings open and Mrs. Dodd lifts a broom from where it hangs on the wall. I hunch into the shadow of Johnny's boxes. The baby is too quiet. She isn't moving. I reach up for her foot, dangling there, and close my fingers around it. Mrs. Dodd leaves the door open while she sweeps the floor.

I rip the taped photo out of the book and put it under my jacket, careful not to poke her with one of its sharp corners, close the box, and tiptoe over to the bulkhead. "We're going home now," I whisper to her.

Above us, Brian says, "It's not that I don't like it, but I'd rather be here. I like it better here. Why can't Johnny come home?"

"I said no before and I'll say it again. Let me spell it out for you and your mother. N-o. Did you hear me?

"What?"

"Yes, sir."

When I push the bulkhead doors, they rattle a little but don't budge. I do it again. We are trapped in the Dodds' basement and I can't hear the baby breathing. My head throbs. Is Mr. Dodd going to kill the baby, too?

Using my fist, I hit the bulkhead down the middle, where the two doors are locked shut. I can't tell the difference between the pounding of my fist and the pounding inside my head. All I know is that I have to get out. "Please live," I say to her over and over.

Mr. Dodd's boots clomp across the floor like they're made of bricks.

"Is that Johnny? Where's Johnny?" Mr. Dodd yells. "I thought he was upstairs."

"He is," Mrs. Dodd says, standing at the entrance of the basement. "He's sleeping."

"You better go check, because someone's down there making a helluva lot of noise."

Please let me out of here. I have to take her home now. I suck in my breath. I don't know what else to do; I start bargaining. Let us out of here alive and I swear I'll do anything. I'll never listen in on anyone again, I swear.

"Well, it's not Johnny," Mrs. Dodd says. "Maybe it's a raccoon."

"That'd be a helluva raccoon," Mr. Dodd says, poking his head down from the kitchen. "Somebody's down there. Somebody broke into our house. Do you know anything about this, Brian?"

"No, sir."

"Maybe that's why Johnny was making so much fuss before," Mrs. Dodd says.

"That's right. He knew. He knew someone was down there," Mr. Dodd agrees. "Brian, go get Mossy."

"What?"

"You heard me."

"You can't just shoot someone, Dad."

"Go get Mossy. Someone's down there and I'm going to find

out who it is," he says. "What are you standing there for? Go get her."

Mr. Dodd calls down, "Whoever you are, you better show yourself because I'm coming down with a shotgun."

He's going to shoot us just like those squirrels he has hanging in the garage.

"Whoever it is knows we're coming down," he says, "because now it's quiet. Listen."

I push against the doors with all my strength, but they don't budge.

"Why don't you call the police?" Mrs. Dodd whispers.

"I don't want the cops over here. Where's Brian?"

Brian is running downstairs. "I can't find Mossy. I don't know where she is," he says out of breath.

"What are you talking about? She was right in the dining room," Mr. Dodd says, clumping off.

"I checked there and she's not in my room either."

"Where'd she go? Who took her?"

"I don't know," Mrs. Dodd says.

"Brian?"

"I don't know, sir."

"What about Johnny?"

"Johnny's asleep. He doesn't have Mossy," Mrs. Dodd says.

"Maybe she just got up and walked out the door." Mr. Dodd punches something, like the wall.

"What if whoever is down there took the gun?" Mrs. Dodd asks.

After a minute he says, "Let me think."

I keep my hands on her. She can't die.

"Come on, son, we'll use these. Here. Now let's move."

"Joe," Mrs. Dodd gasps.

They must have carving knives or baseball bats. A gun would be better. Getting shot would be better than being stabbed or clobbered. Either way though, Mr. Dodd is going to kill us. There is nowhere for us to go. Unless Brian stops him, we're going to die. I curl into the shadows beneath the bulkhead.

On the white tip of my Converse sneaker there is a drop of dried blood. If I say I have a baby, maybe he won't kill us—who could kill a baby? But what if he attacks us as soon as he hears my voice?

Footsteps are coming down the stairs, thumping soft like Rabbit. Then a door opens up there and someone runs across the yard, someone who is breathing like a vacuum cleaner. Help, I mouth. Please help us, I don't want to die.

"Check under the stairwell," Mr. Dodd whispers, "behind the boxes. Hurry up."

Brian scurries around, shuffling boxes.

"Anything?"

"No, sir."

"Well, keep going. I'll follow you."

They're coming. One of them kicks a box. What is he going to do to us? Then they both come into view at once. It looks like Mr. Dodd is holding a frying pan. I scramble backward, turning away from them, opening my mouth to scream. I don't know if anything comes out before a thundering slapping noise comes out of nowhere and next thing the bulkhead doors are flung open and light falls on me like a blanket. All I see is white.

Through the white, Johnny's eyes peer down on me. The

pear tree rises up behind him. When he smiles light seems to fall from him onto us. His skin is translucent, like the baby's, with tiny purple veins coursing down his forehead. His teeth are beautiful white. When he spreads his arms wide against the sky, his bathrobe opens. Pale flesh is pulled tight over his bony ribs.

"Johnny," Brian calls.

Mr. Dodd's beady red eyes glare and he lunges toward me. He is going to kill me. She squirms on my chest. Who will take care of her? I can't leave her, I can't die. Through the bulkhead doors, past Johnny, and above the pear tree is a blue line where the sky must meet heaven. That must be where I'm going.

Then, Johnny thrusts his arm out, his hand almost touching me. I leap toward it. Mr. Dodd is breathing right behind me. I hold on to Johnny's hand, hot and smooth. He pulls up and we glide out of the basement, into the sun.

"Johnny, my son, my son!" Mrs. Dodd runs across the lawn to Johnny and throws her arms around him. "Johnny!"

I bolt past them to the middle of the lawn. *We are alive*.

Mr. Dodd's hands are around Johnny's neck and he is shaking him back and forth. Johnny's bathrobe whips this way and that like the wind is blowing it on a clothesline. Why doesn't Mr. Dodd come after me?

"Joe—stop it, Joe!" Mrs. Dodd cries out. Brian tries to pry his father's hands from Johnny's neck. "Stop, stop!" Mrs. Dodd pulls Johnny around the waist.

Grimacing, Mr. Dodd elbows Mrs. Dodd away and keeps shaking his son. Brian piggybacks his father to yank him loose. They are a tangled-up mess with Johnny in the middle, being flung back and forth. Then Johnny's legs buckle. He caves in at the waist and collapses in his father's hands. Mr. Dodd lets out a squeal and finally lets go, and Johnny falls to the ground like a sack. Mr. Dodd steps back, tucking his hands away, and whispers, "Oh, no. No."

Mrs. Dodd kneels beside Johnny, crumpled up on the grass. Mr. Dodd says, "Say something, son. Say something."

"Johnny," Brian calls in a high voice.

He saved us.

"My baby, my baby." Mrs. Dodd lifts Johnny up by the shoulders and rocks him back and forth.

Mr. Dodd drops to his knees. His eyes tear up. He cups his face in his hands. "What have I done?"

"Is he—" Brian calls out. "Check his pulse."

"No, no," Mrs. Dodd howls, rocking back and forth. "My son."

"Look at me, son. This is your father. Open your eyes. I'll do anything in the world if you open your eyes."

Brian kneels down beside Johnny. He takes his limp wrist in his hand and presses a thumb there.

Mr. Dodd says, "Please, son, you can live at home with us. We'll be like we used to."

Mrs. Dodd throws herself on to Johnny's chest. "Please, please," she cries. "Johnny."

"He's all right, Ma," Brian tells her.

"Say something, son."

When Mr. Dodd closes his eyes, Johnny opens his.

"Johnny!" Mrs. Dodd cries.

"Thank you, thank you." Tears roll down Mr. Dodd's face. The Dodds make a circle around Johnny.

. . .

"SHIP!" TERESA is trying to run across the Dodds' lawn, but her high heels sink into the wet soil, squishing and sucking with each step.

"I found her! Here she is!" Teresa yells to Trudy, who breathes heavy as she follows behind.

I wave and start toward them.

"Ship!" Teresa calls again. She comes toward me, one stuck heel at a time as if she's in slow motion. Then she is here. I turn to the side and keep my arm across the baby so Teresa doesn't throw herself around me and smother the baby. She says my name over and over. "Oh, Ship, come here, let me see you. I was so worried about you. What happened?" Trudy is here, too, blubbering on both of us. She can't speak, she's crying so much.

I am home.

"You're safe and sound. Oh, Ship."

"Come on, let's all go inside," Mr. Dodd says quietly. "Give him a little push, Brian."

With her eyes half closed, Trudy takes deep breaths and strokes my hair. "I was so worried. I bet you thought it was too late for an old prune like me to worry about anything else."

"You're not an old prune," I say.

Johnny half screams, half howls.

"What's that?" Teresa asks, her head swinging around. "We heard all the yelling before. Who is he?"

"Is that Mrs. Dodd?" Trudy asks.

"Let's carry him," Mr. Dodd says. He hoists Johnny's arm up on his shoulder. "Brian, take the other side."

"My sons," Mrs. Dodd says.

"What did she say?" Teresa asks. Her arm tightens around my shoulder. "Is that her son?"

"Yes," I whisper.

Johnny's head whips around to face the plastic snowman standing in the middle of the green lawn. Helen is hiding behind it. Johnny waves and the sun blazes down on his pale skin.

"What's the matter with him?" Teresa asks.

Mr. Dodd turns around, and seeing only us, frowns and turns back to Johnny. Long vowel sounds roll out of Johnny's mouth. In the middle of the gush of sounds, I hear him say, "Sorry." Then I hear it again, clearer this time. *Sorry.*

"What is it, son?"

"Johnny?" Mrs. Dodd asks.

"What is it now?"

"He said *sorry*," I yell.

"What?" Mrs. Dodd asks.

"Johnny can't talk," Mr. Dodd says.

"I heard him."

"Ship heard him," Brian says. "She can hear everything. He said it. He said *sorry*."

Johnny looks up past the pear tree. From up there we all must look puny. What would have happened if he hadn't opened the bulkhead doors? Did Brian tell him to?

"Son, you don't have to be sorry," Mr. Dodd says. "You didn't do anything."

"It was my fault. Everyone knows that." Mrs. Dodd covers her face. Her words come out muffled. "No one had a seat belt on."

"I should have been in the front seat, Ma."

"Now what are they saying?" Teresa asks.

Helen crosses the yard to stand with us. She doesn't even know her baby is right here beside her. The right side of her sweatshirt is soaked. "Who is that?" she asks.

"Brian's brother," Trudy answers.

"No, no . . . the brakes . . . I should have—" Mr. Dodd says. A sharp sob cuts through him and seems to split his body in half. "I'm sorry, I'm sorry."

Teresa claps her hand over her mouth. "We need to go now." She lifts one heel out of the wet grass, then the other.

Trudy's breath comes thick and slow while Helen's is quick and uneven like she can't catch it. The baby is warm underneath my bomber jacket. Helen reaches under her sweatshirt to shift something into place. The baby's lips make tiny sucking noises, opening and closing. I have to feed her.

Click, click, that's what I hear, but I can't tell where it's coming from anymore—maybe Johnny or Mrs. Dodd or Helen—or all of them, and me, too.

"It's all right, Ma," Brian says. "Come on." I try to listen for the sound of his heart beating—I know it like the sound of my own—but he's too far away. I look at Johnny one last time. He lies in a heap like the white dog in Sammy's parking lot.

Mr. Dodd kneels beside him. "I'm sorry, son. I'm sorry." His sobs come like belches.

Teresa presses me forward. Without another word, we file across the Dodds' yard.

When we get to the woods between our houses, Teresa asks, "Did you know about him, Ship?"

"No."

"He hasn't been living there, has he?"

"No. Englewood."

"Oh. Poor Brian."

"The poor brother," Trudy says.

"Poor Mrs. Dodd," Teresa says.

"That's right."

Teresa slows to Trudy's pace. "Why'd they keep it a secret?"

Maybe they'll move again and put Johnny in another hospital in another state. The photo of him inches up my chest as I walk ahead.

Helen catches up to me. "Did you do it? Did you give her to Father Hannah?"

"No."

"WHAT?"

Helen has no idea what it's like to carry a baby around, to feed her, sleep with her, and listen to her breathing.

"Where is she?" Helen turns to me. The branches of the pear tree hang like huge arms over us.

"Look, that branch must have been hit by lightning on Friday." Teresa points.

We stand under the splintered, creaking branch as it balances on the branches beneath it. When the wind blows, the branch works like a seesaw. It is going to break—not now, but soon. The next storm or the storm after that. I shouldn't have come home. I shouldn't have brought her home. How am I going to tell them I have a baby and that we have to keep her? What will Teresa do? Now I have to take off my bomber jacket and show them the baby, Helen's baby, who I've been carrying around for two days.

Her body tenses up against mine, and she sneezes—the littlest muffled sneeze, but a sneeze. Then again. They stare at me.

"What was *that*?" Teresa asks.

"It sounded like someone sneezing—like a *baby* sneezing," Trudy says.

"That's what I was thinking." Teresa frowns with her hands on her hips. "Ship, what do you have under there?"

"We have to keep her, we have to keep her," I say, turning to our house, counting the fifteen steps between the pear tree and the kitchen as I take them.

"What did you say, Ship?" Teresa asks, following me. "Ship?"

I keep walking. She knows. She doesn't know what she knows, but she knows. The kitchen shelves, counters, and tables are bare. There are no pies, no danish, no sweet rolls, no bread, and no cookies, only a light coating of flour on the seats of the chairs, underneath the toaster and coffee maker, and on the floor. Helen has disappeared.

I saved her, I tell myself. I unzip my jacket. Under the kitchen lights, the baby's pink head is slumped on my chest. I let the jacket slide off behind me, then begin to unravel Helen's blanket from around her.

"It *is* a baby," Teresa says. An odd laugh comes out of her, a cackle. Her hands rise to cover her face; then she seems to be tipping over.

"A baby," Trudy whispers, gripping the kitchen table.

They stare at the tiny shape emerging from the cocoon of blanket. "My God, Ship, whose is it? Is it alive?" Teresa sucks in her breath, then looks around the kitchen, confused. She reaches out to touch the baby, then pulls back. "Is it real?"

I nod. "She."

"What do you mean? Where did you get her?" I've never heard her talk so loud.

"I found her in the woods."

"You what?" She steps up to put her fingers on the baby's neck.

"On Friday afternoon, I heard something crying. I found her in the woods behind Jimmy Joe's."

Teresa's head bobs side to side like she doesn't know what to focus on. Then she hits the counter with her fist, one, two, three, four times. The floor creaks under Trudy's weight as she looks from me to Teresa. With her teeth pressed together, Teresa says fiercely, "You can't just take a baby, Ship. What if she died? Have you taken her to a hospital?"

"No."

"What have you been doing with her for the last two days? Whose is she?" Her voice rises higher still. "We have to call the police."

The baby's eyes open, then close. "But she didn't die," I say. "I saved her."

"She's a newborn. She could have died. Do you understand that?"

"Yes."

"You didn't report her to the police or anyone?"

"No."

"Whose is she?"

"She's mine."

"She's yours?" That shrill laugh comes out of her mouth again. "You had a baby in the woods, then you found her there?"

I don't say anything.

"What have you given her to eat?" Teresa asks.

"Some milk and water."

"Do you have any idea what this means?" The baby lifts her head slightly toward Teresa.

"Can I see her?" Trudy touches the top of the baby's head. Her finger runs over the soft center of her skull.

"We have to take her to the hospital. Now." Teresa turns around. "Where's Helen? Helen! Get down here right now."

Helen has been standing outside the kitchen door. Her eyes, red and puffy, lock onto mine.

"Is anything the matter with you?" Teresa stares at Helen.

Helen shakes her head.

"Do you know anything about this?" Teresa's gaze shifts from me to Helen as she paces the kitchen, her high heels going *clackety-clack-clack*. "Ship, do you have anything else to say?"

She brushes her hands over the bare counters. "All right, I'm calling the police."

"No," Helen cries. "I mean, you can't."

"And why can't I?" Outside the pear tree creaks. "Why can't I, Helen?"

"Because—" Helen's face falls into her hands. She whispers, "It's my baby."

"She's yours?"

Trudy's hand covers her mouth. Helen keeps her hands over her face. Then it's quieter than it's ever been in here.

"You left a baby in the woods?" The words drop like stones. "*Your* baby?"

I can't see her face, but Helen's whole body shakes back and forth with her crying.

"Do you know what you've done? Do you? Answer me right now, for God's sake."

"I didn't just leave her. I was going to come back for her. I mean, I did go back for her, but Ship already found her. It wasn't very long." She lifts her head. "You had Ship in the back of our car. I was right there. She was fine for hours. And you said she would have been fine for another day, too."

"That's different! I never left her. I was there in the car the whole time. I fed her and took care of her," Teresa yells. "And I didn't have a choice. My God, listen to yourself. How could you?"

I cover the baby's ears. Helen drops her head to the kitchen counter. When Trudy steps toward her to console her, Teresa puts up her arm to stop her. She turns to me. "Why didn't you bring her back here when you found her?"

"I did. You weren't here."

"I haven't been home that much." Her palms run over the counter. "Why didn't I know? I should have known."

"Thanks to me," Trudy cries, looking down, shutting her eyes. "Because all I think about is dying."

"It's not your fault, dammit." Teresa looks up at us. "Look, I'm sorry I haven't been a better mother and I'm sorry you never had a father."

I remember how much I missed her and I say, "You're a good mother."

Teresa's lips part slightly.

"I didn't want anyone to find out. I didn't want anyone to know," Helen cries.

"How could I have been so stupid?" Teresa says. "Thank the Lord nothing happened to her."

"What are we going to say?" Helen says.

"We're going to say you had a baby. We're not going to say anything about leaving the baby anywhere. If anyone asks, the baby was born right here in this house. End of story. Is that clear? Helen? Ship?"

We nod.

"Did anyone see either of you? Does anyone else know?"

"No," I say.

"Owen knows. He's the only one."

Teresa draws in her breath.

"He doesn't want anything to do with it."

"Well, I do. I want everything to do with her," Teresa says. "Now, Helen, take your baby, we're going to the hospital."

"What is everyone going to say?" Helen lifts her head off the kitchen counter.

"I don't think that matters right now, Helen. Right now there's only one thing that matters. Why don't you stop thinking about yourself for once?" Teresa puts her hands on the sides of her head. "She needs to be fed. I think you should feed your baby, Helen."

"I can't." She stands straight. "I don't know how."

"Come on, take her. You just have to put her to your breast. She'll know what to do. Go ahead."

"Do I have to?"

"Yes."

Helen takes the baby from me, holding her out like she's going to drop her.

"Hold her close to you. Here, sit down. Sit here. Like this."

Where the baby was is a hollow, like my chest has been carved out. That's how it was when Brian first left. Or maybe it was always there. Maybe it's part of me and this is why I found her. I breathe into that hollow, filling it up with my own breaths. Everything is not ruined. There she is. Here I am.

I push the photo of Johnny down, tucking it into the top of my jeans. I wonder if they're going to take him back to Englewood State. If they are, I'm sure Mr. Dodd will take the side roads, and if they pass someone from town, what will they do— duck his head below the dashboard or put a hat on him? *She's* not going to be a secret. That's why I heard everything. I was supposed to find her and bring her back.

Outside, the broken branch on the pear tree groans. Helen is feeding her baby. "Are we going to keep her?" she asks quietly.

"Yes," Teresa says. "We're going to keep her. She belongs to us."

"You're a grandmother," Trudy says.

"You practically are, too."

"What's her name, Helen?" Trudy asks.

A name. I close my eyes and see myself when I was little, curled up inside that dog, smelling of earth and sun, the sun leaving, but the warmth still there. The pads of his paws softer than anything, his tail thumping and his heart beating—I was alone and part of everything around me. I remember spelling my name in the dirt. I learned to spell by tracing letters on the tabletop sprinkled with flour or sugar. Teresa made the letters and I traced the words over and over: Teresa, house, pie, pear tree, Trudy, butter, sky, Helen. That day I wrote *Ship Sooner*, that's what I remember.

A fly is buzzing. It stumbles, rattling against the window, knocking to be let out—a prick inside my ear. A thin, hollow cry. Then something like a stone smacks against the pear tree, falls through the branches, and thuds on the ground. And another. *Listen.*